Wasp Days

Wasp Days

Erhard von Büren

Matador
9 Priory Business Park,
Wistow Road, Kibworth Beauchamp,
Leicestershire. LE8 0RX
Tel: (+44) 116 279 2299
Fax: (+44) 116 279 2277
Email: books@troubador.co.uk
Web: www.troubador.co.uk/matador

ISBN 978 1785892 783

British Library Cataloguing in Publication Data.
A catalogue record for this book is available from the British Library.

Printed and bound by CPI Group (UK) Ltd, Croydon, CR0 4YY
Typeset in 11pt Aldine by Troubador Publishing Ltd, Leicester, UK

Matador is an imprint of Troubador Publishing Ltd

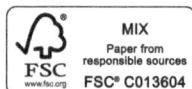

MIX
Paper from
responsible sources
FSC® C013604

'When I was younger I could remember anything, whether it happened or not; but my faculties are decaying now and soon I shall be so I cannot remember any but the things that never happened.'

Mark Twain, *Autobiography*

Contents

I

Annemarie, Erica, Elizabeth, Cecilia, et cetera

'What thou lovest well remains,
the rest is dross …'

Ezra Pound, *The Pisan Cantos*

1

Annemarie

Ah, Annemarie, it really wasn't that bad with you! "Come on, keep me warm a bit longer," you said, your voice soft and mocking, very womanly, very experienced. So we lay together a little longer, let cigarettes and shower be. "Whatever happens, I don't want another baby," you said. The pill didn't agree with you and condoms turned you off. Ah, Anna, ah, Marie, ah, Annemarie, it really wasn't that bad with you. The smell of wet plane trees wafted in through the window from the Predigerplatz. A rainy day. It must have been a Saturday afternoon towards the end of May.

That's how it flashed through my mind, bright and clear, like something said out loud. I could have taken it down as dictation. At the same time I was perfectly aware that the thinker of these thoughts was a forty-five-year-old husband and family man, a civil servant at his desk behind the plastic and steel lending counter in the library. It wasn't quite proper, but real enough, no doubt about that, and rather banal.

It was during the first week of the holidays that those old love stories came to my mind. As in the past few years, I had remained at my post in Wangen, deputising for the

3

boss: I don't like taking my holidays in summer. Eva was in the Engadin with our younger daughter. The elder one, Lydia, was in France with her friend, and she still hadn't sent us a card.

I don't know why I suddenly remembered Annemarie. It can't have been for lack of business at the library: in the first few days of the holidays in particular, lots of people who hadn't yet left – and also lots who wouldn't be leaving – came to return their books and stock up with fresh reading matter. And since the staff had been reduced by a third – as always at this time of the year – those who were left were kept very busy, including me. For when Odermatt, the boss, is away on holiday, I'm the one who's in charge. Not that it worries me, we're a good team. Still, there was no time for daydreaming.

Things just happened to come into my mind. There must have been some kind of Jamesian stream of consciousness law – what a tongue twister! – behind it.

That Saturday afternoon at the end of May. Or some other Saturday afternoon under the sloping roof in the Froschaugasse near the Predigerplatz in the middle of Zurich. In the idiocy of youth.

Actually, I'd first met Annemarie in an attic flat halfway up the Zurichberg, at the Naefs' place. Gerhard Naef was a fellow student of mine, married. In my second semester I'd stayed with him and his wife for a couple of days while looking for a room, and since then I occasionally babysat for them.

The little boy I had to mind never gave me any trouble. He slept soundly – I was there purely as a tranquilliser for his parents. If only my own children, later on in Paris, had been such good sleepers. Whining children are an abomination.

Whenever I went to the Naefs' place to babysit, I took along some work; in those days, in the enthusiasm and earnestness of youth, there was so much that urgently needed to be summarised, excerpted from, or at least read. Yet more often than not my diligence soon flagged: the Naefs' flat featured a television. I couldn't resist. Television – or the bookshelves. Gerhard Naef was a precocious, precociously married, precociously full-blown petit bourgeois with all the frills – from the broom cupboard and the TV unit right up to his own special library. Other people's bookshelves with their motley collections have always fascinated me. I'd rummage through the books, dip into a volume, put it back in its place, rummage again, read. With the exception of Anderegg, whom I didn't get to know until later, I've never met anyone crazier about books than Gerhard and with the same urgent need to possess them. Incidentally, it was thanks to his passion for books that he'd met his wife – she was a bookseller.

But what's the connection between Annemarie and my babysitting?

I was at the Naefs' again one evening when the two of them – they'd been to the theatre – brought home a woman.

"And this is our tried and tested babysitter," said Gerhard.

"I could do with one too," she said. "Could you lend him me once in a while?"

That's how we were introduced to each other.

The Naefs offered us punch, the winter speciality of the house whenever they'd been out and I'd looked after the baby. Their friend took one sip, and then changed over to rosehip tea.

No, I wasn't particularly struck that first time. She seemed so much older than me. Not unattractive certainly but much older, somehow more mature. Thirty. Married, separated, divorced. There was an ex-husband, there was a child. The child, a boy, had already started school. She seemed to be so much further on in life. I felt embarrassingly young.

Didn't she belong to another generation, or almost? In any case, we definitely didn't belong to the same age group. Immediately all those learned expressions came to mind – from age group and age cohort to cohort analysis and cohort comparison. Whereas Annemarie had been born just before the war, I was a post-war child. The first time she went to the cinema, James Dean was still alive and they still made real Westerns; the first time I went to the cinema, James Dean and Westerns could only be seen at revival screenings. And then there were the many roles Annemarie had already played and which – in their gender-specific adaptation – still lay ahead for me.

Besides, there was Erica, my girlfriend, and she definitely belonged to my cohort. That consideration alone was enough to prevent me from paying much attention to the new acquaintance. Looking back now, it seems strange. But that was how I saw it then.

Perhaps it was just that I lacked the courage to

imagine, even for a moment, that a woman as obviously experienced as Annemarie could possibly take an interest in someone like me.

How do love affairs end? How do love affairs begin? The most trivial things will do. It catches you the way you catch a cold, and if you're out of luck it's the flu. Things like the weather, draughts or cold feet might play a role. Yes, the climate. 'April is the cruellest month, breeding / Lilacs out of the dead land, mixing / Memory and desire …' Mixing memory and desire … or does he mean longing? Lilacs out of the dead land, the cruellest month? – No, it can't have been April, more likely the end of May, at the earliest. For the moment anyway I was still sitting in the Naefs' flat, and not even the beginning of a beginning had been made.

Even so, what the Naefs told me about the dark-haired woman stuck in my mind. It was after she'd gone and, ensconced in armchairs – the four-piece easy-care suite had also been a must-have from the start – we were rounding off the evening with a last glass of punch. Her name was Annemarie and she was a kindergarten teacher, they said. She'd been living apart from her husband for the past three years, had got divorced a year ago. That was after five years as the main breadwinner of the family while her husband was still a student at the university. Shortly after her husband's graduation they'd separated; he was the one who'd run off.

"Make sure that nothing like that happens to you," I told the Naefs. I was reading Durkheim at the time and I knew that morality was to be regarded as a thing. Any uncalled-for remarks were thus purely theoretical and not to be taken personally. But the Naefs protested all the same and had to be placated: they knew what a pessimist I was.

In fact, the two of them still live together, the same as ever: I don't want to paint too black a picture! And in the meantime the little boy I so often used to look after has become a lawyer and is already living his own tried-and-tested micro-family life. The Naef family life cycle is characterised by its ideal-typical clarity and simplicity.

Now I might have been a bit of a pessimist, but the fact remains that the Naefs had started out in personal circumstances very similar to those of dark-haired Annemarie. You didn't need Durkheim's *Rules of Sociological Method* to see that. It was an established fact that in student marriages – where she works, while he studies – as soon as the husband graduates there's a crisis. It was evident that this was so. Why it was so would have been worth investigating. Not that it would have been of any help to the people under investigation: they'd have sorted their lives out long before.

Since my arrival here in Wangen, the library has acquired every single report published by the Swiss Federal Statistical Office. Who knows what purpose those figures might serve one day? The boss, a classics scholar, doesn't concern himself much with such things. But he doesn't have any objections either.

"Things are much better for me now that my divorce has come through," said Annemarie. "Moneywise too, since my beloved ex has to pay alimony."

8

She worked as a kindergarten teacher in a village on the eastern shore of Lake Zurich. One third of the population there had always been wealthy, two thirds were nouveaux riches, newcomers – a ridiculously low tax rate, of course. But we have that sort of thing around here too. And then they come along from those classy neighbouring villages, expecting us at the municipal library to provide them with coffee-table books on the remotest parts of Africa, America, Asia and Australia, together with the most up-to-date travel guides so that they can plan their holidays for free. To him that hath shall be given. And it would never occur to those posh councillors from the villages around Wangen to pay the town an even halfway adequate sum for the use of the library. We have to go begging every year, yet we hardly get a mention in their budgets.

So Annemarie had a job in one of those poor rich villages. And of course they hadn't been able to make up their minds to have a regular two-year kindergarten there. Why should they? All they allowed themselves was a one-year kindergarten with a part-time teacher. After all, mothers had enough leisure time to look after their children, and there didn't seem to be any women there who needed to go out to work. If there were any, it was up to them to see how they could combine a job with having children.

Anyway, the sixty per cent job came in handy for Annemarie. It gave her more time to look after her own child, and she didn't have to depend on her mother so much any more.

"I come around here nearly every Saturday. My kid joined the scouts last autumn. He's a cub. They meet over there on the Predigerplatz. I take him along and pick him up afterwards. So I thought I might look in. Nice to see you."

It was her, paying me a visit two or three weeks after that evening at the Naefs'.

I invited her up for a cup of coffee – we were still down at the main door. She suggested going to the Café Marion, she'd treat me. "From there I can see when the cubs get back. They usually drift back around five."

That sounded harmless enough, and so it was. *L'amour, l'après-midi*? Oh no, far from it, things didn't happen that fast. It took quite a long time for it to turn into a love affair. And if those afternoon meetings had gone on in the same manner for a few months more it would probably have developed into a friendship without ever having been a love affair.

I lived in the Froschaugasse, in an antique dealer's house. I shared a flat with three other students. The four attic rooms with pitched ceilings were rented individually. At the weekends I was often alone in the flat, the others went home.

How I'd run down the stairs – and then there she was, at the door. Her round face, broad forehead, owlish eyes. I remember my surprise. In those days I seldom had visitors – except for Erica or the Naefs hardly anyone ever called in.

"We used to live in the Spiegelgasse, down there on the way to the Neumarkt," she said. "That's why my son prefers going to the cubs here rather than in Altstetten. Two of his friends from kindergarten are in the same

10

group. Admittedly, bringing him here every Saturday is a bit of a strain, I travel around quite enough as it is. On the other hand, I get to have an afternoon in town, on my own. I can shop around: I don't have enough time during the week. Sometimes I just go for a stroll."

She sat there opposite me, talking. She'd had her stroll and done her shopping – toys from Pastorini's – and by four o'clock she'd found herself back at the Predigerplatz. Why not pay the babysitter a visit?

Some time later she came by again. After a while she came regularly. Every Saturday afternoon. The bell would ring, I'd run down the steps, we'd take a little walk through the Niederdorf, then sit down in a café near the Predigerplatz.

It was like in a Rohmer film, and indeed it was she who took me to see those French films, a few weeks later and always in the afternoons.

"A woman with a wide range of interests, and always very busy." That's what Gerhard Naef had said that evening after Annemarie had left.

I admired her.

She had her profession, which she carried out with enthusiasm. She was a single mother and she did twice as many things with her child as the Naefs – the two of them together – did with theirs. She ran a proper household, she enjoyed cooking, and her son often took his friends home for meals. She was her own dressmaker. She devised and constructed wooden toys for her kindergarten: marble runs, picture puzzles, spinning tops, xylophones.

Yes, she was clever with her hands.

She went to art galleries and museums. She read fiction and psychology, and she always talked about what she'd read with such fervour that I felt guilty at not finding time to read the book in question.

She believed in astrology. I kept silent on that; I avoided getting involved in conversation on the subject. I sensed that there was no point arguing with her about Virgo, Aries, Aquarius. Viewed from a folkloristic-sociological standpoint, her astro-sympathetic system might certainly have been considered rather special.

She was religious, of the Protestant variety. But it caused her pain to think that by divorcing she had done something that she felt could only be justified by means of Roman Catholic casuistry. But she never said anything bad about her former husband.

There were a lot of things in her erotic repertoire that up to then I'd only known from books. She was familiar with the preludes of the *Kama Sutra* and applied them, with improvisations and variations. It's not for nothing that kindergarten teachers are said to have lots of imagination and to delight in play. It was doubly true for Annemarie. Without Annemarie I'd probably have continued for many a year to be as artless, bashful and quasi-chaste as a James Fenimore Cooper hero.

Oversexed? Not at all! She might have been rather over-eager in her attempts to give yet more pleasure. She herself seemed quite easily satisfied. But what Masters and Johnson Tirisias will investigate, calibrate and measure that for us?

When she met that man Ulrich, the goldsmith, at the opening of a Tinguely exhibition over at the Zurichhorn, it became evident that I'd been nothing but a stopgap. Ulrich was older than her, I was much younger. There's a time and a place. Time for a severe bout of jealousy – that was part of it too.

Annemarie concealed nothing. When I timidly mentioned the matter, she insisted on discussing it right to the bitter end. And, in one of her generous, broad-minded moods it was Ars Amatoria one last time. It was clear that that would definitely be the end of it.

She was rigorous in her own way. And she wasn't afraid of using the word love, not in the beginning and not at the end. "If love doesn't grow, you see," she said – yes, I saw – "it's better to part before it starts declining." Before love starts declining: oh, Annemarie, that's the kind of thing you used to say! Never again would I meet anyone, any woman, who said things like that to me.

2

Erica

She'd been my classmate all the time I was at primary school in Gonten, and I'd never particularly noticed her – she was just one of the many girls in the playground. Later, she did a commercial apprenticeship in Herisau.

I ran into her by chance at the railway station in Zurich towards the end of my first semester when, for once, I was on my way home for the weekend. She was taking the same train. I almost failed to recognise her.

She said she'd only been working in Zurich since last

summer. No, after her apprenticeship she'd stayed on for another year at the Herisau municipal offices. Yes, she liked the new job. No, she'd been lucky and had found a studio flat almost at once. We talked about flat-hunting. I was busy looking for a flat again, for the second time within six months.

She knew all kinds of things about me, even from the time long after we'd stopped running around in the same playground in Gonten and I was already at the Kollegium Sankt Michaelis while she was at the Benedictine convent school in Menzingen. I, on the other hand, knew very little about her. She didn't seem to mind being quizzed. Trivial curiosity is something I've never been short of.

Was she going home for the carnival? No, she wasn't interested in the carnival, she said. But she enjoyed other Appenzell traditions: the *Alpaufzug* annual procession of cows up to the alps, and also the *Klausentreiben* on New Year's Eve. "Did you know that the Musée de l'Homme in Paris shows *Klaus* masks from Urnäsch right next to masks from Bali and Burkina Faso?" I listened with interest.

The following week I rang her up at her office. There are only so many patterns for getting to know each other.

We went to the cinema together. A revival, I remember, in the cinema next to the Café Select on the Limmatquai: *East of Eden*. I'd already seen the film at least two or three times. It might also have been *Baby Doll* or *The Long, Hot Summer.*

It was love at second sight. Or possibly, as far as she was concerned, love at third sight.

We came from the same village and had had the same teachers for six years; we'd never actually belonged to the same cliques, but we knew more or less the same people. Out of touch for a long time – admittedly, I'd hardly noticed Erica at all before – and then a chance meeting: there was enough to talk about for a start. On top of that, we both came from the Appenzell region and had only recently come to live in Zurich.

I lust, therefore I am. And when going without I am too. And all the more so if it's you who's doing the lusting or the going without. And if, as they say, everything revolves around that one and only point, it would be pure stupidity to feel ashamed when it comes up in one's own vaguely dissolute life. With mademoiselle on the carousel. Slaves to work that we are, slaves to internal secretions and cinema in the head.

A dissolute life my foot! My relationship with Erica couldn't have been more harmless. A visit to the cinema, followed by a stroll through the Niederdorf district. And when the weather grew warmer we occasionally sat down on the steps of the Uto Quay, on the Riviera as young people then called the area between the Wasserkirche and the Bellevueplatz. Then, in summer, we'd go swimming over at the Zurichhorn, hardly ten minutes from Erica's studio flat.

Neither of us had anyone else, we were both of us ready to have each other. But I have to admit that it took me some time to realise what I really had in her.

Delicately built, fair-haired, pale-complexioned. And from May onwards her narrow face was covered in freckles.

She always wore flat-heeled shoes. For a long time the fact that she was shorter than me by a head and a half made me feel awkward.

But her slim neck appealed to me from the start. As did the down-to-earth way she had of talking about her work: office life.

And sometimes a stubborn look would come over her face, like a splash of colour in her modesty.

I acted as though I was experienced in matters of love; she was as inexperienced as I was. When, one Sunday afternoon, we slept together for the first time, it was a premiere for both of us. Something I never admitted to Erica, even afterwards.

"Let me finish my apple first," she said, and I watched her, and she stretched out her half-eaten apple towards me. "Here," she said, and I took a bite. "If temptation grows too strong, quickly drink a glass of cold water," I said citing Bovet, the truly Christian sex education book. "Hush!" she said. Tricky scenes can have such simple dialogues.

She's sitting on the bed with the apple in her hand; munching slowly, loudly; her eyes on something that can't be seen. Sunday afternoon, greenish twilight behind lowered blinds; everything runs its course.

You may scoff, but it was profound and beautiful and unique.

And yet afterwards we had to laugh. The earnestness had disappeared and we felt strangely exhilarated.

Small matters. Erica bled profusely, it was she who had to reassure me. "Having your wisdom tooth pulled out is much worse," she said.

We were sitting in the Bodega. "Is it something we should celebrate?" she mused. Then to herself, gently: "I daresay it was high time for me." Doubtfully: "Did we actually do everything right?" And with blushing resolve: "Hey, I'll get myself a prescription for the pill." Conclusion: "Well, we've got that behind us, and it was fine."

Once again: although it made us laugh, we felt immense satisfaction. Both of us, I assume. The simple satisfaction of having done something complicated for the first time. For two young people from Gonten in Appenzell it was an initiation rite within the conventions of dating, necking, petting, et cetera that was still bound up with all kinds of strong emotions. Beginners' joy at the successful outcome, bashful pride. We'd finally left our early and mid youth behind us. The real life had begun.

Soon our elder daughter will be experiencing something similar, it occurred to me. Oh well, what must be, must be! Everything runs its course.

I felt rather uneasy thinking about it. Perhaps it had already happened a long time ago. I still had the old statistics in mind; according to the most recent Emnid epochal surveys – published in Bielefeld, it's not the kind of thing they investigate in Switzerland – precocious puberty must start even earlier now. Oh well, let Lydia take a bite out of a Granny Smith, it wouldn't be the worst alternative.

Was I being permissive or patriarchal? With sudden horror it occurred to me that at this very moment she was travelling around somewhere in the South of France with her friend, that gangly girl Monica. And the only thing I'd been able to talk them out of – forbidding it would have been to no avail – was hitch-hiking. "But Dad, there are all kinds of interesting places you can't get to by train or by bus!"

"Dear Dad, tomorrow we're going to Monica's godmother's. Everything going fine." That's what she'd scribbled on the card from Avignon. At that godmother's place in Joyeuse – presumably there was a bus that went there – they'd be under some kind of supervision at least; a little anyway, better than nothing, never mind patriarchy and overprotectiveness.

No need to worry, Lydia is a sensible person, pleasantly level–headed, I thought. She was sociable and enterprising and at the same time, I'm glad to say, she also read a lot. Weren't the old Russians on her programme at the moment, *Anna Karenina* and the like? And she was planning to study chemistry – or was it biology? – in any case not one of those flabby humanities subjects and certainly not that scourge of our times, law.

I had no reason to grumble. Other fathers are worse off.

3

Elizabeth

I'd actually had a dream! That seldom happened. Not like Eva who has two or three a night and can tell me all about them at breakfast – provided she's already up.

A woman, walking in front of me in a group of people who all look familiar; a street in the Niederdorf. I catch up with them and look at the woman from the side, a young woman: Elizabeth. I put my hand out to her. A surge of joy, joy in her face too. Next to her, another woman, a stranger, pale. This is my mother, says Elizabeth. In that case we know each other, I say, and take a long look at the woman's face. She also stares at my face, for a long time. We've seen each other before, I say. The noise in the street drowns her reply. I follow the people, uncertain as to whether I belong or not; I keep a few steps behind, then catch up again. Elizabeth walks on ahead of me, I know that she knows I'm there … In a stairwell, high up, alone with Elizabeth, sitting side by side on the wooden step, not touching, feeling attraction, powerful, all-encompassing. I've met her mother three times, I should have recognised that woman in the street straightaway: once Elizabeth was ill and I paid her a visit at her parents' place, another time I picked Elizabeth up to go for a walk, and another time … the house on Central Square is very tall and has bay windows, and in the garden behind you go down a slide … Elizabeth is sitting beside me on the step and I try to get things straight … the woman in the street, I should have recognised her at once … and suddenly, to my relief, it dawns on me: it's because she's aged. I didn't recognise that woman, I say, because she's aged. I see Elizabeth nod, see us both sitting beside each other in the stairwell, and at the same time I know that I'm lying in bed dreaming. And the sentence 'Because she's aged' comes out again through the dream into my awakening. And, with a jolt, this is followed by: and I've aged too. And at the same moment Erica comes to mind: it's years since I last saw her. Still in a doze, I work it out: when did I … it must have been … rang her once from here, from Wangen …

I shook it off and got up.

While I was shaving it came back to me. And it was only then I realised that although I'd dreamt about Elizabeth it was Erica who'd come to mind as I awoke from my dream. And somehow – only somehow – Eva was there too, and someone else too, but who exactly? And Eva was in the Engadin, as she'd been every year for the past few years; the previous evening she'd rung me and I'd told her what letters she'd received, as I always did when she was away for a few days; I'd also read out to her the letter that her friend, the Canadian woman, had sent from Changchun … What a muddle! But it didn't seem to be entirely without rhyme or reason.

Thus I left those I'd loved behind, somehow, somewhere, and they slipped away, although I used to think of them quite often in the beginning, less frequently in the ensuing weeks and months, only intermittently later on, and then hardly at all as the years passed by with noise and folderol.

After one cup of coffee, even after two, that feeling of nostalgia – or whatever it was – still hadn't been washed away. It remained with me all that morning at the library, haunting me. I started drafting the annual report, the first parts of it: statistical information, stocks, user frequency. On his return from holiday Odermatt was sure to find something to cavil at as usual, but he'd supply the foreword nevertheless. It's only the content of life that's noise, it occurred to me, time itself flows on silently from nowhere to nothingness. All afternoon, sentences like that came into my mind. I don't know where I got them from.

"If I was still a bachelor, I'd ask her to marry me on the spot!" This from Gerhard Naef. And he wasn't being ironic. He liked Elizabeth.

The Naefs had been introduced to Erica at the time, it was at their place that I'd first met Annemarie, I also introduced them to Elizabeth.

Admittedly, Elizabeth was beautiful. It was a rare attack of boldness that had made me approach her at the student cellar club that Saturday evening. Usually, beauty struck me dumb.

Later – the time for retrospectives had already come – she said: "You? Shy? You stared at me as if I was some kind of weirdo, or at least the way you kept looking my way was extremely conspicuous!" Whereas I thought I'd only glanced over at her furtively once or twice when the opportunity arose!

And then everything was so incredibly easy. I was bowled over and she beamed. "A priori infatuation, thunder in winter!" someone like Sommerhalder would have mocked. And indeed, it seemed to me like something absolutely out of season, a kind of freak miracle, at least for the first three weeks.

With Elizabeth: that time was the best of those times.

She worked in Basel, for Hoffmann-La Roche. Her parents lived in Zurich, as did her brothers and sisters; she went home every weekend. We only saw each other at weekends. And if we missed one weekend, the following one was all the nicer. Forget-me-not. No, I shan't forget you.

I've never worked better than that winter, spring,

summer, autumn. I was getting on fine with my young Tibetans. Work and discipline for six days. Love on the seventh.

Years later I didn't at all mind staying behind in Paris on my own when Eva, with the child – and highly pregnant into the bargain – went on ahead of me to Switzerland, to Wangen. As though I'd somehow secretly wanted to repeat what had suited me so well with beautiful, quiet Elizabeth.

Elizabeth was a laboratory assistant. None of my girlfriends those days was a student, all of them had proper jobs: Annemarie the kindergarten teacher, Erica the secretary, Elizabeth the lab assistant at Roche's, Cecilia the air hostess, Sibylle the nurse, Linda the bookseller …

And they all seem to have got married shortly after their liaison with me. Annemarie, the divorcee, married that Ulrich from Altstetten, Sibylle married a medical student, Erica an architect; Linda is said to have moved to Germany and married a journalist; Cecilia married one of her pals from the Alpine Club. And Elizabeth? I don't know what happened to her. I could have found out later on by asking either her sister or one of her brothers – one of them must still be living in Zurich.

If, in addition to those main friendships, I count all the fast-friendships, the three-week-infatuations in the intervals and interims, my love life at the time seems to me to have been less a love life than a collector's life. In fact, I've always tried to be normal, and that's why things just accumulated the way they do at that age.

In the fury of youth – that was also when Eva and I got to know each other. And we'll remain together, as far as circumstances permit, right up to the potbelly and wide hips of old age.

So is that the proverbial petit-bourgeois pleasure in juvenile escapades? Gone, never to return, oh sap-green time! A mortified nod. And what purports to be maturation should it in fact be seen as a withering process? – Again, a mortified nod.

With pleasant regularity, from the middle of the week on, I'd start looking forward to Saturday. We often did things with Elizabeth's sister and her husband. Elizabeth was beautiful; Ruth, her sister, was charming. And as autumn approached I began to look forward with rather more interest to those weekends when we planned to go on outings with Ruth and her husband – cinema, rowing, a swim in Lake Türler – than if I was to be alone with Elizabeth at the cinema, in the rowing boat or swimming in a lake. Ruth was witty, she had a lot of stories from her musicians' milieu; a conversation with her was like a game of ping-pong.

Don't fool yourself. That's what Annemarie had taught me. It was only after prolonged hesitation that I applied the lesson. And summoned up enough courage to be mightily sincere.

Elizabeth listened very quietly. Did I think, she asked, that it would be better if we saw a little less of each other in future.

In October she went on a trip to Greece with a tour group. It had already been planned, and I couldn't have afforded the journey anyway.

When, a week after she'd got back, she still hadn't contacted me I started to miss her. And after two more weekends sans beauty sans charm I wrote her a letter.

And the silent woman was again talking amiably to me over the phone. I wouldn't have dared ring if I hadn't already sent her a letter dutifully admitting my fault.

There was a reconciliation – quiet and simple, as things always were with Elizabeth.

And the resulting emotion soon faded into the old tranquillity.

Break-up, remorse, pardon: it could not reasonably be expected to work a second time.

And yet it happened. Although I'm not too sure about the pardon. The remorse, on my part, was there all right. However, it would have been too much to expect of Elizabeth to pardon me a second time, or so it seemed to me.

If I'd bumped into her some time after our break-up, who knows? But she never went down to that cellar club any more. Also she never turned up at any of the places we'd had the habit of frequenting in those one and a half years. Elizabeth was gone. Once, on the Mythenquai, I saw her sister from afar. Another time I nearly bumped into her younger brother on the Bellevueplatz.

Months later – I was already going out with Cecilia – I'd still go to the main station on Sunday evenings and stand where the trains from Innsbruck and Schaffhausen drew in before going on to Basel. I'd go and stand there at various hours, always for very long periods of time. Elizabeth, even if she still regularly came back home to

Zurich from Basel at the weekends, must have completely changed this habit too.

4

Cecelia, sophisticated and elegant

"Do you take something, you know, the pill, something like that?" "Of course I do. How can you ask?" Kissing was nice, what else would follow? It came. Cheerfully she knelt over me and I eagerly snatched at her breasts and the bumps of her spine. The usual turmoil: kiss and counterkiss, couscous with nutmeg. A manual, some kind of manual was being followed, not step by step but haphazardly. Don't tell me your head is switched off during this kind of turmoil. You're awake, quite conscious of what you're doing, even if only vaguely. The little glass egg on its silver chain dangled down between her collarbones. I took a bite at the egg. "Ouch!" she said, and we laughed. And redoubled our efforts. I lifted up the whole jolly little person with my pelvis. "Rocket launch," she said, "don't ruin your back." The glass egg swung to and fro like a thurible above my face. "Caravelle taking off," I suggested; it seemed less vulgar, although calling it a rocket was presumably a compliment and therefore acceptable. Would we share a cigarette after the steep climb, the nose dive and the hard landing, I wondered. With debriefing and fooling around? Would she stay the night? And what if she didn't? The tram stop on the Stauffacherplatz? Or would I, quite the proletarian gentleman, take her home on the last tram out to Höngg? And why her sudden gaiety? And would it last? The sound of noisy kissing brought me back to the physical plane. Human beings, such moist creatures. A log snapped in the stove; she stopped short, alarmed. How on earth had we got onto this bed? A moment ago she'd been sitting in the armchair by the balcony door and we'd been chatting about something or other.

Revival cinema when there's not much going on at the lending counter, for example in the early afternoon. However long ago a thing like that might have happened, suddenly it's there, so clearly and distinctly as to be almost annoying. Revivals? No, video clips. And what are they advertising? Old times, in memoriam Annemarie Erica Cecilia et cetera. Details; strange what gets remembered. Sex in the head, and Freud can't be far off, perseveration and repetition compulsion. Didn't Anderegg too, with his imitation? I've never really trusted those psychoanalysts. I prefer to see daydreams as sociological facts. To balance office life? Didn't Adorno, something, somewhere? Bloch for sure. What about Moscovici? And Bourdieu and Passeron? Hey, where have I landed! Smatterings of knowledge, soaked in a once-upon-a-time sauce.

"I never look at myself between my collarbones and my navel, it's much too depressing. The Lord Almighty wasn't kind to me there, and on top of that they're the wrong shape – no, my love, ever since I turned seventeen I've preferred not to look." Making fun of herself or fishing for compliments? Oh those little sagging breasts that allegedly troubled her and that I then proceeded to praise to the skies. "It's all very well for you to make fun of me," she said, doubtfully; but I persisted in my praise

26

of those little gewgaws. Never has a bosom of such dubious quality been more lavishly kissed, never has anything given me so much pleasure; never has, never will.

It seems that everyone's got their own problems; they keep them to themselves, without other people, even their closest friends noticing! At times Cecilia seemed quite incapable of realising that, in every visible feature – with the exception of that negligeable detail – she was much prettier than the average.

With her long-legged elegance she confirmed every positive prejudice about Swissair-stewardesses. Her face exuded respectability and friendliness, with a slightly Maghrebian-Hamitic, even Asian touch. But she came from Graubünden, on both her mother's and her father's side. And both her maternal and her paternal ancestors had lived in Graubünden for generations – not a trace of Carthage, Tibesti, Huang Shan or Yellow Sea.

Her father was a butcher and a local politician in Schiers.

Respectability and friendliness? In private, she would occasionally let herself go with fine abandon, she'd be moody and obstinate. "Don't I have to pull myself together quite enough at other times? Just think of all the marked friendliness we have to produce in the course of the seven-hour flight from New York to Zurich. When I'm with you I take a break. I can, can't I?"

We only met irregularly. Her complicated flight schedule might have been one of the reasons why. However, the main reason was because she wasn't quite sure that I was the right person for her. I seldom knew in advance when I'd see her next. "Give me a ring," she'd say. "If I'm at home I'll answer."

Trivia, please.

A Sunday in March, one of those rare weekends when she was not on a flight, or skiing in Prättigau, or on a climbing tour somewhere in the Alps. I hadn't known she'd be in Zurich. She hadn't rung till late on the Saturday evening. For Cecilia I was ever ready. She'd taken home US beef from New York, she said. "So that you get something decent to eat for once. To help you get somewhere in life. I'd like to make a boxer of you."

While I was peeling the potatoes and she was washing the lettuce, I regaled her with some grisly details from Sinclair's jungle book, told her about the Chicago of those times and the slaughterhouses there. But then, when she went to take the thus maligned meat out of the fridge – it was no longer there.

Bafflement, incredulity, perplexity. Regine, Cecilia's flatmate, must have taken the delicacy for her picnic in the woods: mixed up the packets, certainly there were still plenty of sausages left.

What should we do now? Make do with someone else's sausages, or a tin of corned beef? Omelettes? Cheese? I myself found it all rather amusing, but the meat mix-up had put Cecilia in a bad mood. And she didn't really relax until Regine had phoned and, with repeated apologies and kindest regards, released the veal sausages for consumption.

"It's something they often do," said Cecilia, meaning Regine and her boyfriend. "Sometimes even in the depth of winter. They walk off into some wood or other and cook sausages over a campfire."

"The ones we're eating now."

"Don't go on about it, I feel awful enough as it is."

"American beef in a Swiss wood. Is your friend's boyfriend a corporal in the army? Or did they both use to be in the scouts?"

She didn't know.

"They'll have to make a massive fire for your thick steaks."

"And they'll squat down beside it in the wet, and still feel freezing cold," she said.

"Back to the woods, to the Üetliberg wilderness."

'Pathfinder, asked Mabel, when shall we see you again?' I told her what Cooper had written about the trek through the forests to the Great Lakes. Down the river in a canoe, red men in pursuit; Lake Ontario, Mabel, besieged in the blockhouse; Pathfinder's honesty versus Iroquois cunning, and the victory of the good and the brave – but no happy end for Pathfinder's one and only passion. In Mabel's heart Natty was but a fatherly friend; for the rest of his life he would send her the finest furs, anonymously. Those splendidly insipid women of Cooper's, not created to stimulate the Cowper's glands, certainly not, that was not in their nature. '... but a tread, whose vigour no sorrow could enfeeble, soon bore him out of view, and he was lost in the depths of the forest.' Cecilia had never seen the Great Lake Ontario or the small Otsego Lake, not even from above, from afar; her Swissair plane only flew as far as New York. And what was it like south of the prairie? Ah, now we were back to the steak, which down in the real Wild West was still buffalo meat, not beef, with buffalo hump considered the best joint by Natty, the Pathfinder, long since become an old man.

Cecilia reached for the flight schedule and an atlas. We'd finished the sausages. The Mövenpick Vanilla Ice Cream was melting. No, she hadn't ever seen the prairie from above either. "There's nothing of it left anyway," I said. "It'll be all fields of maize and wheat now, in neatly checked patterns on the rolling hills, and farmhouses, barns, silos – certainly no buffalo herds. And in place of the wigwams and corralled wagons there'll be mobile homes and Babbitt homes." She looked up from the atlas, took a spoon of ice cream, hesitated, said: "Strange, isn't it, really – here we are sitting in the kitchen near the Hönggerberg, and I see Regine – it doesn't take much imagination – cooking steaks on a stick over a fire on Mount Albis, and your Natty Leatherstocking – or whatever his name is – paddling his canoe across Lake Ontario, and people slaughtering cattle on a conveyor belt in Chicago, all pretty much at the same time. What about that for a flight of thought?" She was astonished at her own profundity.

A Sunday in Hönggg. Trivia. Happiness? It almost seemed so.

"I think you're very nice," she said, "but somehow, you know what I mean, there's just not enough ardour." What could be done? Bide my time and drink wine.

This time she'd taken along a bottle of Californian wine, duty free, and we were on what she called a flight of thought together. I was delivering a lecture on Riesman's other-directed society, the miniskirt and the hula hoop. She talked about her father, the Grisons dried-beef producer she liked going skiing with in the winter. I told her about the Tibetans in Appenzell who – being tradition-directed, *vide* Riesman – hung up provisions of mutton cutlets in their wardrobe and a week later were baffled by the gruesome result.

Dried, roasted, smoked, spoiled, switched, whatever: the meat perseverated.

But Cecilia had something new, and informed me that from May on she'd be flying the Zurich-Beijing route. I added something about the Cultural Revolution. She expressed sympathy with the Dalai Lama's fate. I defended secularism. She agreed that religion was a private matter. I gave her a summary of Schelsky's *Die skeptische Generation.* She genned me up on Mövenpick, Fogal stockings and Hilton hotels. We both scoffed at von Däniken's bestselling astral tripe. "I prefer to believe in the Virgin Mary," she said. "Some of us, even some pilots, you know, have earnest discussions about flying saucers. Nothing but figments of the imagination! Luckily I'm a Catholic. As long as the Pope doesn't proclaim infallibly that things like that exist I don't have to believe in them, do I?"

We often scoffed about all kinds of things, with pleasure. "At least I don't get bored when I'm with you," she said.

Sophisticated. A remarkably unobtrusive style of dress, always in subdued colours. Pale grey culottes or a pale green tailored suit or a pale pink flared skirt. She didn't wear jewelry, except for chains with pendants: the ash-coloured glass egg, or medals of the Virgin Mary or St Christopher. She was a churchgoer – albeit often prevented from attending Sunday mass by her job or her mountain climbing. She never wore a cross on her chain; a cross, flat between her collarbones, would have disconcerted me. I don't like heavenly and earthly love to be too closely associated.

I was allowed to take a bite at the glass egg, but not at the medal of the Virgin or at that of St Christopher. "You're not to make fun of those things," she warned. And when I did so all the same, she pushed me away with her elbows. She sat there, her long legs drawn up, her bony knees on a level with her armpits, sat there silently, naked and grieved.

5

Dorothea, the philosopher

And that was the end of that. No more Annemarie Erica Elisabeth Cecilia, adieu jolly student life in Zwinglian Zurich. Now I was leading a serious married life – consistent with serious scholarship. I had not come to Paris to dig for the sandy beach beneath the asphalt of the Boule Miche, I had no time for complicated amorous relationships – simple ones don't exist. The Swiss Confederation was paying me for high quality work, and I had to rebrand myself as an ambitious young man working as though he'd swallowed a clock.

The two-roomed flat on rue Lacépède, three houses down from rue Linné. At five in the morning I got up – yes, even in winter – and sat myself down with a cup of Nescafé at the still pleasantly bare kitchen table. I progressed methodically, reading and writing, writing and reading, until seven o'clock when the child appeared in the doorway, wide-awake, holding in her hand the picture-book I'd told her bedtime stories out of the evening before – goodbye and amen to work. It was a while before Eva – grumpy, as always in the morning – crossed the kitchen on her way to the bathroom. I cleared the table for breakfast.

Afterwards: off to the Censier reading room. I can't work with children around. I could only stay on in the flat if Eva went out with Lydia in the morning. So I got used to sitting in reading rooms. From sociology-lite to reading-room sociology. Little did I think at the time that later on in life I'd be spending years and years working in a library, as a civil servant.

Twelve-hour days: read and summarise, summarise and read. And as an intermezzo and social event there was Bourdieu's seminar once a week at the Ecole Pratique des Hautes Etudes, and occasionally I'd attend a lecture at the Collège de France. Chunks of social anthropology, ethnolinguistics, Third World demography; cinema and society, society and the economy in China, the sociology of signs, historical sociology, the historical sociology of Catholicism and ethnopsychology; general semantics and special semiotics; and rural, urban, comparatistic, Muslim sociology. Scholarly distractions, I was an inquisitive person. But again my main theme was youth – not young Tibetans in Switzerland this time, but youth in general.

Did those in high places really want to know what made those young people so agitated and restless? Whatever the case, it kept me busy in the reading rooms: Censier, Sainte-Geneviève, Musée Social, occasionally too in the

Bibliothèque Nationale or out in Nanterre, and every day in the early morning and in the late evening in our cramped kitchen in rue Lacépède. I was accountable to the Swiss Confederation.

No, there was nothing wrong with interim reports on restless youth. They'd been available long before 1980. And indeed, long before 1968. It was just that no one had taken any notice of them. And no, there's no reason to lay into the small group of clowns, ruffians, heroes and starvelings doing sociological research under the banner of Tell's crossbow. Sociologists cannot be held responsible for the status of women and the situation of men; or for families and households or indeed young people in the Swiss Confederation being as they happen to be.

So was Dorothea back then in Paris an exception and at the same time the last? In other words, in the past thirteen years have I never kissed anyone but Eva, all contentment and connubial duty? And what would be so bad about that? It would have pleased the great – all is lost – Augustine; and others too. "In that case virtue would be a psychosomatic reaction, so to speak?" Anderegg would ask – a rhetorical question since he already knows the answer. And Sommerhalder would come up with his "Balls, psyche and soma. A petit-bourgeois reaction of the simplest kind". That's all right with me. But what did that have to do with my trifling affair?

The only reward of virtue is virtue, nothing else, says Emerson, freely quoting Spinoza. And according to Spinoza himself, we rejoice in virtue not because we control our lusts, but on the contrary, it's because we rejoice in virtue that we are able to control our lusts.

My flirt with Dorothea the philosopher turned into a bedding with Pandora; my lust was checked, and now I have to rejoice in virtue. And therein lies the tiny difference: Spinoza lives in the truth, I live in Wangen.

But back to married life, to the post-Parisian period of fasting. While you're drawing up a catalogue you may as well make a thorough job of it.

Not really kiss and tell stories, confessional stories at most – forget desire and suchlike. But anyway, three almost-girlfriends, heart-warming affairs, pseudo-platonic. Once on a Swiss National Day in Aarau. And another time when a former fellow student from Zurich even suggested I stay overnight – something I found incredibly moving but which filled me with silent panic. Run from the myrrh chamber, away from the pools in Heshbon – see the Song of Songs, 5:5, 7:4. You really can't be careful enough in these rigorously permissive times.

Oh no, of course I don't step aside or avert my eyes when a beautiful woman comes striding by! And in those strange days in April, May and June in Paris it was really the beginning of the end of the calamity – what ever has become of Dorothea? – when, in the metro between Jussieu and Sèvres-Babylone, I suddenly saw all those lovely faces again: Thy hair is as a flock of goats, that appear from mount Gilead. Thy neck is like the tower of David builded for an armoury. See above 6:5 and 4:4.

Our town is small, everyone knows each other. That, too, inhibits lust. Any stories that might have taken place these last thirteen years can be included in the chapter on trifling matters.

The one or the other of our trainees? Admittedly, now and then there was a discernible whiff – or should I say an aura – of eroticism in the air. But I never got carried away; it came, wafted around, was pleasant, and disappeared again. Occasionally one or the other of the advanced students for whom I ordered books from the interlibrary loan service put me in a bit of a flurry. But from year to year the age difference increases, those young women could now almost be my daughters.

Not having to rouse yourself anew every morning to get down to work has its merits. All I need do now is set off for the library, sit down here at my desk, and deal with the work as it comes in.

Ever since the introduction of flexitime – what an expression – it's the punch clock that supplies my day with the necessary landmarks. Measure and rule: orderliness is the vital nerve of a civil servant's life. I don't want to complain, it doesn't really bother me. The business here keeps me tolerably active. Probably without my tenure as a civil servant I'd just sit around doing nothing. Goodbye academia, it really doesn't hurt that much.

II

Card index of trifling matters

'On the papers were written
thoughts, ends of thoughts,
beginnings of thoughts.'

Sherwood Anderson, *Winesburg,
Ohio*

1
Scribblings

Outpourings on the couch, part confession, part plea in favour of cunnilingus, fellatio; furthermore, a laxative against patriarchal constipation. Or Herzog's crazy letter-writing. Or a hymn to life in the woods. Straight to the heart of the matter, however abstruse it might be.

I've no idea how I could find an excuse even halfway as convincing for my narrative. My wife hasn't left me, nor am I struck with some hypochondriacal malady. No hereditary ills, no alcoholism in the family, no grievances, no midlife crisis. My elder daughter isn't anorexic nor is the younger one a failure at school. And I think Wangen is as good a place as any to live in.

It's only my habit of occasionally writing down the things that come to my mind.

It started in Paris. During my daily sessions of silent study in the reading room. The dissatisfaction and unrest of youth; their radicalism, their revolts, their rebellions; youth between adolescent moratorium and emancipation, between hatred and hopefulness, to have or to be – basic research, meticulousness, oh dear! Everything that had been written on the subject in the past twenty years was to be collected and clearly presented in a scholarly report.

That was the task I'd taken on. Nothing original had to emerge, all that had to be produced was a useful paper: groundwork, spadework.

It was essential to keep to the subject and not allow myself to be sidetracked – or at least not too much. And so I sat there and I read and I wrote. And if something that had nothing to do with the subject came into my mind I wrote that down too. I thought it was the best way to keep those diverting irrelevancies more or less under control.

Cecilia was quite right: within your head, you can get to all kinds of places in the shortest of times. Man, the distracted being. Some praise it as proof of mental agility.

Chat until two in the morning about Meienberg and his Gallic rooster, about Anderegg and his family, about unemployment, Mitterrand, Sommerhalder and other local celebrities. The efficient woman from the Entlebuch. Buy an Apple and you'll get on faster with your research, she said. In any case she's always ready to stay up until two o'clock in the morning. She drinks the blackest of coffees from the smallest of cups, but keeps serving you wine however much you refuse, and only laughs when you remark that you need enough sleep if you're to work the following day. A bleating laugh! Besides that there's nothing you could hold against her.

Beatrice? The historian? Yes, I remember. Her special field was French colonial rule; she'd been sent to Paris by Professor Hofer from Bern. I'd quite forgotten that she, too, had apparently kept me from my work. Chatting till all hours of the night, with a bad conscience at having – without serious reason – left the baby-sitting to Eva for a whole evening. There's nothing about that in my notes, but I remember. A husband with the right sentiments and the wrong behaviour: chatting and drinking wine and staying away from home. Apart from that there was nothing else I had to reproach myself for, no Cecilia et cetera business.

If someone sitting across the table from you loudly sniffs back his snot three to six times a minute – I counted – while immersed in a book whose author and title you can't decipher because his hand is covering exactly that part of the jacket …

Things like that can be annoying, of course they can. But why on earth had I written it down?

The air full of flying machines, like locusts the size of excavators. And the countryside below, hilly, bare, crisscrossed with roads, is full of people. All bustling around, I tell you, it's incredible how many people can fit into a dream. And I myself am standing to one side, on the edge – and yet right in the midst.

No commentary. Not even a hint as to who was supposed to have dreamt the dream. Most likely Eva. Already back then in Paris she used to recount her dreams at breakfast. As entertainment. Sometimes she was astonished by how much had happened during the night. It's astonishing how many things distracted me from serious work.

Or had I just grown weary of it all? Was it a minor insurrection against all the copying and the paraphrasing? Against the required professional detachment, the method, the objectivity, against the constant need to provide references, to find quotations? "Problem reception, my foot," Sommerhalder once said. "Digging up old bones and shovelling them into new graves, that's what I call it." Private scribbling in resistance to terminological hair-splitting, to index-card fingers, and to calloused bums on wooden stools and plastic seats in catalogue rooms and reading rooms? Scrawling one's daily irritation onto the little cards as though it was a Durkheim quotation. It wasn't efficient – at least not against the calluses. Going on walks in the Bois de Vincennes would have worked better.

Was it my own idea? I'm afraid that here too it was Anderegg who put me onto it – in one of his private lectures on the stream of consciousness, free association, language and imitation. Or was it on imitation, play and day-dreaming? Anderegg's digressions! Hardly anything of my own, nearly everything taken from others. May as well admit from the start that it's filched, even if you're not sure exactly where from.

"It's still the best way to relax," Anderegg lectured. "You simply sit down for half an hour in the middle of the day and write down all the things that came into your mind in the last two or three minutes: what you saw, what you heard – and especially, of course, what you thought. You'll be surprised at what goes on in those few short moments while you're there yet far away, half away at any rate. After all, don't we know ever since Freud what an extravagant ragbag of thoughts a serious man busies himself with, en passant, day in, day out. Catch as catch can, it's an occasional pastime I wouldn't want to miss. Why use yoga, Zen or other spiritual exercises to empty your head and make room for the sublime and the profound when all the time, inside that very same head, there are so many curious things awaiting discovery."

Sommerhalder listened with interest. "Live reports from inside one's own skull. Fine, I might try it some time. Thanks for the tip. Although I can already see what'll come from the likes of us: the clucking of a petit-bourgeois hen laying her eggs."

"Quite likely," said Anderegg. "Cartesian meditations will no doubt be the exception."

Whatever you say, you stole it.

We ate onion soup in the kitchen at the Andereggs'. Anderegg loved cooking soup and giving lectures. Was it rue Berthe, or already rue Gaillard in Vincennes? It must still have been rue Berthe.

Glimmer of sweat on the sex-flush patterned skin of her neck; cornflower blue bra and star-spangled stockings, boots, solid ones, more suitable for country lanes than for the Champs-Elysées, and panties that didn't match anything else – why should they? – and specks of dust whirling around in the beam of sunlight, the wail of sirens up from rue Linné – and the frankness between us once we were finally lying beside each other on the bed, for if you let someone take off your clothes you also open up your inner life to their gaze, the closeness was poignant – or am I just trying in retrospect to put a rather more refined spin on vulgar lust?

As recorded on the index card, thesis had to submit to antithesis, or at least to contradiction.

Man, the ever-ready being, ready for active help, ready for a dissolute life, deregulated, freed from instinct and yet driven.

That can only have been Dorothea's influence; so it should be dated somewhere near the end of my time in

Paris. The thing itself and all the minor matters. Snatch whatever has just flashed by – and away with it, behind lock and key. It needn't be the splendidly gloomy 'hell' section of the Bibliothèque Nationale. The closet up in the north room of the attic will do: next to the army clothes, the assault rifle, the two pairs of shoes; no one will ever look for it there!

All those things painstakingly sorted and filed away in a card index? Better not. Admittedly, once, three or four years ago – wasn't it also in July, or the beginning of August? – I did, in a fit of I don't quite know what, have a go at arranging the notes more or less chronologically, which might have resulted in a kind of journal of trifling matters: quiet days between rue Monge and rue Linné. I didn't get very far. Since, in order to arrange them, I had to read all my notes, at least fleetingly, I soon discovered, after due consideration of what I'd read, that such a venture was rather childish or at least juvenile. The thought of all those pubescent diaries that had been collected by psychologists researching epochal typical adolescent inwardness embarrassed me. After all, the man responsible for those scribblings had been over thirty at the time; a sociologist, a university graduate, not an eighteen-year-old gawk; a husband, an experienced market-researcher, a pater familias, a Swiss National Science Foundation scholar. It was not without a strange feeling of anguish that I read what the man had noted in those distant, ever more distant, days: on large-squared paper, *feuillets mobiles* (17x22 cm); on pages torn from 9x14 cm notebooks; on different size cards; on the backs

44

of book order forms – he particularly seemed to have liked those from the Bibliothèque Sainte-Geneviève. Platitudes, platitudes. But on the other hand, that was the intention: I'd only noted down odds and ends, the things that kept my mind off the main thing, off what was important. As I read I told myself that I wasn't concerned with flights of fancy at the time, only with work method. And yet: at a second reading the psychohygienic aspect was unmistakable.

As if I'd secretly hoped that Thoreau's daily jottings had been the model! Vanity, thy name is man!

Principal matters, minor matters. What I was working on at the time was a principal matter, no doubt about that, the Confederacy was spending money on it. And something that was generally recognised as being so important should have absorbed my full attention, sustained my zeal, yes even aroused a passion for work. Up to a certain point that's what it did: although it was a modest project, I did want to carry it out with some distinction.

What I do here in Wangen day after day, dutifully, diligently, is neither particularly important nor very interesting. So that I've already caught myself wondering what's more interesting, the work I have to concentrate on – after all I get paid for it – or all those little things all around me that I'm distracted by: the giggling in the entrance hall, the overheard snatches of conversation, or the bits and pieces of town gossip peddled by my workmate Mrs Kupferschmied. And also the freshest morsels of knowledge the periodicals bait me with, from Archives for Egyptian Archaeology to Zoology,

Swiss Journal of. Or else that most private, distant past, Annemarie Erica Elizabeth Cecilia et cetera. Or then again snapshots of the fashion show staged by our young readers on an invisible catwalk extending from the entrance to the reading room. This summer, shorts are short, as they should be, with a slit on the side up to the hip-bone, meant to make the legs look longer, a classical optical illusion!

No, it's not at all true that readers can't be pretty. On the contrary, library users have their own kind of attractiveness. Which doesn't in any way keep you from doing your work – the more charming a person the more scrupulously she is attended to.

2

'This is the pubalic liberry, Ulysses.

Books all over the place.'

Farewell, Paris and scholarship! Farewell ambition – in case I ever had any. As it is, on coming here to Wangen, my slogan was: The New Modesty. In the meantime I've come to the conclusion that it was nothing but the old timidity. I haven't got the guts to be self-seeking.

Here in the library I am wholly dedicated to the common good, as an assistant I assist research by providing researchers with the books they need. Of course they're mostly only future researchers, or to be more precise, potential future researchers – for who can tell what will become of students in their middle or final semesters who come home to their parents in Wangen in the holidays so that they can work undisturbed on their seminar, licentiate or diploma papers, or prepare for exams in the peace of the provincial reading room?

Admittedly, most of them are studying law – whether that counts as a science or not is another matter. This summer, too, there were seven or eight half-fledged lawyers sitting amid piles of books, battling their way through articles, sections, paragraphs, all exam panic elation and iron-willed staying power. Among them two girls, blonde beside brown.

Our library is only small, but the interlibrary loan service partly makes up for our inadequacy. Whoever comes to me at the loan desk gets any (or at least almost any) book they want within two weeks at the most. Before I started working here, the domestic and international interlibrary loan service only existed on paper in Wangen. I was the one who got the service going. It takes up about a third of my working time, and that in itself goes halfway towards justifying me; there are not many libraries of our size that offer such a service. And it's a much-used service, as is proven by the rising numbers in the statistics compiled annually for the Municipal Library Committee.

Take for example the people from around Wangen who lecture at universities and institutes in Basel, Fribourg, Bern, Zurich, impassioned teachers committed lock stock and barrel to science, as regularly appointed professors or private lecturers: there are at least a dozen of them in Wangen and the neighbouring villages. And of course they're glad to use a library which is so conveniently near, often they urgently need something out-of-the-way, and therein lies my work.

47

Last summer I supplied the lecturer in German studies, Dr Flück, with more than thirty titles on the subject of 'Kafka and Women'. She teaches in Zurich but lives up in Erzelen, i.e. far out in the country.

For the comparatist, Dr Born, I ordered masses of articles from France and Germany: 'The Role of Munificence as the Mainspring and Meaning-giver of Human Existence in 17th Century Courtly Literature' was the title of his course of lectures at the University of Bern the following autumn. The man is also a French teacher at the local Gymnasium, and Lydia says he's said to be not at all bad.

There was a young woman – she often used to come when she was still at the Gymnasium, a Sinclair Lewis reader, I notice things like that – for whom I intermittently ordered things relating to her licentiate paper on, as she confided to me, 'the postmodern representation of foreignness'.

Word has got round that you can get anything you need here, and that there's someone here who can always help you, even if the bibliography you've prepared is flawed. The up-and-coming academics occasionally confuse Sinclair Lewis with Upton Sinclair and the latter with Updike; but perhaps Rabbit and Babbitt – with or without Sinclair – really do have something to do with each other. And recently one of those post-adolescents, who was interested in history, typed 'Warren' into the computer and was quite baffled when, instead of the report on the assassination of John F Kennedy, three novels by a certain 'Warren, Robert Penn' appeared on the monitor, even in duplicate, in American and German – mea culpa:

at the time I'd managed to get a secondhand copy of the German translation. I finally got the young woman the Warren Report via the interlibrary loan service.

Librarians are pernickety. Is that the new humility? Would I at that tender age have spontaneously been able to keep Lévy-Bruhl and Lévi-Strauss apart? Not to mention Malraux, Maurois, Mauriac, or Nohl and Hohl, Broch and Bloch? Only, confusing Andersen, the one with the fairy tales, and Anderson, the American, that's something that wouldn't have happened to me even then. It's quite likely that, sometime soon, someone will come expecting to find a Swiss Federal Councillor under the keyword 'Dreyfus affair'.

3
Chengde

"And how's Eva getting on in the Engadin?" she asked.

"She goes on long walks and our little girl plays the cello."

"Still?"

"More than ever."

"Surely you don't object?"

"Of course not – I'm proud, a talented daughter. People in Eva's family all played an instrument. But Bach suites for hours on end, day after day, that's pushing it a bit!"

"Bach? How marvellous, really, at that age! My son only plays football – though he's very keen too. I don't know where he gets it from."

My colleague Verena Kupferschmied; from the

49

'Books for Young People and Children' department; lively and nimble-witted; and extraordinarily tough when it came to getting her department extended. When I first arrived in Wangen she was in charge of the cataloguing. She grew up here and knows half the town; she also knew Eva from before. They've just recently started going jogging together once a week, down along the Aare, past the allotments, and across the river into the woods.

"When will Eva be back?"

"In a fortnight – unless anything unexpected happens?"

"And what would that be?"

"Nothing of course, you're right."

In a moment we'd go our separate ways, Verena into the cool of the old building, I to the lending desk out in front.

"By the way, Eva got another letter from China yesterday." What on earth made me tell her that? Why should the correspondence between Eva and that Isabelle interest Verena Kupferschmied?

"Oh, the Canadian. Shouldn't she have got back a long time ago?"

"She's staying on another year, goodness knows why."

Relaxed conversation: about the heat the past few days in Wangen in general, about the heat today and here in the new wing of the library in particular; about Eva and our daughter in the Engadin, and finally about the letters from China. We didn't really have much to say to each other, but it was nice to stop for five minutes in the entrance hall and chat, thus assuring and being assured that we liked each other. My favourite colleague! And she, for her part, seemed at the time to appreciate the way I'd initiated her into the mysteries of the computer, and also that while so doing I'd hardly ever lost patience. With Eva I'd have lost patience right away – sensible of her to have learnt by herself. We're too close. A dozen chances a day to get on each other's nerves.

The letter from China had arrived on the fourteenth of July. I remember the date because that day I happened to come upon the Paris military parade on France 2; the show was still on when the telephone rang. It was Eva. I informed her about everything the postman had brought since her departure.

That's what we always do, I only forward what's urgent or particularly interesting; so I have to read or at least scan through everything. And if for once I'm the one who's away, Eva does the same for me. Brazen, I know, but that's marriage.

And what was in the letter?

Chengde was a place Eva absolutely had to visit if she finally decided to come to China. The best way to get there was from Beijing, it was only a couple of hours by train, it was really worth it. One of the Qing emperors had built his summer residence there, with audience chambers, palaces, pagodas, pavilions for diplomats and concubines, the lot. And he'd also had all kinds of different landscapes artificially created, complete with rockeries and lakes. And surrounding it all a Great Wall ten kilometres long. It was a miniature Middle Kingdom, a Manchurian Disneyland dating from the third century before Hollywood. Needless to say, there was also an imperial library there.

The letter was addressed to Eva, no best wishes to me. But what made her mention the library? And she was quite emphatic about it too.

Baedeker's, Merian Travel Guides, Polyglott Travel Guides: here you can take your choice. I looked it up and found something.

The building looks, I read, as if it had only two floors, but in fact there are three, of which the middle one – the actual depository – can only be seen from inside. No direct sunlight ever reaches this room, yet daylight floods in from above, from the third floor; the ventilation is also said to be good so that the room is ideal for storing books. In ancient documents the town is called by its Manchurian name 'Jehol' which is said to mean 'mountain villa for avoiding the heat'.

How nice it would be to be there now, I thought.

Compared to the imperial library in Chengde-Jehol, the building here was a joke: the open access library with its glass façade facing south, the entrance hall with floor-to-ceiling windows facing south-west and south-east, the reading room, too, fully exposed to the afternoon sun. The extension built by the people of Wangen wasn't a library, it was a greenhouse. Tomatoes would ripen here earlier than in Spain. Why haven't we long since set up hydroponic lemon trees in the entrance hall? We could include them in the next budget under the heading 'remediation, micro-climatic'.

4

Foot bath – Adult education college – Firewalking

Now it was even hot in the flat. Sitting at the kitchen table late at night taking a foot bath in a plastic basin of cold water. Lights off, both windows open. Unusual silence inside the house. And outside, the familiar summer night sounds drifting over from Post Office Square. Last buses, mopeds, laughter, a car honks, the sound of drumming on metal. It was extraordinarily nice to have the flat to myself for a couple of days.

Isabelle Jurt, née Wescott; Canadian by birth, married to a Swiss, divorced for some years now; teacher at the Gymnasium: English and French. Eva, who was always on the look-out for people who could teach at our local adult education college, also asked Mrs Jurt. That's how the two got to know each other. There were never any problems, Mrs Jurt was said to be a good teacher. And when one day she decided to start learning Chinese Eva joined her.

"Why Chinese?" I asked.

"Why not?" she retorted.

At least Frau Jurt had a purpose. She wanted to get out of Wangen for a year.

Why did it have to be China, I asked. "I don't really know," said Eva. "Why don't you ask her yourself?"

Not even Eva could manage to organise a beginners' course at our college here. Firstly there were no more than two people who were definitely interested, and secondly she couldn't have found a teacher.

And hadn't tanks rolled across Tiananmen Square

the previous summer when the young people there were trying to catch up on May '68? After that, who'd want to have anything to do with those Chinese? In any case, Swissair flights to Beijing were running at a loss. And although kung fu, spring rolls, acupuncture and soy sauce were still to be found in plenty in the Wangen area, in order to learn Chinese the two women – they were almost friends by now – had to go to either Basel, Bern or Zurich.

For one winter they went to Bern every other week. Then Eva heard from a friend in Zurich that the course at the adult education college there was much better. Isabelle wanted to get ahead faster now, as she already had the offer of a job teaching English at a provincial university somewhere in the depths of what used to be known as Manchukuo. She wanted to be able to talk to the people there not only in English but also in Chinese – at least a little – as soon as she took up her job.

"When Isabelle does something, she does it properly," said Eva. And she kept up with her, went to Zurich with her every week, bought cassettes with shrill-sounding dialogues, practised writing characters, read all kinds of interesting things about Ming, Mao, the Long March and the Great Wall, about the Gang of Four and the Four Reforms; and occasionally she went to the cinema with Isabelle after the course. And the start of Isabelle's job was delayed for another year; the central administration in Beijing worked with exquisite slowness. But that didn't matter because the two friends' progress in Chinese was also very slow: not abacadabra, more like one step at a time.

But then, towards the end of summer – almost two years after the first Chinese word – the moment arrived: Mrs Jurt flew off. Three weeks later we received a postcard from a city whose widest avenue was still called Stalin Street – the Chinese practise ancestor worship. And after another few weeks we received the first letter describing life and work in that town. Mrs Jurt seemed to like it there.

The letters with their remarkable postage stamps – dragons, teapots, Terracotta Army soldiers – arrived at long intervals, but regularly; every two months, the most recent news from Changchun, Jilin Province. And Eva wrote back every two months with little news items from Wangen.

Eva is not the woman to discover her true self in a psychodrama workshop on 'Goddesses in Everywoman'. She has no desire to engage in body-centered awareness work. She makes fun of postural integration, biodynamics, human holographics, Bach flower therapy and rebirthing, matriarchy-focused dream interpretation. Despite all the touting in the small ads Eva does not seek fulfilment, either at an 'earthy, fiery, versatile' weekend in the Calanca Valley, or at a 'creative Lucullan' course in Tuscany. She wants to learn Chinese, the language, not Chinese meditation, neither taijiquan nor qigong energy flow or any other Western adaptation of Eastern shadow boxing. Simply words, sentences. "We'll be the only ones here in Wangen to know Chinese, Isabelle a lot, I a little. Perhaps it'll come in useful one day."

An active rationalist. I've always been lucky with

women. How could I have lived with an Eva who pursued a sideline in astrology!

It had always been clear that she'd be going to China too – not for longer than two or three weeks of course – if only to see if what she'd learned could stand the test of tourism. Eva has always liked travelling. I, on the other hand, prefer to stay in Wangen. A few days in Paris every year, usually in the autumn, is enough for me.

5

Textiles – Satie – Skyscrapers in Chicago – Jazz in Willisau – Cabbage under coconut trees – Fields of clover

… and the navy-blue, white-dotted summer dress; her face, her arms, her legs brown. Constantly in motion, even when seated: first she rested a foot on the stool beside her, next she crossed her legs, then stretched them out in front of her alongside the second stool that served as a table; she spread them a little wider, then crossed them again; and then she stretched herself, rose and took three paces towards the balcony door, before returning and dropping back into the armchair. At times her skirt slid up to a hand's breadth above her knees – she instantly smoothed it down again; then she let it hang loosely between her lap and her thighs; the white-dotted material tautened across her back, bulged out sideways over the chair arms. I didn't look the other way, I didn't specially look, but as I stared at her face, her talking face, I took it all in en passant. You couldn't help noticing. What a bubbly thing, I thought, and so young, so young! Short hair, large mouth, bright red lipstick, her grey eyes disconcertingly still. And her hands too remained remarkably still.

Not an old scrap from my Paris days: the scribblings were still quite recent. Yvonne in her studio between the railway station and the River Aare, textile design.

So it must have been that summer with Chengde et cetera, for up to then I'd only known her as a library user. A woman who read a lot – regularly at long intervals. Our town is small, everyone knows each other.

Whenever there aren't many people in the cinema and the closing credits are running and the lights go on, it's almost impolite not to greet the person who's been sitting in the row behind you and whom you half-know. I nodded a greeting. Nice film, she'd already seen it and hadn't wanted to miss the rerun.

A little later we were standing in Stalden Square in front of the City and the City was closed, and round about all you saw was 'Closing day' or 'Closed for the holidays'.

Did I want to come along to her studio for a drink? The invitation took me by surprise.

She asked me why I wasn't away on holiday. I explained the library's holiday attendance schedule. My wife was used to going away alone with the children. And besides, my elder daughter had got to the age where she wanted to travel around Europe by herself and as she chose.

"Where did you say she was at the moment? Oh, France, marvellous, the south, Provence and all that – but now? At the end of July? Absolutely ghastly! I did it once, years ago, and I swore: Never again! It's a miracle a few hundred people don't get trampled to death every day. Not that I mind lying on the beach, on the contrary. But not in the season thank you. Last May it was the Camargue; a quick decision, as always in such cases: after I've handed in a pile of drawings and I'm completely knackered – off I go! – to lie on the beach at Les Saintes-Maries, reading. Reading's what I do when I'm not doing anything. I got through three fat books, didn't manage to finish the fourth, unfortunately – it's lying around here somewhere, it's a pity, I'd have liked it. But something else came up, I'm like a hen, I pick something up, give it a peck, run on to the next thing – yet that book I started on my last day would have been enthralling, I often had to laugh out loud, and that's always a good sign, getting absorbed by some outlandish story as though you were at the cinema, forgetting everything around you, the people, the weather, mealtimes …"

Did I want to listen to some music? She'd bought a CD last Saturday that she liked a lot. Satie, did I know him?

The wine was good. But even if it hadn't been very good I'd have praised it. I wondered why she'd invited me – the question irritated me. They said she was very successful as a textile designer, that she worked like mad. Besides that I hardly knew anything about her. We'd never talked longer than two minutes, a couple of sentences when she came to the library, a couple of sentences across a table in the pub. Whenever I saw her she was with the same man, a handsome fellow who could sit there for a whole hour without saying a word.

So she talked all the more.

She poured wine, shoved another CD into the player. Satie had been pleasant, now it was time for jazz.

"… Crazy, isn't it? Anyone who plays the sax like that must practise an awful lot, hours and hours every day, I should say, just for his technique, to keep up to scratch. Listen to that – there – and now – quite stunning isn't it? The drive, the energy! I go to the Willisau Jazz Festival every year, never miss it, it's usually fantastic you know. You see someone there on the stage, he looks like a butcher, and then he draws out such tunes from his bass! It really has to be experienced to be believed. Those musicians are practically married to their instruments, you see it immediately, they're in complete control of their instruments, even the way they hold them in their arms, fascinating …"

I've only ever been to Willisau once, for two hours just after midnight, during manoeuvres at an army refresher course.

Why did she talk so much? Now the topic was a couple who'd recently invited her to a meal: supper followed by a slide show.

"… we spent at least three hours watching those slides, mainly skyscrapers in Chicago – he has to fly there on business two or three times a year. Whenever he can arrange it he takes his wife along. Not only to Chicago, by the way, he takes her along to Hong Kong, Singapore, Boston or Tel Aviv too – it's one way of taking a holiday isn't it? He finds a cheaper flight than the one his company pays for, and the price difference goes to pay for his wife's ticket, partly at least. Clever isn't it? And then they take photos: skyscrapers, and skyscrapers mirrored in the façades of skyscrapers, and street canyons, real canyons cutting through skyscraper landscapes – and motorways, motorway bridges, motorway interchanges, motorway loops – and squares, then skyscrapers again, and squares again. And never a human being, or hardly ever, at most a tiny individual or a small group of people far away in the background or out of focus in the very front edge. And do you know how they do it? – You'd better not ask me why they do it! – They get up before dawn and go out with their cameras, always the two of them together; the only time cities are empty of people is very early in the morning. They always set out with two cameras, but they photograph exactly the same things with each camera so that if anything goes wrong they'll still have a decent picture on one of the films at least. They never take people, as I said. By the time people have come out on the streets the two of them are already back in their hotel fortifying themselves with coke, coffee and cornflakes. Nothing but architecture and nature – only a tiny bit of nature. Some people are strange, aren't they? …"

I assented.

Wine, Satie, jazz, before and after midnight, and talk, talk, talk. A dozen years ago the situation would have been clearly ambiguous. And now? What did it mean? That too, probably. Yes that too!

But she went on talking regardless.

"… as for me, I take photographs too of course, when I'm on holiday and abroad, but without their sense of purpose; actually I only do it to please my father. My father's diabetic, you know, so he doesn't dare go abroad any more; that might seem unreasonable, after all there are doctors everywhere and he's got the thing well under control, and yet he simply doesn't feel comfortable about it, and so he told me that, since he didn't have the gumption to travel all over the world himself, I might at least bring him some pictures of my journeys so that he could see what it was like in the places I'd been to. My father's old-fashioned. He likes leafing through photo albums. So why not afford him the pleasure? I start taking lots of pictures as soon as I'm away, and then of course I have copies made for myself too, but to tell you the truth I hardly look at them. At least I don't stick them into an album, I'm not that type of person, I stick them in an old envelope and shove the envelope in between my books and forget all about it. It's a pure fluke if I ever come across it again. Would you like to see where I went last year? Quite exclusive: the Seychelles. It's the first time I've been able to afford a holiday so far away. Actually, it wasn't really that expensive, one of those off-season special offers; they just have to have a minimum number of tourists so that they can keep the hotels open. Our little town here's all very well, we have everything we need, it's perfectly okay, but at least once a year you want to see something different instead of the usual faces, the Aare and the mountain …"

She'd already risen and gone over to the bookshelves where she started ferreting among the books, talking all the time, looking back over her shoulder. "Ah, here we are!" She came back holding an envelope. "Do you really want to see them? Honestly, you don't have to."

"Don't make me ask," I said. "Show me."

"There, palm trees," she said, "the white beach, coral sand, that's why the colours are so unfamiliar. And there, under the palm trees, look closely, here you can see it close up: cabbage, planted in a neat circle around the palm trees, you freak out the first time you see that: cabbage beneath palm trees! Everything grows perfectly there, any amount of vegetables, sweet potatoes, lettuce. The only thing they have to import is rice. I had the beach more or less to myself, five minutes from the hotel, just a stroll through the palm grove, I usually spent the whole day lying on the beach, reading."

"Ah, that's why you're so brown."

"No it isn't," she said. "That was last year, not this year. This year, as I've already told you, I only went to the Camargue, Les Saintes-Maries, hardly a week, in the middle of May. And by the way, the title of the book I started reading on my last day there and that I enjoyed so much is *Bluebeard*. Do you know it? Of course you must, you're a librarian."

I only knew what was in the blurb, I countered.

She didn't believe me. Should I – without waiting to be asked – have recommended *Hocus Pocus, Breakfast for Champions* or *Slaughterhouse 5*? I hesitated. She, however, had no scruples and commended Michener's *Texas* – or was it *Caribbean*? – some thick book anyway for her slender woman's hands on the beach. For several months the book had ranged between eighth and third on the *Spiegel* bestseller list.

The most popular books of the year – indeed, we have those too; we buy them judiciously to provide high-quality entertainment for appreciative people of all ages, the authors Aitmatov to Zeindler, the publishers Haffmans to Heyne. After all, Cooper's novels about Indians also got to be bestsellers back in the year dot thanks to his publisher Sauerländer.

"May I?" I bent down over Yvonne's work-table which was covered with drawing-paper, drafts. "I'm just making a new start," she said. "I don't know yet if anything will come of it. Probably they'll think it's too gaudy."

"What about that?" I asked, pointing to a cardboard folder at the other end of the table.

"If you're interested …"

A3-format pages, each one filled to the edge, the colours flowing into each other; at first glance I thought they were flower patterns. But when I inspected the pages more closely I discovered a dense profusion of tiny figures: mythical creatures on one page, geometrical designs on another, and on a third all kinds of plants, then again writing, calligraphy – and on several pages a strangely natural-looking combination of the lot.

"Scrap," she said. "Things that the two companies I work for can't use for their textiles. I don't even bother to send them things like that any more; I know what kind of things they'll take, I don't want to make a fool of myself."

I asked if she had any more I could see.

She jerked her head towards the cupboard. "There's a whole lot in there. I don't know why I keep all that stuff. But of course I'd like to see people walk around in clothes like that. Now I'm going to make myself a cup of coffee, espresso. Do you want a cup too?"

It was a pity that Eva wasn't at home. On my return, some time after midnight, I'd have had something to tell her. She likes that: being woken up and hearing the news.

Yvonne? Oh, her! A textile designer? Where do you train for that? And why did she land up in Wangen, after Zürich and Munich? Oh, a love story. And she told you all that? And I'd have added that I'd always known that she talked a lot, but that I'd been astonished that she talked that much. And all those cardboard folders, piles of them, with the sketches inside, scrap she'd said. She was as good as any of the most painstaking Appenzell Bauernmalerei artists. Fields of clover, heather, menageries, Bosch and Breughel and Grimm's Fairy Tales in miniature. You could paper our art museum with it. And the way she seemed to get lost in all the details – but systematically, on A3 pages crammed to the edges …

Now that I know that over there between the station and the Aare, at a long table overlooking Rüti Bridge, there's someone busy drawing, I eye the material of the blouses in the library more closely. Just in case those goblins and elves, strawberry-red and lime-green, might after all be having a picnic on one of the backs bent over the card index drawers.

What I saw again and again, and even long after Eva had returned, was the flash of a dark-blue white-dotted skirt swinging in from the entrance. Freely quoting Malamud: I didn't need to close my eyes to see it.

6

Quiet days in Wangen – View from the bridge – Buying books – Pigeons – Hands – Journeys in the mind, et cetera

But Eva wouldn't be back for a long time yet. No Marie-Jeanne playing the cello up in the attic room, no Lydia down in the kitchen holding forth on organic vegetables and Tolstoy and techno.

I was still alone in the flat, free to take a footbath in the kitchen without being disturbed, free to watch old films until two in the morning. While the others are away on holiday I take a holiday from the family.

At night there was no one in the house besides me and Mrs Zwigart. Mrs Zwigart often watched television with the window open. The noise of traffic up from the ring road and across from the Postplatz didn't disturb her: she was deaf in one ear, half deaf in the other. She was getting on for eighty, still enjoyed life, but was very forgetful. On several occasions Eva had had to rush downstairs, alarmed by the smell of burning: Mrs Zwigart had a habit of putting the meals-on-wheels dish to heat on the lowest flame, then sitting down in front of the TV and completely forgetting her hunger and what was in the kitchen. It was soothing to hear her pottering around her flat.

How nice to know you're being useful: looking after books, library users, and old women.

How the days go by – I don't even dare set an exclamation mark any more. Something happens, and then something else, nothing important, I hardly notice. Standing on Rüti Bridge I look down along the Aare. Natty Bumppo and the Mohicans: there they are paddling against the stream beneath the overhanging boughs of ash, past the allotments, past the concrete building of the municipal pumping station …

On Thursday, my day off, I went to Zurich. Searched through the antique bookstores in the Niederdorf for German translations of American novels, and found

Sinclair Lewis' *Anne Vickers*, published in 1933 by Rowohlt; I also happened to find *The Hills Beyond* by Thomas Wolfe, a touching sample from the early days of paperback.

Folklorists are old fogeys, quite harmless; collectors, backward-looking nostalgics, in keeping with the Wangen mentality: it's always been that way; that's the way it's always been; that's always been the way it's been.

Apparently there used to be a fountain in the middle of the square – a pity I never saw its feathery plume sheeting out to rainbow iridescence. What you now see, instead, is the alternating play of red and green lights at five different spots. Eva was right to plump for triple glazing when we did our renovation; soon afterwards the underground carpark was built, on four floors the size of the square. What remains is the pigeon plague: overfed and brazen, flocks of them near the benches at the two bus stops. And on Saturday evenings the second generation of Gastarbeiter race around the square on their mopeds. Another good reason for triple glazing! City pigeons and foreign workers? Thinking with your gut instead of using your head: spontaneity can be terrible. Incidentally, Marie-Jeanne makes just as much noise with her cello; young people are, above all, a noise problem.

They scratch their throats, their necks, their sides. They toy with their hair. They prop their chins on the backs of their hands, fingers clasped, both elbows spread on the table. They fiddle with the beer mats or their cigarette lighters. They stare straight across the room. They laugh, nod, talk, insist, lean forward, turn back to those sitting next to them. They put up a hand, they wave something aside. Ash blonde beside henna red, curly beside straight, pageboy bob beside feather cut beside braids. They cling to their cigarettes. Or their glasses ...

Six hours of sleep, no more, she said, blowing smoke out through her nose and her mouth. Otherwise, you know, she said, I get too deep into my subconscious. He admitted that he slept much longer, eight hours at least. That's unhealthy for sure, she said. If I happen to sleep that long I feel shattered the next day. The healthiest thing would be to do the same as cats: they sleep in snatches throughout the day, never more than an hour at a time, it's a proven fact.

... town on the River Aare, town at the foot of the mountain: intrigues, careers, cliques – everything so pleasant, so straightforward, at least that's what you'd think. And yet I only see a small part of it, and hardly see through anything. What I know, I learned from Eva or Mrs Kupferschmied. Even Ursula Odermatt, the boss's wife, usually knows more than I do – and she's a stranger here too, only moved here three years before me. A sociologist's eye? You make me laugh! If something's not in a book – with footnotes please – I simply don't see it.

Down in the hall, near the stairs to the stack room, you chat with your colleague about your daughter who plays Bach. And at the same time your elder daughter and her gangly friend are sitting beneath the plane trees eating ice cream, and the next moment you yourself are lying on the banks of the Rhone near Avignon, and you see the dishes piled up in the kitchen of the youth hostel – Avignon or Sète? – and the voices you heard in the entrance hall of the Sainte-Geneviève library in Paris mingle with the

67

sounds in the hall of the library here. 'It avails not, time nor place – distance avails not.' The way things were, how they might have been, the way things are, the way they'd be if … Whatever flits by: recorded. A modest vice, a minor foible.

Eva's sure to be going. She flew to Africa on her own, she flew to India on her own; the year before last, she took Lydia and Marie-Jeanne to Iceland. As for me, I haven't even been to America. But Altamont, Concord, Brewer, Zenith and Yoknapatawna County around Jefferson are close at hand: all I need do is delve into the bookshelves. If I were to take the plane and go there with Eva it might damage my inner picture of the region. Or Brooklyn, the tree in the back yard, the girl Francie on the fire escape; the ferry. No doubt, as soon as Eva's back from the Engadin she'll book a flight, Swissair, Lufthansa, China Air; autumn in Changchun. Or go there on the Trans-Siberian, ten days by train. That'd be okay for me too, sedentary person that I am.

Ah, Annemarie! Bosoms, tiny, see Cecilia; Chengde, Chinese, College of adult education, Compulsive repetition, Cooper's heroes, the Cowper's glands; Dorothea; Erica; F for Fall for, Fasting, Footbath; Holiday photos; I for Ithaka or Isabelle or Index of trifling matters; Jazz, see Willisau …

It's easy to think up things like that; a silly game on the short way down from the computer at the lending desk to the time clock next to the cloakrooms.

Marianne cf. Annemarie; Numerus currens, from Nowhere to nothing; Orderliness is the key to science; Pop and Paris and a Petit-bourgeois (that's a living contradiction); R for Rubbish,

68

Rule and measure; S for Sex life lite, willing Stopgap; Thot, with the head of an ibis or a baboon; Unique copy; Videoclip; Wangen, Winesburg; Yvonne's field of clover, Youth …

File it or tear it all up?

Throwing away the whole pile of scribblings would be a true act of humility.

III

Paris lectures

'You shall no longer take things
at second or third hand, nor
look through the eyes of the
dead, nor feed on the spectres in
books ...'

Walt Whitman, *Leaves of Grass*

1

How I came upon the Tibetans

Why did I choose the Tibetans? Because I knew two at school and used to give one of them private tuition.

When, in 1961, the first large batch of Tibetans were settled in Switzerland, it was the mountainous cantons that were favoured, among them Appenzell Ausserrhoden and Appenzell Innerrhoden.

I was fascinated by the immigrants from the distant highlands. Previously I'd been interested in Indians and Blacks – thanks to James Fenimore Cooper and *Uncle Tom's Cabin* – now my interest was focused on the Dalai Lama, Lhasa, reincarnation, and the Chinese. It was the Tibetans in Appenzell who gave me the idea of studying ethnology.

What else could have given a factory carpenter's son in Gonten, Appenzell Innerrhoden, such an idea? If you choose an unremunerative profession you may as well choose one that's wholly unremunerative. That's something my brother, a car mechanic at the time, the owner of a garage now, has never been able to understand.

The private lessons at least earned me pocket money; my little café au lait stranger's foster parents paid me well. He learned German eagerly. However, I didn't learn anything much from him about the barren highlands in

China's Wild West. And the library in Appenzell wasn't much help either. There was nothing available on the subject besides Hedin and Harrer.

At that time you still couldn't do ethnology at Zurich University. You could do folklore studies, but only as a subsidiary subject. And since a new professor had just been elected for sociology I chose sociology, although I hardly knew what it was. Which explains my subsequent astonishment.

Sociology plus folklore studies plus psychology divided by three: didn't that result in something like ethnology? In fact I only took psychology as my second subsidiary subject; I've never really trusted the thing.

As an Appenzeller in Zurich I was singularly aware of the Tibetans in Appenzell; during the whole of my first year as a student I felt a bit like a Tibetan myself.

My father had barely been able to afford to send his child to the Gymnasium; with only his carpenter's wages he couldn't possibly pay for a university education. That had always been perfectly clear. So I worked nights at the Sihl post office, five nights a week during the whole of the holidays and the occasional week during term time. Those nights suited me. I'd never thought of asking for a grant from my canton. Why on earth should Appenzell Innerrhoden finance a degree course in sociology!

It was only in the second half of my third semester – you remember a thing like that – after I'd attracted attention with a paper on Schelsky's *Skeptische Generation,* that I applied for a grant. For in the course of the brief tête-à-tête following my presentation, the professor asked me about myself and I had to mention my father's profession and my night work at the post office. The professor gave me a letter to attach to my application. It worked. The following year I received two thousand francs. The people of Central Switzerland are renowned for their thrift. It was perfectly in order to make no exceptions for a sociology student, even if his subsidiary subject was folklore studies.

That, incidentally, was a subject I sorely neglected – my first subsidiary subject continued to be my work. Not at the Sihl post office any more: I now had a job as an interviewer for surveys. The work was less arduous and the pay better.

Schelsky's *Skeptische Generation* had another effect.

Up to then I'd been regarded by sociology students as a folklorist, consequently not to be taken seriously. On the other hand, as a sociologist I remained an outsider among the folklorists; besides, I'd never concealed the fact that Hopi Indians interested me more than local history museums. But now that a titular professor had graced my presentation with a couple of laudatory remarks, the sociology students, at least, accepted me as one of them – more specifically, I was introduced and adopted as a man capable of writing stylish German.

Students came to me for advice on how to polish up their papers. I was a willing assistant. The sentences I helped formulate were considered elegant without being flashy. I systematically consulted all the Duden dictionaries: the sentences should be reasonably correct at the least.

That was during the peaceful period with Erica. Ah, Annemarie …

And so I grew to feel at home in Zurich.

I'd worked on that Schelsky for four months, yet ultimately it was no more than a summary of the most important theses of the book, each supplemented by a couple of lines of critical commentary. I'd polished the thing until it shone. It would have been humiliating if my paper hadn't attracted attention.

The short stocky professor with his peasant's head and his peasant's hands. He was conservative, as befitted a sociology professor in Switzerland, even long after 1968. Thanks to that kindly man – I hardly knew him – I might almost have become an egghead on Tibet issues, an authority in the field of multicultural socialisation, an expert on youth matters.

Oh, I was lucky.

Meanwhile, quite a few of those who were at university with me have become precisely such eggheads, experts and authorities – with the result that there's hardly anything left over for the next three generations of students. Emmenegger advises high performance sports clubs in Magglingen; Plüss is introducing feminism into the Federal Military Department; Nora-Maria has made his name in the field of sociology of the household: Kudrun has been doing research on nationalism for the past fifteen years in Geneva; Bernstein – as I heard by chance – works as an executive for a company leasing surveillance systems to major chainstores like Manor and Migros; Tania has been recruited as an assistant manager at the Federal Bureau of Statistics; Thomas is a marketing strategist for the Ringier media company. Who says sociologists are useless? They are eminently employable, by the Swiss automobile clubs no less than by the Central Office for Refugee Issues.

I progressed tolerably well with my studies, one seminar paper per semester. And when I got to the stage where I needed to find a topic for my dissertation, the Tibetans in Appenzell once again came to mind. And since I'd attracted the professor's attention at a seminar on youth, it was easy to draw the right conclusion. Tibet and youth: young Tibetans in Switzerland; add a couple of technical terms like dysfunctional enculturation, anomie, identity divergence – and the project could be submitted.

The professor said the topic was a trouvaille. "We could do something interdisciplinary with it." Interdisciplinary studies had just come into fashion in Zurich. "Get started," he said, "then we'll see." He dismissed me with a friendly smile.

A year later there were three of us working on the young Tibetans. Psychology and folklore studies had been added to sociology. And by the time I was writing the fair copy of my dissertation – another year had gone by – there was a pedagogy student working through the material we'd collected. Little was known about Swiss youth; soon almost everything would be known about Tibetan youth in Switzerland.

My professor was in charge of coordination; we didn't give him much work, I myself only consulted him once, and the others were looked after by their own professors.

The assistant at the Institute of Sociology, an Israeli, was the only one who helped each of us, again and again, with statistics and also with advice on computer programmes. And there are still people who maintain that in our country research is done inefficiently!

In any case, the project had tangible results, two licentiate theses and two PhD dissertations. The young Tibetans had helped four young Swiss students gain academic titles, and nearly helped one of them embark on an academic career.

The Israeli, by the way, who was mathematically inclined, named us the 'Gang of Four'.

Nonetheless, our work was to serve as a model: interdisciplinarity – pursued with youthful vigour and also with the whole-hearted support of the sociology professor and his forward-looking colleagues in the other subjects – continued to be put into practice. And once again the fieldwork area was the Appenzell. The subject: Cleanliness. From the chamber pot (ethnological aspects of the chamber pot with particular regard to sphincter training in early childhood) via class-specific attitudes to tidiness and cleanliness, through to basic disposition and obsessive-compulsive character, everything was investigated ethnologically, sociologically, psychoanalytically and pedagogically before being consigned to paper with scientific rigour.

A clean job.

Once, when I told Anderegg's wife Valérie-Anne about it she said that listening to us one might get the impression that we'd only ever dealt with trivial matters in those Zurich days. "*Rien que des futilités,*" she said. So I had to put her right. "*Futilités*?" I asked, getting into my stride. "Are displaced Tibetans in Switzerland a trivial matter? Is Tibet a trivial matter? You and your *grande nation* may make fun of *ma petite Suisse*, but that doesn't make us, with our modest conceit and our highly industrialised pedantry, either *négligeables* or a trivial matter."

That said, Anderegg's wife still didn't know what I meant. I doubt if I knew myself.

2
Wohlwender and Co

What can you do with a PhD about the Tibetans in your pocket?

There wasn't a big choice. Wohlwender, Perspectives and PR, Applied Social Research. It sounded good but it was only the office I'd worked for before, part-time as a student, doing interviews for marketing surveys.

It was a two-person enterprise, the owner and his secretary. Now I was the third person, the bringer of an academic title into the firm. I wasn't the boss's partner, but I straightaway became the vice-boss.

Our main customers were cosmetics distributors, textile companies, and a supermarket chain. In a fit of complacency or self aggrandisement we might have said that what we did was basic research: practice-oriented pilot studies for marketing problems and advertising optimisation … yah, right: marketing perspectives and PR. For you need to know what people don't know, and then you need to know what they do know, so as to make the thing you want them to know as palatable as possible.

You can only distribute goods that people want to buy, and the only things people want to buy are those they feel they need; but people's real needs are those of which they have been made fully aware, and that, in sum, is the signal feature, the badge of honour of true advertising, its glamour, its radiance, its son et lumière – in short, advertising enlightens.

In fact I enjoyed it. Three elegant rooms in the upper Niederdorf district opposite the Great Minster, with a view on the River Limmat.

Wohlwender, in his early fifties, shrewd and smart, a jack-of-all-trades. And what we did was not completely superfluous. We certainly prevented two or three flops a year.

I called it sociology-lite.

3
How I got to go to Paris

After I'd been working for Wohlwender for three years we – my small family and I – moved to Paris.

It had all happened very quickly. At the beginning of March I chanced to meet my former professor at the entrance to the Zurich Central Library. "What are you working on at the moment?" he asked. Slightly embarrassed, I told him. He asked me why I'd never been in touch in all that time. I looked at him inquiringly. That Tibetan business had been interesting, he said, he was surprised that I'd simply disappeared afterwards. A good thing he'd bumped into me just now. He'd been playing with a certain idea. I was to come round and see him at his institute. Yes, he still had his office hours at the same times.

The business with the Swiss National Science Foundation – a research grant, initially for two years – wasn't my idea. It wasn't my fault that the kindly gentleman with his peasant's head and his peasant's hands was biased in my favour. As a conservative specialist in social change he probably found it rather touching that an offspring of the lower classes had graduated from his institution. And just as the professor had considered my Tibetans topic a trouvaille at the time, now that I was to engage in advanced research he again left it to me to suggest a suitable project.

In Zurich the so-called restlessness of youth was being investigated empirically; the Swiss Confederation, Zurich canton and Zurich city had already granted the necessary credits. "We'll fit you in there," the professor decided. "You can contribute something theoretical."

From Gonten to Appenzell, from Appenzell to Zurich. Wasn't it high time I went abroad? Even if the subject was youth in Switzerland.

Foreign languages have never been my forte. I could read English fairly well, specialist texts at least; my French, however, was hopeless. Whenever we had a client from the French-speaking part of Switzerland I had to call the secretary or even ask the boss for help.

Ergo, it had to be France, to improve my French.

That was not a scientific reason, not empirically scientific nor theoretically scientific. However science might still provide adequate reasons for me to go there.

And Eva was also in favour; she'd spent her two semesters abroad in Paris and had good memories of her time there.

Nevertheless I still had to find an explanation for my choice of Paris as a research location.

Durkheim came to mind. But he had died in 1917. And had he ever written anything specifically about youth? The more recent big names came to mind: Ariès, Aron, Foucault, Lacan, Lévi-Strauss. They could hardly serve to justify a stay in Paris for research on youth, rather for general studies or a university of the third age.

In the *Handbook of Empirical Social Research*, volume 6, I finally found a couple of names that pointed to France, from Abboud through Marrou right up to Zazzo. Unfortunately many of them were psychologists or educationists rather than sociologists, but on the other hand, with youth as the subject everything had always been mixed up together anyway, and if I wanted reasons for going to Paris I couldn't be too choosy.

First the place, then the persons, finally the topic.

What best matched present-day youth problems in Zurich? Those long-past riots in Paris in 1968. It was obvious. It hit you in the eye. And there were sure to be enough leaflets, pamphlets, analyses, discourses, reports, articles, memoranda and memoirs still around for the matter to be treated using nothing but desk sociology. For me on the River Seine, jolly riots in retrospect; for my colleagues on the River Limmat, everyday discontent live.

Why is student unrest always considered to be so important? Back then in France the elation collapsed like a punctured balloon as soon as the petrol stations ran out of petrol. And the outcome? An increase in the minimum wage and one and a half reforms in the field of education. And all the left-wing professors packed away to a new university hastily erected in Vincennes on a site belonging to the army, for the matter had to be settled without delay. After all the tremendous excitement, back into the old rut. The French remained Catholic, about seventy-six point three per cent of them.

I know it can be seen another way. Those who were directly involved have created their own passion story out of it, their October-Revolution-in-May, their 'something completely different'. And because hardly anything at all happened in Switzerland at that time, at least nothing half as important as what happened in Paris, people here in the Mittelland have, in the course of time, dreamt up parallel events. The Globus riots in Zurich and a few demonstrations and an increase of one point five per cent in the number of eighteen- to twenty-four-year-olds who're interested in politics, big deal! In comparison, the 1980s riots caused more of a rumpus. Yet they too are long forgotten by now.

So, what was my conclusion? Clearly I didn't really fancy doing research on May 68.   ʼ

A pity! The violent unrest in Paris at that time would have gone so well with the vague discontent of Zurich's youth. New insights gained through comparison and contrast.

So, what else, if not that? It really wasn't easy for me to find a topic this time.

While I was working on the young Tibetans, colleagues had often asked me why I was interested in the tiny group of Tibetans here and not in the many Italians; it was much more urgent to interview the children of foreign-worker families. No doubt, and no doubt it stood to reason that, after having worked on that minority among minorities, I should take the second generation of our Italians as my topic.

However, without field studies there could be no pretence of even a semblance of methodical correctness. And field studies were out of the question, that was settled. This time it was to be desk sociology. From sociology-lite to desk sociology, it was logical, especially as an elegant writing style had been my trademark all the time I was at university.

But I couldn't do desk research on the second generation of our immigrants, if only because there was no ready material available. You can't summarise and critically arrange material that doesn't exist. And that was something I happened to know, thanks to my journeyman's piece on the Tibetans: neither the Department of Home Affairs, nor the Department of Foreign Affairs, nor the Federal Office for Industry, Trade and Employment, nor the Swiss Federation of Commerce and Industry, nor anyone else for that matter, had ever commissioned a study on foreign youth in Switzerland. Our immigrants would all disappear, sometime, somewhere, somehow. What did the Swiss care if the children of Italians didn't know what kind of Italo-Swiss they were. If I were to plump for the serious topic I wouldn't be able to copy anything from anywhere.

So one thing followed from another.

The Maghrebians in Paris corresponded to the Italians in Zurich. And although fieldwork in Paris was out of the question for me – insufficient knowledge of the banlieue patois, not to speak of my total ignorance of Arabic – I had reason to hope that French sociologists had already produced some systematic work on their foreign workers and guest workers.

It would have been a nice topic. I sounded it out for a couple of weeks and even went to Paris for a few days to look up the literature, only to discover that there wasn't much source material I could have copied from. The French, too, left the problem to the police, to pedagogues and social workers. So the Beurs in the banlieues were ejected from my shortlist.

Well actually, also because of the topic. Why fool myself? Only an ass could create a link between adopted Tibetans and the Italo-Swiss and then get from the Italo-Swiss to the Beurs in Paris – and all that for a paper on tiresome Zurich juveniles.

I was seized by panic. I almost wished I'd never met the professor that day at the library entrance. Market research was a tea party by comparison.

No field research; no minorities; neither an overly specific youth group nor an overly general one; extensive within reasonable limits, just manageable; and the topic had to be spontaneously understandable so that I wouldn't have to lose time pondering on what to make of it; and no sociological jargon please, just a liberal arts paper, plain and simple, critically hermeneutic; trivial but deep.

You just have to keep on thinking: there's always something suitable around, somewhere or other, and sooner or later you'll hit on it or stumble across it. The trip to Paris had been worth my while. On my return journey, between Vesoul and Mulhausen, the solution occurred to me: *Youth in Transformation* would be the title and main keyword; *New historical-sociological contributions* the explanatory subtitle; then the humble phrase that credits a young academic, *A critical reference bibliography.*

As the words ran through my mind I saw the peasant face of the professor who'd have to champion my application: his expression undecided, wavering between pensive lip-pursing earnestness and an understanding smile. Oh, he was not incapable of irony, that man. And he would, I could be almost sure of it, give his assent. He'd like the 'transformation', also the historical perspective. "I look forward to seeing what you make of it," he'd say.

And that's how it turned out.

4

6 rue Lacépède, Paris 5ᵉ

But first of all we had to find a flat in Paris.

Eva took on the job. She went there twice, for a couple of days at a time. I remained in Zurich, staying at home to look after Lydia – Wohlwender was always generous when it came to children and family. Incidentally, he didn't in any way try to hinder me in my Paris plans. "Scientific research, youth," he said, nodding in his jovial way, "can't have any objections to that. And when you've had enough of it, give us a call; the company will still be here, or so I hope."

By the beginning of September Eva had found something. "It's tiny," she said on the phone, "but that's how things are here. I think it might do." She described the flat in such detail that I could have drawn the groundplan. "In any case, the location is terrific, right next to the Jardin des Plantes: the ideal playground for Lydia."

My French had improved – I could now read Bourdieu – but it was nowhere near good enough for me to dare to negotiate a tenancy agreement with its small print. Eva managed everything, I could rely on her.

At the beginning of October we drove to Paris in a packed car. We'd already moved house twice in Zurich, so we had plenty of practice.

Rue Lacépède, an attic flat; a greyish-green copper roof on the outside, flower-patterned wallpaper inside; draughty in winter, hot in summer; but it would be very pleasant here in the temperate seasons.

The staircase was steep and narrow with roomy landings; the bars of the bannisters wobbled; oaken steps, well trodden. "Broken, broken, broken," said Lydia the first time we climbed up. Later on, she never tired of clattering down those stairs.

Two rooms and a kitchen, everything small; and at one end of the corridor, a kind of alcove that could be regarded as a tiny room; the shower and washbasin could only be reached through the kitchen. The squat toilet in the stairway, half a flight down, had to be shared with an old lady, Madame Malochet, who was mistrustful to start with, but eventually became very attached to us.

One of the rooms overlooked the inner courtyard and the tin roof of a little two-storied house; the other room and the kitchen both looked across to other people's windows, into other people's flats. And on the left, in the gap formed by rue Lacépède and rue Linné, you could see the trees of the Jardin des Plantes.

Lydia wanted to know the name of each of those whose tops – already changing colour – we could see from our kitchen table. It kept us busy the whole of one early Sunday afternoon. We went across, we came back, we went over again: the great oak at the park entrance, the maple next to it, behind it the robinias, an elm, several poplars, plane trees – and those right back there on the right must be the two larches and the Corsican pine.

As a rule, Ikea, ABM or Möbel Pfister were not good enough for Eva; in Paris, however, she even managed without Habitat and we bought folding chairs, imported from Czechoslovakia, at the Monoprix on the Avenue des Gobelins; we bought foam mattresses, made in Taiwan, at Le Bazar on rue de Rivoli; and at the nearest hardware store, in rue Monge, we bought tubular steel twin beds that could be shoved one beneath the other. I've never been able to understand how people can take furniture seriously. A table, a chair, a bed, a cupboard, all of the simplest design – that's to say, the design doesn't matter, all that counts is that the furniture be available and that it be functional.

In Paris Eva was undemanding. "It's only makeshift," she'd say showing a visitor the cupboard and the kitchen shelves I'd carpentered, unwillingly and without the right tools. "He can do it if he wants to. His father's a carpenter." Good middle-class respect for manual work. Had they but known!

In those first few days, Paris seemed like a scrap heap to me: cars parked nose to tail all along the streets; the streets themselves dirty, grey; in front of the shops, cardboard boxes, crates, piles of rubbish; messy façades, peeling paint, decrepitude; people hurrying past beneath a smoky sky.

But the Jardin des Plantes appealed to me from the very start. It was only a few paces from our flat to the entrance north of the labyrinth. The colder it got the fewer the people taking a walk there. The long avenues gave me the feeling that I'd come out into the open air.

5

Anderegg

Most of the people Swiss people get to know in Paris are Swiss.

He scrubbed away at his jacket, wetting his finger with spit and rubbing the material near the front buttons whilst listening attentively to the lecturer. And he was the first to have a question ready when, after the introductory exposé – 'Youth myths in the interwar period' – the discussion began.

He spoke several times. What he said met with interest. The man seemed to be highly esteemed in that circle. He spoke softly but with assurance, now slowly and thoughtfully, now fast and with lively gestures, and with a St. Gallen twang in his French.

After the discussion when I was putting on my coat out in the corridor he came up to me. "I think we know each other, at least from afar."

He was right.

Swiss people in Paris who know each other from Zurich call each other by their first names.

Hadn't we attended the same seminar for a semester? Something about youth, already back then; one of the few psychology seminars I'd attended regularly. I vaguely remembered his presentation. Something about role play, role choice, role compulsion, non-conformist behaviour?

I was right.

Afterwards, he told me, he'd graduated on the topic of play.

He invited me for a glass of beer on the Place Saint-Sulpice. I said my wife and child were waiting for me in rue Lacépède. He had a small family too, he said. We could get together. Why didn't we come to an early supper next Sunday.

From Jussieu to Sèvres-Babylone; there you change trains and continue in the direction of Porte de la Chapelle; Pigalle, Abbesses. We'd set out after Lydia's afternoon nap and – it was Eva's suggestion – wanted to take a stroll in the Sacré-Cœur district beforehand.

Dodo – metro – a short walk: that was the Harder family's Sunday routine; one day here, another day there, field trips in Paris. During the week too sometimes. But then Eva had to manage on her own. Lydia wasn't an easy child at the time, daredevil one moment, querulous and withdrawn the next, full of qualities most worthy of pedagogical attention.

Rue Berthe, a narrow street on the steep hill below the Sacré-Cœur. The flat was big by Paris standards, big enough for Anderegg's little family, much too small for Anderegg's books.

The four rooms were a library. Even the narrow entrance hall was lined with crammed shelves – they extended right into the kitchen. Wherever there was a wall there were bookshelves. Books everywhere, even under the beds: Anderegg had had flat wooden cases purpose made, complete with castors and plywood lids.

"I need them all," he said. "The only reason I go to the library these days is for the periodicals – and also to find out what else might come in useful and consequently needs to be bought at the earliest opportunity. You see, I always have to have everything I need for my work ready to hand; so I immediately buy anything I think might contain material connected with what I'm working on at the time. And strangely enough I'm hardly ever mistaken, I always find something or other that can be used sooner or later: an argument, a footnote, an example. Not surprising really, considering that everything – or almost everything – has already been written sometime, somewhere, somehow. And of course it's handy if I can simply pick up the book in question without having to thumb through piles of notes and extracts and fascicules first. It's saved me a lot of time, it's really worth the expense. You should at least always immediately get yourself photocopies of anything you've unearthed. What I then do is staple the pages together into booklets." He reached into the shelf behind him and showed me some: "It's handier that way. I've got to know a couple of good second-hand bookshops by now and I've already unearthed the rarest of tomes: a first edition Gelb and Goldstein, Kurt Lewin in French,

91

Husserl's *Vorlesungen zum inneren Zeitbewusstsein* edited by Heidegger, Halle 1928, published by Niemeyer, some yearbook or other. In Paris you'll find everything, like in Ali Baba's cave except that things are not so conveniently all together in one place, you'll have to run around a bit. If there's anything special you can't find let me know, I'll help you if I can. By the way, have you got yourself a pass for the BN yet?"

Once, years before, I'd already had some business with the Bibliothèque Nationale – there were exiled Tibetans in France too. Anderegg gave me the right tips, so that by the following Tuesday I'd already obtained admission to the reading room.

Lydia also enjoyed being at the Andereggs'. While we chatted on about libraries, flats, second-hand bookshops, Cacharel, Foucault, La Samaritaine, Zurich, she and Anderegg Junior built the Eiffel Tower. And afterwards they looked at picture books together; yes, there were masses of children's books there too.

6

Censier or Life in reading rooms

However, I didn't go to the Bibliothèque Nationale regularly. It was a long way away and after I'd had the bad luck for the second time running to find all the seats in the reading room already taken although I'd got there in good time, I switched to a less frequented library.

Sainte-Geneviève: the high hall with its twin vaults and the pale light shining down from the arched windows, and the cast-iron columns, and the staircases and galleries, and all the green glass lampshades, one at each workplace, pentecostal flames distributed with Cartesian precision throughout the depth of the room. And you come out of the building to smoke a cigarette only to find yourself standing in front of the Panthéon. Which is enough to send you back to the hushed gloom after half a cigarette.

When Lydia was awake she wanted something. When she wanted something she made a noise. My quiet presence in the flat in rue Lacépède annoyed her. Whenever I spent the day at home, proper work was out of the question.

Fifteen minutes on foot. It wasn't Anderegg who'd given me the idea, it was something I'd found out for myself. At the Sainte-Geneviève, too, seats were in high demand; but as most of the users were younger than the ones at the Bibliothèque Nationale they didn't come in hordes until after ten o'clock, so before ten I could take my pick.

You couldn't leave your seat for more than half an hour; if you stayed away longer it was considered to be vacated. I don't know how or if they checked; but there was a notice on the wall so I kept to the rule.

By the afternoon, unoccupied seats were almost as rare as at the Bibliothèque Nationale; I had to hold the fort. On the central landing of the twin stairs leading up to the reading room there were vending machines selling bouillon and coffee in plastic cups. It wasn't easy to hold out in the afternoons between one and three.

But the seats in those distinguished reading rooms are always astonishingly comfortable: the small of your back is supported by the rounded backrest, your buttocks on the precious wood are held in concavities shaped to satisfy every anatomical and physiological requirement. What's on offer to our learned bottoms here in Wangen doesn't come anywhere near the old standards: metal and plastic, plywood at best.

After a few weeks I abandoned the dignified atmosphere of the Sainte-Geneviève. Censier was even nearer, only five minutes from our flat.

No individual table lamps, only neon lights in plenty, high up in the ceiling. No choir stalls for diligent scholars, but simple school chairs for young adults instead. So as not to be boxed in by those young people I usually sat right at the end of a row of tables.

The people at the Bibliothèque Nationale reading room were over thirty years old, many of them considerably older. At the Sainte-Geneviève the ages were mixed. At Censier you found undergraduates. It seemed to me that working on youth in the midst of youth was appropriate.

But above all, I always found a seat there. The reading room was as big as four gymnasiums, and apart from the furniture and fittings it also looked like an oversized gym. Incidentally, I did my PT in the Jardin des Plantes, jogging through the tree-lined avenues.

The building could have served as something else: a gym, an indoor swimming pool, a warehouse, a shed for trolleybuses. That was its special charm. And in summer the hustle and bustle on the steps outside, on the forecourt: the snack stalls with their smokey grills and the smell of merguez sausages. The young people fetched the water for coffee and mint tea from the nearby toilets. Campus party and required reading, Gauloises, chewing-gum, exam stress.

I was happy there. There was never any hassle at the lending desk. The library had a basic stock of sociology classics. For specialist literature, however, I had to go elsewhere: Censier was not a place for discovery, Censier was a place for work.

My excursions to the Sainte-Geneviève library, not to mention the Bibliothèque Nationale, were reduced to once a week. Getting out to Nanterre – where, in 1968 in one of the big amphitheatres of the Faculté des Lettres, the revolution had almost been triggered off – was a full-day study trip. I set off by metro shortly after six in the morning: Jussieu – Sèvres-Babylone – Gare Saint-Lazare; from there I took the Maisons-Laffite train and got out at La Folie. Then across to the university, where the cafeteria was already open. Now I had a whole long searching-reading-copying day ahead.

"You'll find everything in Paris," said Anderegg. "What's not in the BN will be in the Musée Social. Or in the library at the Collège de France. Or in the Mazarine, the Forney, the Américaine. In the Bibliothèque de l'Arsenal I chanced upon a couple of old books on the evolution of Chinese characters; who would have thought it? You'll find everything, but it'll be a tedious business. That's why I've started buying all the books I need. Admittedly it's rather expensive."

I only consulted, I didn't buy. A bed, a table, a chair, a book: just one of each – that's how simple life should be.

7

Imitation, imitation!

"We know next to nothing about the original. For where would the beginning be? Apes already did it, and it's not without good reason that even today aping behaviour is regarded, if not as the actual basis of social interaction, at least as one of its basic patterns. Demonstration, imitation, archetype, prototype, stereotype, reality and model: what is related to what and how is it related? The emergence of Chinese characters, by the way, provides an example of eminent heuristic value in this context. But hieroglyphs, magic, sacred dances, in fact every kind of rite or ceremonial, should also be taken into consideration. Or the child's first imaginings, understood as deferred enactive imitation. Not to forget mimesis in art theory, methexis in Plato's cave, mime, mimicry, computer simulation, stock market crashes, cinema."

That was Anderegg's great topic at the time. According to him, without imitation there'd be no language acquisition, no language, neither society nor the individual, no art, no kitsch, no science, neither simple manipulation nor feeling of elation. Imitation was a foundation, consequently it was a fundamental concept – or vice versa if you like. It was the be-all and the end-all, the alpha and omega. It was the *a posteriori* to every *a priori*. It was not the whole, and yet it was one of those parts of the whole without which the whole would not be possible. It was a condition of the possibility that … Somehow, I never really understood how, it was less transcendent than transcendental, not so much existentiell as existential, either way and vice versa too: in any case it was something meaningful that was worth investigating.

Anderegg took on the job.

He enjoyed talking about it and would rapidly get into full swing. One idea would lead to another, and on to a third, and then from the third or fourth he'd jump back to the first.

It was entertaining. I liked listening to him.

… for example love and passion, don't they lie at the heart of fifty per cent of all novels? In imitation of what though, that's the question, considering that about half of all women go out to work – here in France at least – and the other half are busy doing the housework and looking after the children; as we all know perfectly well, having been amply informed by your fellow sociologists. And yet women hardly ever feature in our novels as anything but sweethearts or lovers; work and marriage automatically imply expulsion from the Eden of literature – or from the limbo, or purgatory, depending on how you see it. And I'd venture to claim that that's how it's always been. Green Henry and his Judith at the registry office is something Gottfried Keller spares us. And even when married life is not completely excluded, it's only the getting to know each other stage, the courtship with obstacles, that provides the really moving parts: will they get each other? – not a hope – not likely – at best if – too late now – yes, at last! It just goes to show how romantic even realistic fiction is. And when all the preludes to matrimony have been played through and can no longer be used as a suspense generator, as a reading stimulus, it's adultery, with variations, that will be resorted to. Prose just doesn't seem to manage without poetry and drama. Even at its most sober it's all storms, lightning flashes, thunderbolts; you're standing with one

leg in the extraordinary and the other in the metaphysical, nothing but passion and fate, a choice between gherkins and candy! Why do generations of readers gorge their way through such mountains of pickles and sweets? But there are still theorists who contend that literature reflects reality! If you say so, but in that case Carnival is a true reflection of life. No, no, the question is this: what is being imitated? Diversity and miscellany are certainly not depicted, more likely a scanty selection from the patterns that happen to be in vogue at a given moment, a couple of passion templates, which are then reused with admirable perseverance; remakes, remakes – call them archetypes if you like, but not samples of no value, goodness me no, on the contrary, added value, high quality, full of the best sentiments – or stuffed with sentiment, boiled sweets with soft centres, and now they're all sucking them and have that rapt, vacant, daydreamy expression as they bow their heads over the printed page; Brecht was right, smoking should be allowed in the theatre, distantiation, distantiation! As for the cinema, the basic menu there is even mushier, even more cloyingly sweet, and why one particular flirt plot should become the model for a dozen others is not of course only a question of individual psychology, since the social and the societal are involved from the start, so that, actually, sociologists too should contribute to the debate – but such things don't seem to interest them. I suppose they're right in a way, it's better for them to confine themselves to statistics, structures and curves; I just like speculating …

He probably continued in the same way for quite a bit longer, I didn't dislike listening to him.

Everything Anderegg wrote showed his extraordinary erudition. The conversion of his flat into a library wasn't simply a fad; it was required by his method.

Whenever he came across anything in his reading that seemed to be important for whatever he was working on at the time – or might perhaps want to work on some day – he immediately marked a narrow strip of paper with the keyword and stuck it in between the book pages. He'd never do any reading without a supply of inch-wide paper slips at his side. And there was scarcely a book on the shelves that didn't have several dozen of those bookmarks protruding from its pages; they peeked out from the tops of the serried volumes, one little bunch of paper slips after the other.

Not for Anderegg card indexes, excerpts, summaries, overviews, outlines: he skipped all that. When he was ready to move on from reading to writing, he first went along his shelves, grabbing a book here a book there, looking through the keywords on the bookmarks, replacing one book, taking out another. Whenever he found something he thought might be useful he'd put the book down on his big worktable. Book upon book; pile beside pile; soon there were also towers of books covering the floor around the table. Everything was rebuilt several times, books were removed, others added, the stacks shifted. Humming and talking to himself, Anderegg would make his way through the piles he'd arranged; he'd consult the notes scribbled on the bookmarks, scan a page, turn over, curse; look for something again, put the book aside.

"Sometimes it takes days and days," he said. "My son hates it, as he's not allowed to come into the room at those times. But what can you do? He likes handling books, just like me, and he'd muddle everything up. Some time soon we'll have to move, I haven't got enough space here."

As soon as each and every book was in its place he'd

start writing. "What I'd like best would be to type it all out in one go," he said, "and never give it another look. Unfortunately that doesn't work."

"*J'sais pas comment il l'fait, mais il le fait*," said Valérie-Anne, his wife.

"Actually all I do is copy," he said. "And if I hurry, sometimes a kind of spontaneity ensues that's rather refreshing."

A blend of his own eloquence together with quotations, explanations, commentaries with cross references, see above and see below. His texts were never easy to read, full of 'on the one hand … on the other hand', 'alternatively', 'insofar as', 'whereas', 'basically', 'partly … partly' …

Did he really only copy? He might just as well have claimed the opposite.

I tell it as I see it, that's to say I tell it and I write it down as it appears to me in all its complexity, and as it appears to me in my spontaneity too; for matching up words to things is something that can't be forced; the only way it can happen – and unfortunately it often doesn't – is in the quasi-playful encounter or failed encounter between the object and the observing seizing verbalising subject. And traces of this correspondence or failed correspondence, of this aleatory matching, should also still be discernible in the text, particularly there, in fact. For anyone who is intensely interested in the thing will immerse himself in it, at least partly, will allow himself to get absorbed by it, and then, in his hasty, provisionally formulated jottings, he will see the thing itself, unfocussed for the most part admittedly, with only certain details fully illuminated and precisely captured. There's nothing I loathe more than pretending I know something precisely and definitely; taken as it is, in all its nuances, in its diversity, even the simplest thing can only be described approximatively. So I'm all for approximation, suggestion, circumscription; the field is so vast, the essential thing is to immerse oneself.

Anderegg in top form. It's quite likely that he occasionally got on my nerves with his jargon even then. Was it in the flat behind Abbesses metro station? Or already in Vincennes? Or even in the house in Montreuil that he later bought? I helped him move house twice, each time it took almost a week, what with all the books; he didn't feel he could trust ordinary removals men with his collection.

Anderegg's father is an architect, a specialist in the restoration of churches and monasteries. Anderegg himself studied architecture to start with, but after two semesters he changed over to art history and archaeology, and finally settled for psychology and German philology. So in spite of being an efficient student he'd turned thirty by the time he graduated with a PhD with his essay on play.

This dissertation had already been a major project; it was not only a psychological treatise on play but also a detailed historical-cultural-aesthetic, analytico-linguistic epistemological, theological, ontological, anthropological analysis. It had attracted attention and he'd been offered an assistantship at the Institute of Psychology.

"In principle I was interested," said Anderegg, "on the other hand the job would have involved considerable teaching duties. I'm better with books than with people. Why would I want to bother myself with students?"

He went to Paris. Six months later he married a French woman there.

"We got to know each other at the cinema. After one café au lait everything was clear. There was no need for me to consult secondary literature. When it comes to matters of life and death it sometimes happens that I'm capable of great resolve."

Although he'd turned down the assistantship in Zurich and his father was of the opinion that he'd paid quite long enough for his education, it was self-evident to Anderegg that he would continue to pursue his studies. His mother supported him on this issue. She had a sideline managing real estate, had only this one son, and was proud of him. She opened an account under his name and made regular deposits. The articles that appeared regularly in the specialist journals gave her confirmation that she was successfully sponsoring research and science.

Valérie-Anne too had no objection to his being an independent scholar. She did the accounts for Cacharel and enjoyed the work; she didn't mind having to help finance the household. She admired her husband.

'Imitation and Dream', 'Imitation as the Foundation of Learning', 'Mirror Stage and Body Image', 'Imitation, Action and Action Science', 'Homologies between Mental and Social Structures', 'Mimetism and Provenance', 'Centrality and Psychosis', 'Departure and Homecoming as Identification Patterns in the Nineteenth-Century Bildungsroman': unperturbedly thorough as he was, he was drawn from one theme to the next. His *Summa Imitatio* is still awaiting completion.

8
Sommerhalder

"Neither God nor a boss, nor a steady girlfriend, nor a permanent editorial job: the Virgin Mary, free love and freelance! Life is too short to squander on a secure income."

I got to know Sommerhalder at Anderegg's. Anderegg liked cooking, and however congested with books his flat might be, he didn't only invite small families to his dinner parties. Sometimes there would be more than a dozen people sitting around the big worktable eating their way through the menu. When Sommerhalder was there he was always the centre of attention.

He was a historian and a journalist, an ad hoc foreign correspondent for Swiss newspapers. He specialised in portraits of great men – there were many in Paris. But from time to time he also took on Swiss notables: cantonal councillors, members of parliament, board members, all sorts of public figures, particularly from the cantons of Central Switzerland.

"Seen from Paris, those politicians – the Hürlimanns, Wallimanns, Oechslins, Kälins – look rather special. That's the alienation-effect."

Judged by Swiss standards he was bold, or even brazen. He wrote in a dry, laconic style; his short sentences were sharp, they hit their targets hard.

During our first winter in Paris, whenever Sommerhalder visited the Andereggs he took along with him the daughter of one of those ill-used men from Central Switzerland: a lively girl, full of enthusiasm and studious zeal. Later on he told me: "I might know some interesting little things about him now! However I can't use them, I'm in love with his daughter. Youth is ungrateful. Fathers have a hard time. Love is made in heaven."

Just as operatic tenors can bawl out their arias in the most impossible postures, Sommerhalder was capable of mockery whatever the situation.

During our second winter in Paris he frequently came to the Andereggs' in the company of a woman named Charlotte. Her father was a banker in Lucerne. And it was because of banks – South Africa, etc. – that she had rebelled against her father, not in public but all the more violently at home.

It was something Eva knew.

"As far as age is concerned, you're halfway between me and my father," Charlotte had apparently said to Sommerhalder, "So whose side are you on? You've got to decide!" Youth is difficult, fathers have a hard time.

This time Sommerhalder hadn't come by a new girlfriend because of a father he'd portrayed. His reputation alone, as someone who relished attacking Central Swiss gentlemen, had been enough to arouse Charlotte's curiosity, so much so that she'd gone to see him in Belleville. "I understand about as much about banking," Sommerhalder told her, "as any old dimwit from the backwoods of the Entlebuch – i.e. nothing. I've only ever studied a bit of history. Go to the Berne Declaration, they have the facts there." Of course in private he sided squarely with Charlotte in her quarrel with her Lucerne family.

He wrote poems about her. Previously I'd never personally known a man who wrote poetry. And who also recited it. Charlotte was celebrated in unrhymed, unmetered verse: head, heart and hand; she'd come to Paris to perfect her French. *"Jésus cuit à l'ail*: that's what my poems are like, a kind of sausage you can buy here in Belleville, artisanal, filled with bits of bacon, gristle and lots of cabbage."

Anderegg, however, found they contained sundry traces of Heine, Whitman and Brecht.

"If you say so, it must be true," said Sommerhalder. And he related – Sommerhalder always had stories to tell – how he and Charlotte, on a night stroll near the Canal Saint-Martin, had been threatened by a young Arab:

"There's this haji waving his pistol around right in front of my nose, I already see my tiny brain flying through the air, smacking into the wall, horrendous! The funny thing is, I don't feel in the least bit frightened for myself, my only concern is for little Charlotte – you never know, headlines in the *Vaterland*: Banker's Daughter Attacked. The fellow curses and swears at me as if I was the world's scapegoat incarnate. I can only understand half of what he's saying, he's that drunk, perhaps he only wanted to have a chat. But why did he have to choose us? Do I look like a racist? Like a neocolonialist? Of course not. Scandalous ingratitude, that's what it is. When you think how I've always stood up for those frustrated creatures! Even at home in Einsiedeln I try to promote understanding for him and his likes – unfortunately that's something the fellow can't possibly know. Sexual repression I'd say, a clear case, the women in Paris are a provocation for these Maghrebian hajis.

They haven't yet become inured, as we have thanks to our early diet of *Lui*, *Penthouse*, *Big Ben*, *Playboy* … The only thing you can do is keep calm. And in the end he drifted off, his pistol back in his plastic FNAC bag. An interesting experience, but no repeats please! We washed down the shooting gallery scare with two cognacs in a bistro on rue de la Grange-aux-Belles."

Quiet days in Belleville. "I'm living here in the midst of Armenians, Poles, Vietnamese, Yugoslavs, Turks, Portuguese, Jews, Algerians. Most of them are French by now of course. One more foreigner doesn't stand out. There's a newsagent near the Couronnes metro station where you can buy papers from all over the world, from the *China Daily* to the *Neue Zürcher Zeitung*."

For a while he lived in a hotel that was the epitome of a zero-star hotel. His room was on the third floor at the end of a corridor next to the shared toilet and shower. "Having to put up with the perpetual sound of gurgling water has its advantages. It means I can make as much noise as I like without disturbing anyone. But I had to complete the furnishings: a telly, a hotplate, and a camping table for my typewriter. I need the hotplate for Nescafé and couscous, the telly for the political press conferences here – of course I don't go along myself, I'm not that daft!"

Anderegg had his imitation, Sommerhalder had his petty bourgeoisie. At least that was his favourite topic for a time. All around the Lake of Lucerne there was hardly one great man who wasn't a petty bourgeois.

"History is a series of class struggles: that's the

classical theory. I'm a vulgar Marxist, you see. Switzerland is so boring because it hasn't got a history any more. And Switzerland hasn't got a history because it hasn't got any classes any more. And there are no classes because there's only one big one left: all of us are – or would like to be – petty bourgeois. And even people who have no desire to be petty bourgeois already are; and people who think they're no longer petty bourgeois still are, all the same. Switzerland is middle class, full stop. Müller, the office worker in the block, has his car and his stamp collection; out in the leafy suburbs, Gerber the office manager has two cars plus his big model railway, set up in the attic above his double garage; Pauli the banker has all those appurtenances too, with the addition and perhaps the burden of a rustic cottage in the Ticino or a farmhouse in Tuscany. Potted plants, flowerbeds, lawns, rose pergolas or crazy pavements; photo albums, original prints or machines by Tinguely: it all boils down to the same thing. And they're all hard-working and conscientious and occasionally they're smart alecs. But they don't overdo things. And they'd all like to be nice and kind, and then they're outraged if someone disagrees with them. And they have doubts about whether what they're doing is right: sensible half-hearted doubts, one's moral health shouldn't be put at risk for too long. And of course you'd fancy this and especially that, but luckily you're inhibited. I'm a petty bourgeois myself, very much so! My private history is full of soul-searchings and pricks of conscience. May I really? Or shouldn't I have? Those girls from Central Switzerland who're so curious about this old windbag here in Paris and who turn up wanting to put on the femme-fatale act – but no, they don't really want to, it just happens, and that's exactly what makes it petty-bourgeois."

Attentive female faces stimulated Sommerhalder. It was the same with Anderegg. As long as there were women in the audience, neither of them ever failed to deliver on irony and argument.

Valérie-Anne was usually present, but she didn't really count for Anderegg as he had her as a listener every day. On the other hand she certainly counted for Sommerhalder – the aloof Frenchwoman from Lille, come from the northern provinces to the capital to keep the books for Cacharel and to marry a man who was crazy about books.

Usually Eva was there too. She counted for Sommerhalder, she counted for Anderegg.

Probably it was thanks to her that we got invited.

9

Beatrice – amœbas – Adalbert

"What I had for lunch today was really disgusting again. It's almost always the same lately: if I cook something myself I can hardly get it down, I throw half of it away. But the canteen grub isn't up to much either."

Beatrice, the historian; also one of the people who occasionally turned up at Anderegg's eat-drink-talk sessions.

"Really, it wouldn't be a bad thing if I managed to find myself a rich man to fund my research. So far, the ones I've met have always been the wrong kind: small fry with financial problems worse than my own – or else they were dependent on daddy, a frightful situation I happen to know only too well. I've only ever once met a man who was good-looking, who was clever, who found me fascinating – yes, honestly – and on top of all that, who seemed to have money. And liked spending it. He took me to the La Louisiane, and at the weekend we escaped the Paris heat for the Pas-de-Calais, went to Le Touquet and took a hotel right on the sea-front, and he insisted on paying for everything, no stingy talk of emancipation or anything like that. But the regrettable detail I was unaware of at the time was that his cheques weren't covered. And that, of all things, had to happen to me! It's enough to make me weep, even now. That was the end of my libertarian dream of the kept woman sacrificing herself in the name of progress and science!"

"Those nasty Frenchies," said Sommerhalder. "I bet he was a Frenchman. Swiss men don't do things like that."

The grand confessions continued with vinous candour across Anderegg's large table.

"Lately I've felt as if I was riding a rollercoaster, down one moment, up the next, then down again, tossed around this way and that. Sometimes life makes me want to puke, the next moment I think it's okay. Like now, for example. Old Anderegg's a really nice chap. Although it's a beastly shame that he's so much better at cooking than I am. A clever man who's a good cook: Valérie, tell me how on earth did you manage to hook him?"

'Peaceful penetration or military subjugation. The establishment of French supremacy in the Ivory Coast up to 1914': Beatrice's subject. After graduating from the

University of Bern – she was from Schüpfheim in the Entlebuch – she went on to Paris with a recommendation from her professor and a grant from the Swiss National Science Foundation.

Later on, in Wangen, I ordered the book for the library. No doubt it's right to use federal moneys to promote research on topics other than the monasteries of Central Switzerland or young people around Lake Zurich. Penetration, subjugation, ivory: the title alone could make you envious.

According to Anderegg Beatrice is now working in the Army archives, not in Bern of course. Another one to have got stuck in Paris!

She was a plump woman with a bleating laugh and a passion for Apple computers. Her hunt for a rich husband was her running gag.

She didn't seem to need any sleep – a candle burning at both ends. She could be as dynamic at two in the morning as if she were still twenty. If she'd been at the Andereggs' and was driving you home – and she always insisted on driving you home in her battered Renault – a lengthy stop at her place in rue des Ciseaux was unavoidable.

She didn't mind baby-sitting for us. And then, when Eva and I arrived home from the Cinémathèque at half past eleven, Lydia would still be up and would have had an entertaining evening too.

A militant socialist, the daughter of an upper class family, handing out flyers between the Jardin du Luxembourg and Saint-Germain-des-Prés. Apparently, she once said to Anderegg: "It's also partly thanks to me that Mitterand got elected."

How intimate was she actually with that doctor, also a Swiss expat in Paris, a specialist in tropical diseases, in particular parasites, worms and suchlike?

His name was Ryf. He came from Bern, had studied there and in Lausanne, and had subsequently spent several years in Africa, in the true spirit of peaceful penetration.

At the Andereggs' I hardly ever talked to him – which wasn't surprising considering that I generally said very little whenever there were a lot of people there. I preferred to leave dinner table conversation to Eva: she always had and still has a talent for it.

Once Ryf invited us to a meal: chicken in salt, a recipe from the Sahel.

Beatrice picked us up. "That way you won't need to search around. It's in a new quarter, you know, difficult to find. "

A high-rise building south of the Place d'Italie. Second floor from the top; a sparsely furnished flat. At first Lydia didn't dare go out onto the balcony; far down below, a muddle of old houses and building sites; a view over the Paris skyline as far as La Défense and, when you looked right, as far as the strip of green formed by the Bois de Vincennes.

The chicken was in the oven, the vegetables in the pressure cooker. The doctor, busy with sauces and salads, would not tolerate women in the kitchen. I was the only person allowed to stay and watch him. I asked him about Africa – the most obvious topic – and about amœbas.

He told me that, even after they'd been cured of their amœbic dysentery, quite a few tourists suffered intermittent relapses with all the symptoms. However, in such cases pathogens could hardly ever be found, no matter how meticulous the examination. Lately, two hypotheses were being considered: it was an allergic reaction to the bugs one had had, perhaps also to the antibodies against them; or else it was a psychosomatic complication. From a purely medical point of view, the allergy theory was the more interesting of the two. Anderegg, with whom he'd discussed the matter, even found the case extremely interesting as an example of how a healthy body continues over a long period to imitate what it did when it was sick. However, for him, the practitioner, that was a bit too philosophical: he tended to consider the pathogen-free dysentery relapse as psychosomatic. And that in itself was no trifling matter – the disagreeable state of feeling you had something, yet you didn't have it. Exotically trivial, harmlessly dangerous, excruciatingly pleasant: enterocolitis at its most exquisite.

In the jungle, in the bush and in the desert he'd brought his parasitological knowledge to his African colleagues. Here at the Val-de-Grâce his skills were getting their final polish, for the time being. Did I know that fecal problems were endemic pretty well all over Africa, not only in the French-speaking parts?

Another fascinating story concerned the incredibly long worms which, even in state-of-the-art medicine, have to be carefully pulled out from under the skin and rolled onto a reel like a thread, a process that takes several weeks.

He chatted on, very much the pragmatic scientist. I listened.

Then the chicken was ready, baked brown inside its white crust of salt. The vegetables were cooked. No need to worry about amœbas, salmonellas, etc. Water-melon was served as a dessert.

All that was a long time ago. Our second summer in rue Lacépède, late summer. We returned on foot down Boulevard de l'Hôpital, Lydia half asleep on my shoulders. Unimportant things that have stayed in my memory. Why those and not others?

Swiss people in Paris often invited each other to meals. Apart from Anderegg, no one cooked anything fancy: since most of our friends lived in makeshift households it would have been difficult anyway.

"There you have it: social conditions in the metropolis similar to those in Witiko's Bohemian Forest," remarked Anderegg. No one besides Sommerhalder and Eva understood what he was talking about. "That's where Adalbert Stifter, with his customary meticulous attention to detail, describes how the people in the great forest visited each other on winter evenings and were offered bread, salt and water – very rarely wine, as far as I can remember. In old Adalbert's other books, too, people are very frugal: they serve up cold meat, or a glass of milk, or a little bowl of strawberries. And you all know my theory as far as that's concerned: hardly anything around that hasn't been done before. But who'd have thought that we, the Swiss in Paris, would take Adalbert as a model for our visiting habits."

10

'Some were amusing, some almost beautiful ...'

… never uniquely in the present but always retrospective and prospective too, the construction of consciousness, Husserl help! Retentions and protentions, reunited in the now of the impression, lectures Anderegg. Review, preview, Sunday Review, *says Sommerhalder.*

In the kitchen in rue Berthe? Or later on, in Vincennes, rue Gaillard? Or was it already in the house in rue Desgranges?

And if you look more closely it becomes evident that he's an artist. Ultimately his research is of a poetical nature. It's just that he isn't aware of it, or else he's pretending not to be. Lyricism is a constitutive element of all his journalistic attacks. His commitment arises from his imagination, his reportages are more metaphor than mimesis.

That was Anderegg on Sommerhalder, no doubt about it.

Oh yes, he's certainly entertaining. But not very sound. Attempting to grasp the course of history through individual biographies is a critical-historical method that's completely out of date, it's as if the Annales *school had never existed. Sometimes I'm ashamed to admit that we went to the same university! And besides, the man has rather too good a nose for things that are fishy – as though he was all too familiar with them himself. Incidentally, it doesn't bother me in the least that he's a macho. Smooth and round and fidgety people like Anderegg tend to get on my nerves much more.*

Beatrice on Sommerhalder and Anderegg. For a time the three of them were inseparable. Saying all kinds of nasty things about each other can be a sign of friendship.

114

Other people collect butterflies, matchboxes, beer cans, perfume bottles, cretaceous snails. Why shouldn't I collect sentences? They came to mind as I sat in the Censier reading room. What she'd said about him, and what he'd said about her. And what they'd said about themselves.

... No, I'm not a pacifist. Wars get waged anyway. I get involved. There are plenty of neutral hypocrites as it is ...

... Women are difficult to satisfy, that's a fact. Usually a phallus isn't much help. A pity, it's mortifying for the owner, but facts are facts ...

... And if a thing can't be forced, I won't be hurried. And besides, every day is a new day and each day can take you a step further; all you have to do is buckle down ...

... Surely all our calamities provide adequate proof that there can't be only one god, even if he's lord over any number of angels, saints and devils. The muddle that prevails down here can only be explained by the existence of a legion of gods. A world above and a world below and, for all I care, all kinds of worlds in between, full of demigods and three-quarter gods – not to forget the goddesses! God Almighty! those Greeks were really wise. For them the squabbling, the spite, the vindictivenes – in short the whole mess down here in our vale of tears – was accounted for by the squabbling, the intrigues, the devastating outbursts of rage up there. As good an explanation as any.

Andereggian argument; it's unlikely that he believed in it himself.

... and isn't all our endless chatter – you can hardly describe it as anything else – isn't it in itself an imitation of the world? Our gossip, merely a poor copy? The sound accompanying the fury? The small words for big matters, the big words for small ones, who

knows? The world as compulsive verbosity and imitation: it seems to apply to me anyway. On the other hand we might also ask ourselves if silence too couldn't be understood as a mystical form of imitative interiorisation of the world.

Well, one thing was certain at least: I couldn't ever complain that I hadn't met remarkable people in Paris:

Anderegg amidst his piles of books.

Sommerhalder with his girfriends: "It's none of my fault if they rebel against their fathers."

Plump Beatrice of the bleating laugh, self-mocking and exuberant.

The overseas aid workers, a married couple, he a former Swiss army instruction officer who'd converted to Caritas, she a domestic science teacher who'd worked for the Basel Mission – three years in Borneo.

Sister Yolanda, PhD, a Cistercian nun from Fribourg, a boarder for a few winter months at the Palais de la Femme on Place Voltaire, to be seen daily searching out patristic subtleties under her green lamp at the Bibliothèque Sainte-Geneviève.

The UNESCO official with his wife and baby.

The Romance scholar, a woman from Zurich, who was writing a structuralist dissertation on Bernanos' *Sous le soleil de Satan.*

The Swiss-dialect writer from the Oberaargau.

The art-historian and sociologist, the only son of an artist, in Paris since 1968, an odd-jobber and world-reformer who'd rather have been a professional jazz-trumpeter.

Valérie-Anne's office mate, the lover, companion and

daughterly support of an impresario, she twenty-five, he well past sixty – "the best man imaginable".

The sculptor from Basel who had his decorative windowpanes on show at an art gallery in the sixième arrondissement.

The grammar-school teacher, a mathematician and casual organist, on sabbatical leave – wasn't his wife called Gertrude and wasn't she a nurse?

The applied linguist who translated French bestsellers into stylish German and, as that didn't earn her enough to live on, worked as a waitress at a vegetarian restaurant in the Marais quarter ...

It was touching to see how urgently the Swiss in Paris sought friends. But such sociability was also evident among other foreigners.

In the playground of the Jardin des Plantes Eva got into conversation with a young Quaker woman from Ohio who attended classes at the Alliance Française in the mornings and for the rest of the time worked as a nanny to two American children; the three of them often came up to our flat.

The English sinologist whose flat we'd taken over was back in Paris the following year, together with her Tunisian boyfriend, and wanted to know how we were getting on. Whenever she came to Paris for a couple of days from London – or was it Leeds? – she dropped by; she took us to a Chinese restaurant behind the Gare de l'Est and talked a lot about the status of women during the Ming dynasty.

The German sociologist at the Bourdieu lectures, very eloquent albeit with a Teutonic accent in his French

– which he made up for by stressing all his final syllables – occasionally turned up late at night for a glass of beer.

The other sociologist, a Greek who'd evaded conscription during the military junta by coming to France, and who'd married a French woman from the Dordogne, took Eva and Lydia on his forays through the Paris fleamarkets: he earned his living as an antique dealer.

And the Yugoslav in the flat below ours, married to a German woman from the GDR who was a filing clerk at the Goethe-Institute, invited us out to the country a couple of times. He worked as a carpenter during the week, and spent every weekend building a house near Château-Thierry. Later on he occasionally gave Anderegg a hand with his renovations in rue Desgranges.

Then there was the Faulkner specialist, a woman from Hanover; and the German Jew from Heidelberg, and the Italian from Turin – and Dorothea, of course.

And that long-term political science student, also a North German woman, said by Sommerhalder to be a man-eater who'd gobbled up fellow students galore – and yet with Anderegg and Co she was a paragon of discretion and reserve – who, to everyone's surprise, told us one evening about some hanky-panky that had come to an embarrassing end. For, a day or two later, her copain had phoned her in a fury: did she want to kill him? His chest was so bloody and bruised he'd had to go and see a doctor; she ought to have known that you couldn't touch, and much less bite, someone like him *sans précaution*? "How was I to know he was a hemophiliac? He never told me, the silly nitwit!"

Things were more difficult with the French, even when they lived in the same building. If it hadn't been for Lydia we'd never had got beyond a nod and a hello even after months. But Lydia clattered down the stairs and laughed. The clatter may have been annoying but her energy was impressive; and if she got ticked off she didn't answer back but simply looked puzzled. Soon she knew all our neighbours, including those in the rear building, and the old couple on the ground floor of the lodge in the courtyard, and the concierge's daughter, and the two children the concierge had in day care. Even the xenophobic monsieur on the upper floor of the lodge – who habitually grumbled about the foreign riff-raff peopling the neighbourhood – said that we Swiss were an exception: already in our first winter, on the Feast of the Epiphany he brought us a large round cake with a golden cardboard crown.

So it was usually Lydia who was the first to make friends with the local people, Eva saw to it that good relations were kept up – and I enjoyed the benefits.

No, we certainly weren't unpopular. Not only did Swiss expats and other foreigners drop in, we also had visits from old Zurich friends. And Eva was always so welcoming that they preferred to stay with us for two or three days rather than take a room at a hotel; they seemed to find the cubbyhole with its skylight at the end of the corridor quite comfortable enough.

It wasn't until we were in Paris that I realised how many good friends we'd had in Zurich. Even Wohlwender's secretary turned up, together with her husband, and filled a whole evening with her account of the latest hits and flops in the advertising field. All those people had come to Paris for some important reason, used the occasion to pay us a visit, enlivened our social life and messed up my work routine. For of course I was only too willing to be a tour guide from time to time and show my guests things they wouldn't have seen otherwise: the Canal Saint-Martin with its locks and bridges, the roof terrace of the Samaritaine department store, the already scruffy new university out in the Bois de Vincennes, the Place des Vosges at midnight, the Passage du Caire, the Cinémathèque, the Café Procope and – obviously – the Jardin des Plantes with its joggers, alpine garden and bear-pit.

11
Anderegg in Wangen

"A lot of cultural activity here? You must be joking! Who's interested in culture? Bratwurst and beer in the market square, that's what appeals to people. Only a tiny minority want anything else. And that's a good thing: it's why minorities are tolerated. For guest performances of Dürrenmatt's *The Visit*, the theatre's sold out: Güllen, and then Güllen again. For anything else our baroque theatre's half full at best. Or take concerts: Haydn et cetera and the hall's half empty too. Imagine what it would be like with Schönberg and his like, or even with a composer who's still alive! The only things that really pull in the crowds – thanks to Puccini and minor Pavarottis – are operatic aria recitals featuring second-best heroic tenors from nearby foreign countries. And medleys from *The Beggar Student*, *West Side Story*, *Cats*. And even that wouldn't be possible if the performances weren't sponsored by Migros and the two major banks that have branches here."

That's what I told Anderegg last time he was here on a visit. Anderegg often comes to Switzerland, and on his way to St. Gallen occasionally makes the detour via Wangen.

It was the last week before the holidays; this time he'd even taken the whole family with him, to the great delight of our daughters. Even as he parked his car beside our house he was struck by the noise and the crowds of people. "A festival? We must go and see," he said.

He'd always had a weak spot for such things. He never failed to celebrate the Fourteenth of July, the whole works. And immediately afterwards, the First of August: the house in rue Desgranges overcrowded with homesick Swiss, the garden decorated with red paper lanterns, a tiny firework display – left-overs from the fourteenth of the previous month – and raclette accompanied by white wine from the Valais.

And so, ploughing a way through the late-afternoon crowds, I introduced him to our local market festival: Hintere Gasse, Untere Gasse, Kirchgasse, Prisongasse. The usual things were on offer: Indian bedspreads and blouses, Native American jewelry, leatherware from Africa, bars of soap containing alpine herbs. The stands of the local boutiques displayed last season's non-sellers.

Anderegg spent a long time rummaging in the book boxes, and was delighted to find two Imago volumes that had been missing from his collection. The detour via Wangen had been worthwhile!

Altogether, Anderegg was very pleased with Wangen. We drank Solothurn *Bürgerwein* out of plastic cups, and he raved on about the towns at the southern foot of the Jura. Admittedly, he didn't actually know any at first hand, but he'd always read so much about them: reviews of film festivals, literary festivals, political, cabaret, jazz or chanson festivals, biennales, premieres, open-air events. "That's the difference between medium-sized towns in France and small towns here," he said. "A small Swiss town has certain things, indeed has had them for ages, that a medium-sized French town can only dream of. Politics and culture are linked, they influence each other – but there's no need for me to tell you that – and there must be all kinds of models; a town like this one here – you said yourself that it's conveniently small – would be perfect for a detailed dynamic structural analysis: cultural variety and open-mindedness interpreted as an isomorphism of sociopolitical relationships. Hasn't it been done yet? Small-town sociology as it were. I'm sure something interesting would come of it, all that's needed is a bit of research. That'd be something for you, don't you think?"

The world exists to be investigated.

Anderegg the inspirer!

I'd have liked to have told him to leave me in peace. He was always so persistent in his attempts to get me to do something serious!

"Here you have everything anyone could possibly want," he said. "A history museum, an art museum, a theatre. Not to forget the adult education college Eva keeps going so well, and of course the library – it's enough to make anyone envious."

When a man from Paris heaps praise on Wangen who am I to complain?

"Such cultural vitality and diversity," he said, "is surely a sign of political diversity too, for example flourishing political parties and a lively interest in the *chose publique* in general."

There was something in that, and Anderegg's conclusion did not necessarily show that he, as an expat Swiss in Paris, had become rather starry-eyed about Switzerland.

No, people here were not entirely uninterested in politics, I said. But in my view it would be a bit of an exaggeration to say they were very interested. At any rate, only about two or three per cent of them ever attended municipal assemblies.

"What! You still have municipal assemblies here?" Anderegg asked, much taken.

For someone from Appenzell who happened to end up in the Mittelland, I said, this ancient relic from the past, with speeches pro and contra, hands up and vote-tellers, had a certain charm. But for most people the ritual was only of middling interest. And when, rarely, there was a ballot-box referendum on some municipal business, hardly more than a quarter of the electorate fulfilled their civic duty. In recent years there'd been only one issue that had really got people going: a tax on rubbish bags, and they'd voted it down. But to get back to the political parties: they still existed, in fact there were more of them than ever. The liberal Yellows had new rivals in Blocher's Party and the Freedom Party; the former Progressives had merged with the former Greens and had together become multi-coloured; women joined the elections with lists of their own; the red of the Reds had faded into pale pink or mingled with yellow to become orange; only the Catholic Conservatives hadn't changed, black was their colour and black they remained. As a folklorist, a Catholic and a native of Innerrhoden, I should actually have joined the Christian People's Party, I said. But, conservative as I was, I'd hung on to family tradition and joined the Socialists. In Gonten my father had always been considered a crypto-socialist; I'd gone on to become a regular member of the eternal minority, but we did, at least, have a hundred members here in Wangen. Of course, at meetings there would only be about twenty. And on the First of May, the most important day of celebration and folklore in the workers' calendar, only about twenty turned up at the parade: without reinforcements from the neighbouring villages, and without all the Kosovo-Albanians, the Kurdo-Turks, Italo-Swiss and Hispano-Swiss, I said, we'd have to march through the town in a straggly line of twos to make it look anything like a demonstration. After all, a day off is a day off – off onto the motorway and into the country. But even for the little group of stalwarts who listened to the speeches on the Klosterplatz, it was the merry sequel, sitting and drinking in the former indoor riding hall, that they liked best and that was certainly more important than the part it was their duty and honour to attend. "Whatever way you look at it," I said, "the biggest party in these parts is the Bratwurst and Beer Party, you can bet your life – or a pot of mustard – on that."

"As is demonstrated *ad oculos*," said Anderegg, looking around him. And indeed, faces shone, conversation was animated, the atmosphere festive. "A profound analysis, simple and true."

Not much discernment required, I said. But something it had taken me a long time to realise was that anyone who wanted to become something in this town – a town councillor or a cantonal councillor, a judge, a clerk of the court, a street-sweeper, anything like that – would be well-advised to join the local swimming club. He didn't have to do much swimming, it was enough to be a member and to take part. I didn't know why, but that's how things were in Wangen. Not that it was absolutely essential, not quite, but being a member of the swimming club helped. Of course you were not informed about this at the municipal office when you registered as a new resident. It was something you knew, or else you found out somehow or other. I'd learned about it from Eva, and my colleague Mrs Kupferschmied had confirmed that it was true. Nobody was able to tell me why it had to be the swimming club and nothing else; but never mind that, what was significant was that at the swimming club it was again the Bratwurst and Beer Faction that set the tone. Most likely it was the same at the Rotary Club and in the Grand and Subordinate Lodges, in the brotherhoods, the association for the promotion of tourism, the carnival cliques, the rifle clubs, the drummers associations, the pontoniers club, the chamber of commerce and the trade union branches, in general and everywhere. The B&B Faction called the shots; they might well be the silent majority, but that majority didn't want to be distracted from their enjoyment of B and B.

Did Anderegg know, by the way, what books were currently most in demand at our library? Travel guides. Then, a long way behind, love stories, crime, spy stories, science fiction. Then much further down the line biographies of all sorts of stars, and non-fiction à la *Women Who Run with the Wolves*, *Waiting for the 'Big Beam'*, *Strategies for Positive Aging*. After that nothing for a long time, a very long time. Then the occasional Aitmatov, Irving, Böll, Updike, Grass, Gifter and Co. What a pity there'd never been and that there still weren't enough Karl Mays, Achermanns, Simenons, Van Guliks and Woods. However much they and their like wrote or might still write, it would never be enough. Beer literature had always been in short supply.

"The world as repetition and tittle-tattle," Anderegg said. "But Wangen's nice all the same. And why actually are you so opposed to mainstream culture?"

IV

Dorothea or Strange times

'It might have been yeast, they
said. I should have opened a
bakery'

Kurt Vonnegut, *Hocus Pocus*

1

Some long-lasting afflictions:
a brief summary

At Christmas and New Year our small family was still in
Paris. Peace on earth, happiness and health, a settled life.
In mid January I took Eva and Lydia back to Switzerland.
Eva was four months pregnant; I was to stay on in Paris
for a few more months, returning to Wangen for a couple
of days every two or three weeks.

At the end of January I had a date with Dorothea, the
philosopher.

At the end of February – I'd just returned from a
weekend in Switzerland – we met each other a second
time. Couscous near the Canal Saint-Martin; mint tea in
rue de la Harpe in Dorothea's flat.

Two weeks later two lady doctors, independently of
each other and in the space of three hours, come up with
the same diagnosis: candida albicans.

Paris life is such fun; I apply the prescribed ointments,
I ring Dorothea. I do not postpone my next trip to
Switzerland; I need to talk to Eva.

Back to rue Lacépède and seclusion. At the Clinique
Tarnier in rue d'Assas the fungal infection is declared
cured. But I am not fully reassured.

With reason as it turns out: the fungal infection may

have disappeared, but only to be replaced, a few days later, by a kind of discharge. There can be no doubt as to the cause, but the germ has yet to be identified.

That takes time.

Officially the bug is named trichomonas vaginalis: the prescribed ointments had impeded swift identification, but now at last it had come out into the open. They'd had to grow cultures in special media; a differential diagnosis, they don't mess about in rue d'Assas.

This time Dorothea's reaction is less philosophical. Only Eva in distant Wangen remains unperturbed.

Allegedly the pills work. However the embarrassing symptom persists.

New cultures have to be raised; but nothing develops, neither trichomonads nor diplococci, nor enterococci, corynebacteria, candida or anything else.

Easter in Paris; Whitsun in Wangen.

Meanwhile the national institute on Boulevard Saint-Jacques is looking for chlamydiae, and, to be on the safe side, the surgery in rue d'Assas prescribes tetracycline for eight consecutive days.

Fair copy completed during quarantine; birth of Marie-Jeanne.

In spite of the tetracycline my eyes have become inflamed, and whitish stuff collects in the corners at night. But no, it's not in spite of but because of the antibiotics, says the eye doctor in rue Parrot, conjunctivitis caused by an allergy, and besides it's also due to the weather. I have my doubts.

On top of that the following ailments make their appearance, some simultaneously, some consecutively, some before and some after Whitsun: an inflammation of the right auricle salivary gland, eczematose eruptions in the sternum region, sore throat, ear-ache, stomatitis, stomach cramps and back-ache.

A week after Marie-Jeanne's birth I receive the result of the chlamydiae test: negative. The tetracycline treatment had been unnecessary.

After disappearing for about five days around Whitsun, the discharge reappears, albeit irregularly and not as heavy, definitely unspecific. Where there's nothing, nothing can be found. Although you can't be absolutely sure about the latter part of the sentence. In Paris as elsewhere medicine does not function according to the Cartesian principle. Where there's no proof it makes do with probability. The body is a complicated machine, small deficiencies can always be found here or there.

"Don't pay any attention to it, just forget it," says Eva in Wangen. And in Paris a young lady dermatologist prescribes Valium for my nerves.

I always prefer lady doctors to male doctors. When examining you they're discreeter and friendlier, and they're always ready to prescribe further tests. "They won't find anything, Monsieur, but at least we'll be reassured."

2

Night programme on the couch and Squirrel
Meadow – Jetset and kite-flying – Young travellers –
Harissa – Dirty old men

Exquisite nights on the couch in Wangen. No one else in the house: Eva still in the Engadin with Marie-Jeanne, and Lydia not yet back from France. The things you could listen to on France Culture after midnight when there was nothing but trash on all the TV channels! Broadcasts on Benjamin Franklin and lightning conductors; on Henry James' correspondence with his family, with a delicate hint that James was homosexual; two talks on the history of family values; a heated discussion on the role of money in psychoanalytic practice and – at the approach of dawn – three instalments, one after the other, of the radio adaptation of *Les Mystères de Paris*. Replete with culture, I drank a cup of coffee at the kitchen table before finally going to bed. It must have been a Wednesday: on Wednesdays in the summer holidays I'm not on duty until the afternoon.

Oh yes, it was during that summer that I so often and so clearly recalled that other summer, the strange last half summer at the very end of my time in Paris. Annemarie, Cecilia, et cetera in Zurich; Dorothea, their successor much later on in Paris, was bound to come up.

To bed at five in the morning, or else in the office by six, flexible working hours. It's nice to get something done before the others arrive; and besides, nothing does more to improve my standing with the janitor than being there before half past six to help him air the building. The last to leave in the evening, the first to arrive in the morning, there's no easier way to cultivate the civil servant image.

Across the ring road, along the monastery wall, then straight through Squirrel Meadow and on to the library. Between six and seven every morning Jumbo jets high up in the sky score vapour trails in the blue. "Flying's boring," is what Eva always says. "Your journey doesn't really begin until after you've arrived." Cecilia never said anything else either: routine, routine. Up and away, nonstop to America. Some day. With Eva as a guide. She'd be familiar with my curiosity about Concord and Cooperstown. And she'd be able to cope with a man who doesn't know how to behave in the company of people who're accustomed to transatlantic flights, four-star hotels and menus in French. Luxury makes me feel ill at ease, it's almost physical; not that that's a virtue, only an Appenzell idiosyncrasy. And without someone like Eva, things would be much worse. From time to time she drags me along somewhere or other; but a dinner that costs more than twenty francs still gives me stomach ache. Flying to America for no real reason would be a luxury, no doubt about that.

But why, of late, did the Jura mountain peaks in the cool morning air always have to look like those mountains in China, Huang Shan, Tai Shan: sacred and sketchily painted?

China? America? Neither nor. Two days in Paris will do. Ismael sailing out to sea; Harder getting onto the Paris train, sentimental, but it helps. At the Gare de l'Est I'd take the first hotel in sight, sit for hours in sad cafés or go to the cinema.

Across Squirrel Meadow, travelling in the mind was as far as it went.

And anyway Lydia had come back from her holiday and I had my paternal duties. She talked and talked all evening. And the following evening she wanted to do couscous the way she'd been taught at the youth hostel in Arles.

Monica, her friend and travelling companion, had also been invited. Merguez sausages, however, were nowhere to be found in Wangen.

Life in youth hostels. So the one in Sète still existed, on the hill above the old city, not far from the port. But the one in Arles was no longer on that dusty square with its plane trees where people used to play boules far into the night. And apparently the one in Avignon was no longer on the island between the two channels of the Rhone. I told them I'd stayed there for a week: a ramshackle villa right on the shore, autumn, my first journey abroad, a long time after my Matura. No, not on my own. Monica, cheekily, immediately wanted to know more. "I hope there's nothing you need to keep secret," pursued Lydia. And so, a homage to Erica, nothing in the least unseemly. They both enjoyed that. "And you won't let me do hitchhiking!" said Lydia; which gave her the cue to admit that, actually, they had stood on the roadside with outstretched thumbs a couple of times.

By the way, they hadn't gone to Avignon for the theatre festival but simply to get to know some interesting people, if possible French guys for a change: in Sète and Arles they'd always only met Germans. "And, did you?" "Not one," said Monica, "worse luck. What a bore!"

She was the one who did most of the talking. Lydia only watched as her dad strove to hit the right note for conversation with young people. I wasn't in a position of authority here, I wasn't sitting behind the desk at the library, I couldn't just be the civil servant calmly and politely holding his ground.

Avignon had been full of culture vultures. That or

scruffy drop-outs. Culture vultures or drop-outs. No, nothing in between, unfortunately, at the most a few dirty old men in the bistros and cafés in the town centre. "I suppose you mean harmless old men of about forty or so," I suggested. "Something like that," she said.

The ideas young people have these days! Never trust anyone under twenty. They travel halfway around Europe with the pill in their sponge bags – and, let's hope, with condoms too. But you never know.

I'd better not say anything. And certainly not in the form of fatherly advice. In any case they already know everything, or almost. Even my younger daughter, who recently described with amusement how their religious knowledge teacher – he's the person in charge of AIDS education at our Gymnasium – used the sawn-off end of a broom-stick to demonstrate the use of condoms. It's never too soon to teach young females the significance of symbolic castration.

3
Paris-Wangen return

I'd read and precised all the books and articles. I'd cleared up the questions that I'd set myself on the topic. Drafts of my report were at hand. All it depended on now was my staying power while working on the final copy – half of science is doggedness, and half of life is plans.

"You'll get on better if you stay on here in Paris," said Eva, "and you can come to Wangen as often as you like."

"Of course I can. But it's not very gentlemanly of me

to be sending my pregnant wife on ahead, especially as it's to a flat that has yet to be renovated."

"Don't worry, everything'll be all right. Pregnancy isn't an illness. And anyway I'll enjoy organising the conversion. It's not much, anyway."

"What about Lydia?"

"A father who turns up every three weeks for a couple of days and then disappears again could be rather interesting."

"I'll miss Lydia."

"Really? Lately she hasn't been able to do the slightest thing without annoying you."

"The one thing doesn't exclude the other."

"Granted, your speciality! But let's get back to the facts. How do you expect to work in peace with a squalling baby in the flat? Remember, babies tend to be loud."

"I hope to have finished by then."

"Indeed. Well I wouldn't be too sure about that. No, it's getting too cramped here, my tummy on its own is too big for this flat. And it's not worth trying to find something else for such a short time."

We'd always planned to go back to Switzerland. But did it have to be Wangen?

Towards the end of our second year in Paris Eva's father had told us that he wanted to sign over to Eva one of the flats in the town property he owned. For tax reasons; being a banker he knew about such things.

"It's an old house," said Eva, "lovely but rather run-down. However, if part of it is to be officially mine, as it now seems, I'll be able to take care of it. We could even move into the flat ourselves. What do you think? Or would you rather go back to Zurich?"

Probably I'd go back to working for Wohlwender. Wangen wasn't too far from Zurich. Not too far from Bern or Basel either. Actually Wangen was quite well situated for market research.

I'd never wanted to have a house of my own. But a flat of my own in an old building, I wouldn't mind that. And anyway, the flat didn't belong to me; those property dealings were Eva's business.

Eva didn't insist on moving to Wangen. As far as she was concerned, the fact that her family lived there was more of a deterrent than anything else: although she got on well with her mother, she quarrelled with her father almost every time she saw him.

We certainly couldn't have foreseen that Wangen public library would be looking for an extra librarian that autumn and that I'd hear of it.

But back to Paris and to my medical history, in chronological order as far as possible.

4

Rendezvous

Rue de la Harpe. I knew the street because of the cinemas there. The building was easy to find. A Greek restaurant on the ground floor, a dental surgery on the first, two doors without nameplates on the second floor, likewise on the third and the fourth. The staircase smelled of onions and roast meat. I went back downstairs and reread the names on the letter-boxes: third floor on the left.

I rang the bell.

The front door led straight into a small cluttered kitchen. Beyond the kitchen there was a short corridor with three doors. I've always liked viewing other people's flats.

What would I like, coffee or tea, something else, a glass of wine?

I suggested going across to the Marais. She put on her jacket.

Outside I asked her how she'd managed to find this flat in the middle of the Latin Quarter. She asked me how long I'd known the Andereggs. I asked her how much longer she was staying in Paris. She asked me if Eva had already gone back to Switzerland. For a while we talked about nuclear families, only children, pregnancies, Anderegg's four-year-old son, my almost five-year-old daughter.

We were sitting in the La Tartine bistro in rue Saint-Antoine. In Paris you never ever bump into people by pure chance. Chance needs a helping hand.

It was a book, Plessner's *Laughing and Crying*, that Anderegg had lent her and that I now thought I needed to consult for some quotation or other. Man, the laughing weeping being. 'Bliss it is to rejoice when a friend rejoices, to weep with him when he weeps.' Thus spake Schiller. And the reason Plessner's book was important for Anderegg, or so he told me, was because laughter and tears are both extremely infectious, especially in youth.

Dorothea never laughed, seldom smiled; she sat beside

me at the bistro table, her face stern as if her lips were always slightly tensed – a pensive pout, so to speak.

The topics of conversation were in accordance. Husserl, Heidegger, Sartre, et cetera. Luckily, in my young days in Zurich, I'd once had to read Husserl's *Cartesian Meditations*. I might have understood ten per cent of the whole. Was it an important tenth or was it a tenth that contained only minor details? I really couldn't say.

Instead I was knowledgeable about the history of youth. And I knew everything there was to know about young Tibetans in Switzerland.

At that Dorothea smiled for once.

She wore her hair in a chignon on top of her head, thick, reddish blonde hair. It was my first time alone with her.

Eva and I had got to know her at the Andereggs', at their last St Niklaus party. That was when they were still in the building in rue Gaillard; as always on such occasions the flat was full of people.

The culinary surprise Anderegg came up with that evening was a mannikin as long as your arm, a so-called *Grittibenz*, made of leavened dough baked golden brown and stuffed with all kinds of meat, veal fillet in the legs, meatloaf in the belly.

As I'd agreed to be the Saint Niklaus I slipped out discreetly during the dessert to get changed down in the basement. Cotton wool beard, hooded cloak, birch rod, bag, book of sins, crozier – everything lay ready in their cellar compartment, Anderegg had even remembered a mirror. Back up to the flat in the lift, and then a bit of blustering. By now Lydia only half believed in it all, but

Anderegg's little son still believed fully, so I tried to be gentle. The performance was a success; childish nonsense and folklore nearly always win applause.

Dorothea did not join in the other adults' strained jollity, she simply watched with a polite little smile on her face. I couldn't help noticing.

Beware of the lean and lanky! That didn't apply here since it was not the case. She was not exactly corpulent, just well built. A parson's daughter from Northern Germany, that's what she reminded me of. Wouldn't that have been reason enough to be wary?

5

Couscous or The misaimed kiss

Two weeks later I rang her again. No one answered. I tried again at different times of the day. The French woman she shared her flat with never seemed to be at home either.

I was curiously disappointed.

If our second meeting had come about without difficulty that would have been that; after all, visiting each other is something foreigners in Paris occasionally do. But phoning again and again and no one ever at home! My curiosity was aroused, a curiosity mingled with annoyance and impatience. So impatient was I, finally, that I decided to go there direct. As if that would have enhanced my chances of meeting her! What was enhanced instead, thanks to all my futile trips to rue de la Harpe, was the appeal of the person it was so difficult to contact.

No one and nothing compels me to write this down, I could just as well let it be. It's only my habit of sitting in reading rooms – Sainte-Geneviève, Censier, Musée Social – making brief summaries of other people's writings on my index cards; collecting key-words and sentences and paragraphs in order to cobble something together that might be read and summarised in its turn; copy work, performed with quiet diligence, nothing of consequence, nothing important, Heaven forbid!

In the middle of February I went to Switzerland, for more than just a weekend this time. The flat renovation was under way. Apart from the bigger jobs, there were several details that had to be planned and Eva wanted my opinion.

She'd designed the kitchen and the bathroom herself and was now kept busy quibbling with the architect. "Whenever there's some tricky little problem, you have to find a solution yourself," she said. "An architect won't do it for you, he doesn't have the time." She went along every day. All the architect had to do was supply the professional plans.

"I want to move in in May, before the birth if possible," she said. "It's nice, it means I'm kept busy. All those expectant mothers with that blissfully apprehensive look in their eyes! And I'm building myself a nest: not much better, is it? I've only just noticed that I didn't have enough to do in Paris. What about you? Are you making headway?"

It had been the right decision to stay in Paris to complete the fair copy, far away from family distractions and the building business. I'd be able to hand in my work in spring. Originally I'd given myself two years; a delay of six or seven months was acceptable.

Why should I go back to rue de la Harpe again? For the time being there were no other quotations that needed checking. I stayed at home in rue Lacépède, steady as a rock, fully aware that I ought to be glad there was hardly anything here to distract me from the purpose of my stay.

One late afternoon, however, I was back in that neighourhood after all. I've forgotten why, but I'm sure to have had a plausible reason, nothing special.

The result was a supper, couscous, at a restaurant on the Canal Saint-Martin. Dorothea took me there. From our table you could see bare trees and one of the locks of the canal in the light of the street lamps.

After a lot of eating, drinking and talking Dorothea suggested taking a walk. Boulevard de Strasbourg, Boulevard de Sébastopol, a break at a bistro then out onto the boulevard again and across the Seine back to the Quartier Latin.

Things were still open in rue de la Harpe. Sweet pastries from the Tunisian on the corner, together with mint tea in Dorothea's kitchen as an antidote to the cold.

Dorothea expounded on the banality of evil and the evil of banality. She put forward the thesis that evil should be equated with lack of thought. Where there was thought, evil could no longer be absolute, it lost its power. And Confucius' beautiful idea that man was compelled, all his life, to carry a coffin under his arm. We lose our innocence at every moment, according to Kant, she said.

As we said goodbye outside the door of her flat, something went wrong with our cheek kissing. Her mouth – it must have been an accident – partly touched mine and we looked at each other. Not for long, the light in the staircase went out. Back to the brightly lit kitchen. We embraced passionately.

The philosopher had a certain idea about me and wanted to get down to business at once, there was no time for further foreplay. We'd talked for a whole evening, now it was time for the silent movie.

"*L'acte gratuit* – is that what it's called?" I asked.

"If you say so," she said.

"It took me by surprise anyway."

She, too, admitted to something approaching surprise. Now we heard her flatmate's footsteps in the corridor outside. Sounds from the kitchen, from the bathroom.

"Do you want to stay?"

I stayed.

She fell asleep, I lay awake. The flat had grown quiet, only the noises coming up from rue de la Harpe lasted a little longer. I saw Eva in Wangen, standing in the new flat in the dusty mess of the renovation work. "We'll be moving in in May," she'd said, "at the end of May at the latest." She there, me here. How many years since I first met her? I counted. And seven years ago we got married. Then Lydia. Lying in bed beside the strange woman, I counted up the years again. The cheek kiss that went wrong, no it hadn't happened on purpose. Not now, at least. And it wouldn't have been necessary either. It seemed odd, odd also what had gone before, the Saint Niklaus party, my curiosity, the Plessner book, my telephone calls, everything. And what would the sequel look like, if there was a sequel? Oh, probably things would just sort themselves out. I noticed with astonishment that I was proud that little Swiss me had managed to have an affair with a German philosopher – after seven years of virtuous married life.

"You're nice and quiet," she said. It was not something I deserved credit for, it was largely due to my Swiss dialect, whose slow tempo affected my High German.

She said: "With you, I know where I stand." But why would I take the long way round when the straight path was difficult enough?

She said: "Someone from a modest background." Meaning that to her I was exotic.

She said: "You're a good listener." Easy enough if you don't have much to say.

"And," she said, "you're not as egoistic as the average person of your sex." How large had the sample been?

She showed signs of affection. She'd call me from her office early in the morning, or drop in as late as ten o'clock in the evening. She procured tickets for the Théâtre du Soleil in Vincennes; she invited me to go to the Cinémathèque with her. There could be no doubt about it: those were signs of interest, perhaps even of attachment.

And not the slightest signs of jealousy when I announced that I'd be going to Switzerland for a couple of days the following week. "I'm not your wife's rival," she said. "You must know for yourself if you want to say anything to Eva. There's only one thing I don't want, and that's to participate in crop rotation." I didn't understand

144

what she meant. Smiling and with a shrug of the shoulders, she said: "Kierkegaard." As befitted a philosopher.

6

Champignons de Paris

I had no reason to worry when I felt the itching: some slight skin inflammation. And was it even really an inflammation, that slight reddening? Perhaps I hadn't washed myself enough, or perhaps too much and with soap that was too strong.

When on the day before my return to Switzerland the reddening still hadn't disappeared I decided to go to the day clinic on Boulevard Saint-Michel.

Afternoon surgery. The previous year I'd gone there for treatment of a septic thumb and I knew that the doctors, who offered moderate priced consultations for students, were always changing. This time it wasn't my thumb and I hoped I'd get a male doctor, not a female one.

A young woman doctor examined me.

It didn't look as if there was anything to worry about, she said, after she'd removed her rubber gloves and was back behind her desk. Probably a skin fungus, *un champignon*. She prescribed two ointments. In addition she advised me to get my partner to come by some time, or to go and see another doctor. Otherwise, no sooner the fungus gone, I might get reinfected. Something quite harmless, as she'd already said, but just to be on the safe side she'd refer me to a specialised service in rue d'Assas. That would be free of charge, by the way.

She filled in a form, sketched the position of the lesion on a prescription form, added her diagnosis, and stuck both slips into an envelope onto which she then wrote the address and opening times of the clinic. "You'd best go this evening." She showed me the shortest way on the map of the sixth arrondissement.

That was at three in the afternoon. I could have dropped in at Dorothea's, I'd have been there within five minutes. Instead I went to the Sainte-Geneviève reading-room and sat there for two hours. It was something I hadn't done any more since Eva's departure.

Rue d'Assas. Again it was a woman who examined me, an elderly lady, grey-haired, stout.

She gave me two ointments instead of those her young colleague on Boulevard Saint-Michel had prescribed. She didn't consider it necessary to take a smear for microscopic examination. But she took a blood sample. Why was that, I asked. Due care. I'd be informed if they found anything, not that they expected to. I could also come along in person to collect the report if I'd rather, in about ten days. And in two months another blood test perhaps, if I wanted. She'd give me the prescription for that right now.

An early evening in February. Tomorrow at this time I'd already be changing trains in Basel, soon after that I'd be in Wangen. In the Jardin du Luxembourg I recapped: two lady doctors had, one after the other, diagnosed something harmless, as they said. The elder of the two could surely be relied on; the way she'd examined me seemed very professional and she'd decided without a moment's hesitation: candida albicans. As far as I understood, it was a kind of fungal infection that often occurred in women.

I contemplated going to see Dorothea at once, but then went straight home. An annoying little matter … I had to tell her that … I couldn't understand how … Nothing to be alarmed about, you just had to … At least you should … I'd already been to the chemists' … Both doctors had said it would be best to …

It required an effort, but I had no choice. I rang her up and said what had to be said, with care.

No, she'd never noticed anything. Of course she'd go and see her doctor within the next few days, no problem.

It didn't seem to upset her. And what about Eva, she asked, and wished me a good journey.

The train journey through the winter countryside, my third return to Switzerland. Seclusion and work in Paris; leisure, wife and family in Wangen. I'd just started getting into the routine, it would have been all too perfect!

"Do you remember the German woman, a reddish blonde, tall?" Eva couldn't remember her. "Saint Niklaus evening at the Andereggs'," I prompted. "You talked to her about Simone Weil's book on the situation of women workers, about fathers and daughters too, and about the real estate business."

"Oh, the philosopher," she said. "What about her?"

I told her the truth.

"You're hardly out of the house and your dear husband starts an affair. And now he'd like to be absolved, is that it?"

When I told her how it had happened she didn't ask

147

a lot of questions. In the end she just said: "It's no use crying over spilt milk. Worse things happen. Just get it taken care of, that's all."

I applied the two ointments, scrupulously following the doctor's instructions: for the first five days only the one, the following five days both.

That was no reason not to see Dorothea again, on the contrary. On the train to Switzerland and during the long night journey back to Paris I'd thought about it at length. I hardly knew Dorothea; only getting to know her better could stop her giving me the creeps.

The café near the mosque. She was sitting in the slightly raised section at the back of the dimly lit room. She immediately asked me how things were going with my family in faraway Switzerland. As in our few previous encounters, her manner was reserved, serious. She showed no signs of embarrassment.

Yes, she'd been to see her doctor. No, nothing special had been found. She trusted the woman, a good doctor.

7
Foreign cultures

A real film plot: action and entanglements such as can only be shown on screen; incredibly fast, thrilling, breathless. Except that this story continued in a way things seldom do in films, all grey and banal with no stirring highs. And what about the lows? No, no lows either, at least not for the time being.

Having to apply ointments to my foreskin three times

a day for nearly two weeks contributed to my dejection. Husband and lover, pride comes before a fall; in my case the pride hadn't lasted long.

Instead of simply picking up the results of the blood test at the counter of the Clinique Tarnier at the appointed time, I took a seat in the waiting room again – better be on the safe side. This time it was a man who inspected me. What exactly had made me come, he asked testily, and dismissed me as cured.

I should have felt reassured now; all that was left was a repeat test in two months – or better, in six weeks. I should be free now to concentrate all my attention on the final copy of my paper.

But on inspecting myself one morning three of four days later I noticed something new. If I hadn't had my suspicions and been particularly vigilant, probably I wouldn't have noticed anything for weeks. Man, the being plagued with glands – but what I saw might also have been some kind of discharge. I knew by now that in females candida albicans often shows up as a discharge. So it had to be that.

Was it really that? Was it even possible? At the Censier reading room I read everything that was easily available on the subject. I hadn't ever consulted that kind of reference book before, and in the end I wasn't any the wiser.

I hesitated for two days. It was Friday evening when I went to rue d'Assas; my last chance before the weekend. There was a symptom, not conspicuous, but medically classifiable nonetheless. I wasn't dismissed curtly, the matter was attended to. No diagnosis yet, but I was to come again on Monday, early in the morning.

A strange weekend and a strange week that followed. On Friday I received the first definite result. A swab under the microscope hadn't been enough, microbiological cultures had been required: trichomonas vaginalis – I'd never even heard the word before, now I also knew the thing.

The doctor, bald-headed, cool and detached, was sparing with information. Metronidazole, the whole dose in one go or else spread over seven consecutive days, I had the choice. I'd already waited long enough so I plumped for the drastic treatment: two plastic mugs of water – and the whole handful of pills was down.

Rue Lacépède. It was a cold, sunny day. Down on the copper roof of the shed below me the pigeons strutted around, strutted out from the shade onto the narrow strip of sunlit roof, returned back into the shade.

I rang Editions Mouton where Dorothea had a part-time job. Could we meet today, the problem was solved, at least half solved. Dorothea received the news in her usual reserved manner. Yes, all right, she'd come by some time in the afternoon.

I finished off various jobs; at midday I took a walk through the Jardin des Plantes; for a while I watched the seal doing its rounds in the pool.

It was late afternoon by the time Dorothea arrived. We sat down at the kitchen table and I told her what I'd found out concerning the new malady.

"Apparently you think it's important, okay, in that case

I'll go," she said. "I suppose it'd be better not to try my own doctor again."

Should I go with her, I asked.

We took the bus: Mosque – Jussieu – Monge – Panthéon – rue Soufflot. And on foot through the Jardin du Luxembourg.

"I detest gynaecological examinations," she said, "particularly when they're done by men."

There were also women doctors at rue d'Assas, I told her.

"What difference does that make?" she said.

Besides, it was possible, perhaps even probable, that they wouldn't find anything to start with. In my case it had taken three tests, the symptoms were very discreet.

"What a word, in the light of the circumstances!"

We laughed briefly, unhappily, as we hurried along beneath the bare chestnut trees, along the Avenue de l'Observatoire, past the Carpeaux Fountain. By now I knew the opening hours by heart, we had plenty of time. We entered the hall, I walked ahead.

She could tell the doctor that she could of course feel free to consult my file.

"What for?" she asked.

Only now did I notice how embarrassed she was by my company there.

I stayed downstairs in the corridor next to the reception desk, feeling suddenly very relieved. As though ever since my telephone call that morning I'd all along feared she wouldn't let herself be persuaded to come to this consultation.

"Quick, let's get out of here!" she said.

"What about the result?"

"Nothing, of course. But thanks to your file I have to take the tablets all the same. I've already got the first dose inside me, they really don't give you much time for consideration. An interesting business, quite crazy, and I let them persuade me! Now I desperately need a cognac. And it's no use telling me the medicine and alcohol don't go together, the woman up there already told me."

Two cognacs in the first bistro on Boulevard Saint-Michel. Outside, the evening traffic through the twilight, inside, the noise of the pinball machine; the noise didn't trouble us, we didn't talk much.

Dorothea had to go somewhere else that evening. "Give me a ring some time," she said. I clutched her shoulder, kissed her cheek; she turned away, stoney-faced, crossed the road at the pedestrian crossing and was gone, without a backward look.

Kurosawa's *Dersu Uzala* at the studio cinema on rue Monge. While the Russian surveyor and the old hunter moved through primeval forest and tundra, from time to time I felt the metronidazole beginning to work: a stabbing sensation first here then there, rheumatic tension in the phallic area, in the whole of my abdomen. The old hunter out there on the screen had other problems, where he lived everything was still nature.

The film was long, I didn't get home until late.

Still Saturday, then Sunday, Monday, Tuesday – on Wednesday or Thursday at the soonest I could go back to rue d'Assas for a check-up. I'd leave here at eight in the morning – or perhaps earlier, consultations began at nine, but you could already sign in at half past eight. Saturday and Sunday and Monday and Tuesday, Wednesday too. I had to get through those days somehow or other.

On Friday night I wrote Eva a detailed account. At least I was getting on reasonably well with my work, I wrote. Everything else was true, it was the only lie; but that was of no account now.

The room that opened onto the back courtyard, formerly Lydia's room. I'd had my table there since the middle of January. The bluish green copper roof of the shed below me, the strutting pigeons.

I lay on the bed with a blanket covering my legs reading Cooper's *Homeward Bound* – Eva had given me the rare secondhand book for Christmas, a sea adventure. I read, dozed off, read a bit more, Cooper made fun of his Yankees, and from time to time I sat down at the table and tried to work for a quarter of an hour, half an hour, lay down on the bed again.

You couldn't go to the cinema every evening.

I phoned my in-laws' place in Wangen, Eva rang back.

The first winter here had been very nice. On Sundays we'd gone on excursions all over Paris, always with a stop at some boulevard café for a drink. Lydia enjoyed those journeys in the metro and the walks afterwards, she seldom whined.

"Do you or don't you want to have this affair? That's what I'd like to know." Her bright face beneath her

153

pinned-up hair. Somehow this affair had started off badly, I said. "You can say that again," she said. "On the other hand bugs aren't as important as all that. If two people love each other things like that are irrelevant. You, however, love your wife – don't deny it. In any case, if I were you I wouldn't deny it, it's half your charm." Her smile as she said this was difficult to interpret; I've never been good at reading people's faces.

With a shock I realised how little I knew about Dorothea. Next to nothing in fact. But had it been any different years ago with Elizabeth, Linda, Cecilia, etc? But then there'd never been any disastrous outcomes, at least not of that trivial kind. And since nothing like that occurred, the unfamiliarity soon diminished. Intimacy must begin somehow, otherwise nothing at all can begin.

But Dorothea became more and more of a stranger.

Could she be trusted? What might she do? It was important for me to know where I stood with her. And the only way to find out was by continuing to meet her. She didn't seem to object. The manliness of man lies in chastity.

What friends of hers did I know? At Anderegg's place I'd only ever seen her that once, at the Saint Niklaus dinner, probably he knew little more about her than I did, and I didn't want to ask him out straight.

On that dreary weekend – I should have been working, but instead I was reading Cooper's homecoming novel – she came by unannounced.

You can't go to the cinema every day. Why not, actually? And afterwards would I go with her to see some friends.

They greeted her effusively. They all seemed to

be French, young people. They sat on cushions on the floor. The walls were lined with brightly coloured cotton drapes, trees of life, made in India. They drank tea, and wine from a litre bottle, and I remember being surprised that the cups and glasses were very clean – as though I'd expected something else.

Another time we met one of her colleagues from the Editions Mouton. "I'm a feminist," was the first thing the colleague said. And when she heard that my wife was pregnant she started to extol natural birth, and in particular home birth. Medical technology was a purely masculine affair, childbearing belonged in women's hands, the gynaecologist clique had wielded power long enough, midwives did most of the work, doctors were useless. She herself had attended several home births. Besides, these days it was better in nine out of ten cases to have an abortion anyway.

I admitted that at Lydia's birth at the hospital I'd nearly fainted, they'd had to look after me more than Eva and the baby. However, the second birth would still most likely take place in a hospital, and I'd be there if I could.

A café-bar near the Bastille; the French woman and I were drinking wine, Dorothea had beer. Next to our table there was a spiral staircase leading upstairs, from where we heard a soprano singing Piaf-Barbara-Gréco evergreens to the accompaniment of an accordion. Although the French woman was rather plump there was something spiky and intrusive about the way she kept on at me. There were rings on all her fingers except for her thumbs, bracelets jingled from her wrists, her divided skirt was held up by a broad belt with silver trimmings.

I wanted reassurance. Once I'd got to know a couple of Dorothea's friends, I'd have reason to feel reassured.

8

Doing penitence and a flying visit – The final copy and quarantine

In the freshness of morning, up rue Lacépède, then left down rue de la Clef as far as rue Censier; across noisy rue Monge and into quiet rue Pascal, up the steps on the right to Boulevard de Port-Royal; past rue Broca and rue Berthollet, past the Val-de-Grâce military hospital; on the right, rue Saint-Jacques and rue Henri Barbusse; and then, on the big crossing, the view down to the metro tracks; it was still a bit too early for the surgery on rue d'Assas. On my way there I always prepared the questions I wanted to ask. On the way back I thought over what I'd been told.

The trichomonads were gone, but there were still signs of infection. The doctors wanted to wait and see, so I had to wait too. "Nothing serious, Monsieur, but it takes time. Drink a lot of tea and come again in a fortnight."

If I hadn't, I'd now be able to … If I could, once again, I'd probably know … The sooner the … If, contrary to expectations … If this, then that …

Heavily, but beaming and with a light suitcase, Eva came down the platform.

"Lydia is well looked after in Wangen, she gets spoiled. My father drove me to Basel last night. I wanted to take a sleeper."

She fancied croissants and we chose a seat at the window in one of the big cafés opposite the Gare de l'Est.

"Embarrassing – why? I just wanted to be sure; quite apart from possible complications in pregnancy. And of course everything's all right. Anything else would have been inexplicable as there'd been no follies I could have confessed to. So that's settled, it must have been your philosopher. Dorothea, a dignified name. For you she's turned into a kind of Pandora – have I guessed right?"

Matter-of-fact Eva!

She'd taken the Thursday night express. "I thought I'd better come."

She refused to take a taxi. She stood there good-humouredly in the crowded metro and told me the happenings of the past couple of weeks in Wangen. As the train came above ground after the Quai de la Rapée and crossed the Seine she said: "It's nice to be back."

In the Jardin des Plantes men in overalls were busy pruning the plane trees; standing on stepladders mounted on lorries, they fetched down the branches with long-handled billhooks. Was it already spring? It must have been the end of March or the beginning of April; only a sprinkling of fresh green on the lawns.

"How are you getting on with your work? A stupid question, of course you're not doing anything. It doesn't really matter, does it?"

She chatted with the concierge; she chatted with old Madame Malochet; in the evening she chatted with the German woman and the Yugoslav. They all seemed happy to see her and asked her how she felt. Even in her first pregnancy, with Lydia, she'd hardly ever felt any discomfort.

Everything was going fine in Switzerland. There was no need to worry about that.

She stayed until Sunday afternoon. We didn't do much. On Saturday Valérie-Anne picked us up, and Anderegg took Eva around his building site on rue Desgranges. They wouldn't be able to move in for quite a while yet. They both talked excitedly about bathrooms, plumbing and electrics, flooring materials, workers in Paris, workers in Wangen.

Now that they'd bought their house in Montreuil it was final: the Andereggs would be staying on in Paris. Now that we were converting the flat in Wangen it was final: our move to Wangen would not be a temporary one. It was easy to talk about houses and flats and building work. I listened to the two of them with something like envy.

A week went by, two weeks, three; there were no new troubles. The same symptoms remained, a little stronger one day, less noticeable another so that I'd already be thinking I'd got it all behind me; but then the old symptoms reappeared.

The sun might be shining in through the kitchen window, it might be raining, the weather might be springlike or again winterly cold, it made no difference. Every day began like the one before: grey. After three cups of coffee I'd go and sit down at the table in the back room.

It was meant to be the speedy completion of my assignment: alone in the flat, no lively noisy Lydia, no child-rearing duties, no table-talk, no bed-talk, no discussions about this or that, nothing, the main business and nothing else.

"I meant to go into retreat, now I'm in quarantine," I said to Eva on the phone.

"Don't exaggerate," she said.

All the trivia during that last half-year in Paris! Disgust mingled with enjoyment as I reread the stacks of jottings from that time. They were undated, but what they contained told me clearly enough when they'd been written, no names, no places, yet I knew exactly. Why didn't I throw it all away? Why did I put the packs of papers back into the box? The malady has gone, but I want to keep the notes, as evidence that I once noted down things I knew I'd rather have forgotten the following day. Record everything, whatever it is. Those obtrusively physical little things – they searched and searched and hardly anything was found. Quite laughable, yet it had unhinged me. Nobody noticed anything, except for Eva, I'd taken the necessary precautions. But I couldn't hide it from myself.

The embarrassing detail that I hadn't held out until, say, May, June or July before getting mixed up with Dorothea, that I'd seized the earliest opportunity, without dithering for one moment; and all for no real reason, no desperate quarrels, no permanent annoyance, nothing. "Straight from Stifter-like peace and harmony," Anderegg might have said, "to the cesspool of vice." "Cockfirst into the pit," Sommerhalder would have scoffed, "typical petit-bourgeois."

L'acte gratuit. If you will. *Gratuit* perhaps, but certainly not gratis. The first step and the second step, and whose fault was it actually? There was no getting away from it. The philosopher would certainly have left me in peace. Ethnologists are said to be passionate collectors, transhumance with bell-ringing in Appenzell, nightmares with obsessional washing in Paris. The melancholy of youth; and age does not save you from folly.

And the worst thing about it all was that Dorothea still attracted me. That alone was enough to scare me. I dared not think of the soft-skinned, buttery-coloured fullness beneath that severe protestant face.

Did I make headway with the final copy? The scribbling intensified. Never have I jotted down more notes on irrelevancies than I did while I was living as a hermit in rue Lacépède.

9

An American in Paris

Wait for a miracle and drink a lot of water. Finally they sent me to the Laboratoire Fribourg-Blanc on Boulevard du Montparnasse. Cultures again; but nothing grew, nothing developed, neither funguses nor trichomonads nor anything else. However my blood still contained a significant number of white cells, which proved there was an infection and that the infecting agent was perfectly disguised.

The woman doctor in rue d'Assas – luckily I chanced to have the one who'd prescribed the new tests – decided that simply drinking water was not enough and that something had to be done. "It worries you a bit, *n'est-ce pas*? *Oui*, I understand. There's still a chance that it might be chlamydiae. We'll check it out." She prescribed an eight-day course of antibiotics and sent me next door for more detailed examinations.

The young doctor there introduced himself as an American who'd come to Paris to do clinical studies on precisely those chlamydiae, as it happened. What was I studying here, he asked. – Ah, sociology of youth, very interesting. In that case I was bound to know all about statistics, he too had to grapple with statistics. Unfortunately, the patient groups in clinical research were often very small, which easily led to mistakes, a real problem for him at the moment.

The man was very talkative, his French was like the French I'd spoken two and a half years previously, albeit with a different accent.

Would I be willing to tell him my story?

He took notes, occasionally asked for more details, nodded, took his time. His notes seemed to be more important to him than the bit of secretion he blotted up afterwards with a cotton swab and transferred into two tiny jars as two separate samples. I could pick up the results in about two weeks, he said, preferably from the Institut Fournier direct. He gave me the address.

It occurred to me to ask why I already had to take tetracycline now, before they had any results.

That was the doctrine here in cases like mine. As so many causes of inflammation had already been eliminated, they were giving antibiotics, the tried and tested dose, for once without waiting for the definitive diagnosis. Low risk, considerable time-saving. And if they still failed to find anything, so much the better. Tetracycline was effective against a wide range of bacteria – and it must have been something or other. In any case, he'd be seeing me again. Follow-ups were important, even if only for statistical

161

purposes. I'd provided a lot of information, nice and precise too; teamwork, something he much appreciated.

That was the official part. But the American was in no hurry, at least he didn't get up to see me to the door, or make a move to shake hands. He remained affably seated at his desk.

How did I like Paris, he asked. He himself really loved it, the architecture, the pictures in the Orangerie, the Centre Pompidou. Where in Switzerland did I come from, he only knew Geneva, he'd been there for a conference.

He was inquisitive, understandably, he didn't want to talk about microbes all the time, any other topic must have seemed preferable. Thus Appenzell, Zurich, advertising and again youth. Appenzell interested him particularly. He'd grown up in the country himself. His father ran a farm in Wisconsin, very flat countryside.

Did I know Madison – or Milwaukee? Not surprising that I didn't. Did I like jazz? There were plenty of concerts here in Paris, the best jazz musicians in America came to Paris, the Parisians were crazy about jazz. Admittedly, he preferred opera, and it was only here in Paris that he'd discovered what opera really was. Yes indeed, the Cinémathèque in the Palais de Chaillot was also wonderful; needless to say, there was nothing like it in the Midwest, in one year here he'd seen more films by Allen, Altman, Pollack, Penn than in all his time as a student in Madison. After he'd finished his investigations here he'd have to go back to Milwaukee, unfortunately, a dump compared to Paris, even if it was a dump with skyscrapers.

162

10

Dorothea's confession

Do you really, seriously think I ingested the full dose of that poison? God Almighty! I wish I had your faith in doctors! I took the stuff again the next day, then I thought it over and stopped. I'm not going to stuff myself with medicine before they've proved that it's necessary. Which they haven't, not by any means. They prescribed those pills on the strength of your file and for no other reason. You keep saying how trustworthy the rue d'Assas people are, but what's trustworthy about that, I ask you? And to come to the crucial point – I didn't tell you before, but I'm telling you now: two weeks ago I went to a medical lab to have the thing reexamined – I know a woman who's a biologist there. Just so you realise that I want to know for myself what it's all about. They did all kinds of tests, and they didn't find a single thing, nothing at all. As a matter of fact, I didn't expect anything else, you sense things like that. It would have been completely idiotic to have gone on stupidly and obediently taking those pills for another five days. Don't trust the doctors. Trust your body."

Opposite me at the bistro table, the evening after the discussion with the American; I wanted to keep Dorothea informed.

The wisdom of the body was a debatable question. But apparently Dorothea didn't quite trust her body anyway, otherwise she'd hardly have gone to the lab where her good friend was employed.

Besides, could she name one good reason why doctors or biologists who happened to be one's friends should be more trustworthy than those who were complete strangers? And anyway, she'd taken almost half of the metronidazole for the trichomonads, hadn't she, and that amount would have been at least strong enough to prevent anything being detected, for a while anyway. I reminded Dorothea how difficult the diagnosis had been in my case. That was precisely the reason they now, and so on and so forth.

She listened, albeit reluctantly.

"Most kind of you to enlighten me," she said. "Just don't try to persuade me to go running to your doctors too. You'll never get me back there again."

What on earth had I expected from that blonde philosopher? What had I wanted to prove to myself? Had the seven years with Eva been too simple? In retrospect, you're amazed at your own desire.

11
Eye pain

"In about two weeks," the young American from Wisconsin had said. Which could also mean in ten days.

Fair copy or life in waiting-rooms. The day clinic for students on Boulevard Saint-Michel, the surgery at the Tarnier clinic on rue d'Assas, the Fribourg-Blanc laboratory on Boulevard du Montparnasse; and now the Alfred Fournier institute on Boulevard Saint-Jacques.

A sand-coloured building on the number six metro line. A newly discovered library would have been a more pleasant place to set foot in. The first time I went I only

164

wanted to explore the neighbourhood. I could easily have taken the metro at Station Monge, changed trains at Place d'Italie and got out at Station Saint-Jacques. But I preferred to walk.

The other times too. For I went several times in vain. Either the American had told me something wrong or I'd misheard him. After ten days there were still no results, and there were still none after two and then three weeks. Those lab tests seemed to be very special and very complicated.

Long walks down the boulevards and avenues of the thirteenth and fourteenth arrondissements. Spring came. Occasionally by eleven or half past I'd mustered up enough energy to check a few quotations or retype a page. Otherwise I sat in the dark at the kitchen window and looked out across the rooftops.

I'd taken the tetracycline scrupulously for eight days. I started to believe that it might be the right thing, that it would be effective, either against what they were looking for or against whatever else it might be.

I'd rejoiced too soon: My eyes were next in line.

For a long time I didn't pay any heed, since there were quite enough other things I had to keep under observation. Then one day, on looking more closely in the mirror, I saw something whitish, yellowish in the inside corner of each eye – was it only a little, was it a lot? In any case it seemed to me that it was much more than what usually gets rubbed out of bleary eyes in early mornings.

I sat down. Got up again and took another look, this time in the round magnifying shaving mirror. I sat down again. Dashed out of the flat, ran down the steps, onto the street and across rue Linné into the Jardin des Plantes. The chestnut trees were in blossom.

So that was it! What they'd been incapable of isolating in the ultramodern Laboratoire Fribourg-Blanc, what they were still looking for with all their high tech in Boulevard Saint-Jacques – had finally been produced by my own conjunctive tissues, the best culture-medium of all. And the eight doses of eight tetracycline tablets each had been absolutely useless. Was it possible? Lots of things were possible. Was anything like that to be expected? Not to be expected perhaps, certainly to be feared.

So pus was accumulating in my eye sockets. And in my mind's eye, very clearly, I saw the infection develop – fungi, protozoa, bacteria – as I ran though the avenues of the Jardin des Plantes trying to muster the necessary resolve.

The same morning I found an eye doctor who took patients without previous appointment, in a side street, rue Parrot, between the Gare de Lyon and Bastille. The waiting-room looked like a living room, cluttered up with old-fashioned furniture and overcrowded with patient people. My turn didn't come until just before noon.

The doctor listened to my story, looked into my eyes through the apparatus; his wife assisted.

It was the weather, he said. I was already the fourth patient today with the same infection. So many things played a part: the dry weather the last few days, the wind at the moment, the dust, and pollen too, exhaust fumes, traffic, it got worse from year to year. And then there were the antibiotics I'd been prescribed, things like that considerably increased the allergy factor.

He prescribed two kinds of eye drops, chibro-boraline and vert sulfo. Nothing strong, he said, and if that didn't do the trick I shouldn't hesitate to come back.

In the following weeks I tried out several other kinds of drops: from the end of May sodium propionate, from the middle of June rexophtal and uveline, from the beginning of August zincfrin. The irritation of the conjunctive tissues persisted, they named it conjunctivitis of unknown origin.

I had long since largely lost faith in that amiable doctor near the Gare de Lyon. I continued to go there but at the same time I consulted the ophthalmological service in the Hôpital Pitié-Salpêtrière. Again and again I'd be there sitting in the big, darkened diagnostic room. The Vietnamese woman doctor prescribed swabs and cultures. The results were negative.

The eye infection did not prevent me from starting on my librarian's job in Wangen. Here in town I also consulted two doctors about my eyes. One of them, the father of one of Eva's former schoolfriends, tried cortisone drops; it was no good. His younger, female, colleague and rival gave me a prescription for new glasses; the new lens did not provide a remedy either.

'What thou lovest well remains …' One and a half years later the infection was still there. And then, when I was almost sure my eyes would always be slightly reddened, it suddenly disappeared. Admittedly, for weeks already the irritation had been very slight, almost imperceptible in fact.

Office life; book dust doesn't irritate your eyes.

The Dorothea-Syndrome; a big word for a small

167

matter. "If you'd cried out your eyes over it in a truly romantic manner," I hear Anderegg say. He didn't say it, couldn't have said it, as he didn't know about the complications, knew nothing at all about the calamity. Anyway, I don't need anyone to tell me things like that, sooner or later I come upon them myself.

That's the trouble with knowledge. You know something, you know it clearly and precisely, but that doesn't help you.

12
Dorothea's eloquence

"Did I hear right? You're criticising me? Fine, you may do so! You're upset by the whole business, I can understand that, okay? But why make such a big fuss! And now you even expect me to put on sackcloth and ashes – that's just crazy! Hey man, pull yourself together! The world – even your little world – isn't going to fall to pieces just because of an itsy-bitsy boo-boo like that. I'm alive, you see, I'm alive, and I still live in hope, you know what that means. A little tolerance wouldn't do any harm. Talking to me about morals! I know my responsibilites. You'd better make sure you know yours too. And above all, stop all those delicate innuendos about who's to blame, it's not a matter for the judges. What kind of person have I got mixed up with? Really, I could be the one asking myself that! But forget it! If you want to go on seeing me, okay, and if you don't that's all right with me too. Go on running after your doctors, I wish you luck …"

Had I really mentioned morals, guilt? Was it a reproach? In passing I'd mentioned my astonishment that she was sleeping with a man again before the little boo-boo, as she called it, had been cleared up. No, I hadn't used the word 'irresponsible', I'd only said her behaviour was 'rather careless'. That was enough to bring the woman – otherwise so reasoned and thoughtful – to an outburst of rage.

It's not what I'd wanted.

Being able to talk to her occasionally, even if only on the phone, helped relieve my anxiety. If I couldn't talk to her any more the uncertainty would increase, I could see it coming. It had been careless, reckless, grossly negligent of me to use a word like 'careless'.

She hung up. The end, over and finished, connection cut. All the effort I'd put in for weeks to keep in touch had been in vain. And the violence of her reaction to my mild reservations was anything but reassuring.

13
Two evils are not enough

Candida albicans apparently, the diagnosis confirmed thanks to successful therapy; then trichomonads, no doubt about it, also successfully fought, apparently; *faute de mieux* they looked around for something else, for chlamydiae finally, at the Institut Fournier on Boulevard Saint-Jacques. That came to nothing too, only negative finds, as I finally learned four and a half weeks and several fruitless visits later.

In rue d'Assas they now refused to do any further tests. Medically the problem was solved. What would the world come to if every man with a slightly irritated Halef made such a fuss!

I had to seek counsel elsewhere.

Madame Gascard on Boulevard Auguste Blanqui. While I was sitting in the waiting-room I heard the receptionist outside phoning; a number of cosmetics were mentioned, together with the results of the respective allergy tests. *Paris Match*, *Jours de France*, *Marie-Claire* lay on the little glass table.

The doctor was young.

I explained my case and showed her all my old medical files.

She listened attentively, read through everything carefully.

"That's quite enough," she said. "We won't have any further analyses done. But I'll prescribe a tranquilliser, you seem to be on the nervous side. Take one tablet in the morning and one in the evening, let's say for two weeks to start with."

She accompanied me to the padded door, shook my hand encouragingly.

In a café on the Place d'Italie I pondered the new situation. That was actually what I'd hoped for, no new conjectures, no new suspects, no new medicine – just something to put my mind at rest. It couldn't have been made clearer.

And I believed it: in blind thankfulness, for two hours. With rising doubts the whole of the following day. With resolute good sense now and then for a few more days too.

But a month later Madame Gascard prescribed a second course of Valium. I'd shown her a rash on my chest, and the beginnings of a rash between my eyebrows. "Eczema,"

170

she said, "probably nervous; I'll prescribe the tranquilliser again, together with an ointment for your skin."

Patiently the young doctor listened to my questions. She stuck to her opinion that there was no need to repeat the tests, the institute on Boulevard Saint-Jacques and the lab on Boulevard du Montparnasse could be trusted.

Fungi, protozoa, bacteria. A single evil wasn't enough, nor were two, a third had to be found. And if not those extravagant chlamydiae that the young American had come to Paris to do research on, what about spirochaetes, why not? Venereal disease, antiquated and famous, treponema pallidum.

Preoccupied as I'd been with my trivial discharge it was an eventuality I'd carelessly neglected. The real disaster and the imminent disaster, the dialectics of disaster; once the real one was over – instead of antibiotics only Valium – it was time to think of what was threatening. For who could subsequently prove that that fungus at the beginning of it all had really been nothing but a fungus? They hadn't looked at it through a microscope, they'd simply trusted their clinical eye. All right, there'd been a blood test, that at least. On the other hand it was suspicious that immediately after the first test at rue d'Assas they'd prescribed a second one for two months later; in other words, those tests couldn't be very reliable.

"But that's how it's done," said Madame Gascard. "It's the routine. *Non, non, Monsieur,* you may rest assured, definitely, as far as that's concerned."

"As far as that's concerned?"

"*Cher Monsieur,* you have a way of misunderstanding people! No, really, there's nothing, *rien du tout.*"

171

Oh dear, serological tests, what indeed could they disprove! Although several weeks had gone by without anything appearing, the disease was still there: the articles in the medical reference books described it in detail. Eczema on the chest and between the eyebrows, erosion of the skin between the big toe and the little one on the right, swollen glands on the left, mouth ulcers, acne on the back: they were all symptoms of the second phase, somewhat atypical because of the medicine I'd taken.

A former intern at the Paris hospitals, a Medical Faculty prize-holder, a member of the dermatology department of the Hôpital Saint-Louis: the doctor here on Boulevard Saint-Marcel was the right man for me, even though his speciality was aesthetic surgery and diseases of the scalp.

A waiting-room like a showroom for furniture design, the medical secretary a hostess in a tailored suit. The doctor I was taken to was elegantly dressed too; with professional friendliness he stretched out a hand, patting me on the shoulder even before we'd got through the door: we understand your problems. I showed him the eczema, mentioned the itch on my back; a further clinical examination could do no harm, a second opinion, due care. Smiling and nodding he looked at the reddened skin. Increased sebum production, seborrhea, a discharge here too. He nodded and smiled, yes, yes, we understand. And we discussed the medical profession's advice concerning the interval between repeats of serological tests; I mentioned the diverse information I'd received from doctors so far or that I'd found in books. He nodded and smiled: "You see …" He specified, he qualified, he explained, he asked me to understand. He almost convinced me. "I have patients," he said, "who lead risky lives. I recommend they do those tests every four or five weeks." At that my understanding turned into amazement, and he noticed. "But of course, that doesn't apply to you. I only mentioned it to show you how widely folks differ."

Other doctors wrote out a prescription and sent you to a medical lab. This man – in his elegant suit, without a doctor's coat – stuck the needle into my vein himself.

The second consultation was short. "No, nothing. That was to be expected. If I were you I'd put the matter aside now, I'd say once and for all."

If he'd only known!

Anyway, he was the last specialist with all the information about my case to be willing to prescribe a further test.

I got additional prescriptions, one a fortnight, from ordinary doctors, usually woman doctors. And just as I went to a different place each time to get a prescription, I also sought out a different medical laboratory each time to take it to. Until I noticed on the reports that for the more complicated immunofluorescence analysis the job had always been sent on to one or other of the same two big laboratories: Boulevard du Montparnasse or Boulevard Saint-Jacques. And at the bottom of the page there was always the same remark: '*persistance d'une sérologie négative*'.

They must have noticed that I'm a permanent client, I thought, a *malade imaginaire*.

That should have reassured me. On the other hand it raised new doubts: Did lab technicians and biologists who considered a patient to be a *malade imaginaire* still take enough pains with their analyses?

There was only one solution: I gave each of the doctors who wrote out a prescription a different name. Only by continually changing my name could I be more or less sure that the people at Boulevard Saint-Jacques or Boulevard du Montparnasse wouldn't skimp the precision work.

Now, with those guaranteed individual negative results, I could ascertain for myself the enduring absence of the third evil. Perhaps two evils, minor though they were, had been enough.

The threat remained slight, in fact it diminished week by week. And the residual risk was something I could live with, at least well enough to make headway with the fair copy.

It was high time.

V

Eva, education, married life

'You never did ask each other
anything, did you? And you never
told each other anything. You
just sat and watched each other,
and guessed at what was going on
underneath. A deaf-and-dumb
asylum, in fact!'

Edith Wharton, *The Age of Innocence*

1

The Assumption of the Blessed Virgin –
The year of the wasps

"Really Dad, you – and to China of all places! I'm flabbergasted!"

"What's so special about it?"

"How can you ask? You've never in all your life been on a real journey, only ever to Paris – and now this! I'd always thought that if in the end you ever did take a plane it'd be to America – to see your rabbits and Babbits and the scenery of some of those Hollywood flicks you're always consuming. It'd be logical, wouldn't it?

"I'll never go to America, never ever. I don't fancy being shot dead on a street corner by the first kid to come along, just because I haven't given him a chewing-gum."

"Are you okay, Dad!"

"Trigger-happy, fat and obnoxious, that's what young people are like over there. As for me, I want to stay alive."

"Sorry, Dad, but you're crazy."

Eva, Lydia, Marie-Jeanne: the family was reunited. Eva and Marie-Jeanne hadn't come home from the Engadin until the last week of the holidays. *Allegro vivace* – the end of peace and quiet.

What remained was the heat, the height of summer.

177

In the library we suffered; we aired the place in the early morning, pulled down the blinds in good time, but it didn't help much.

The end of the holidays. But right in the middle of the first week of term there was already another holiday: Assumption Day. Here in town they had a nice nickname for it: *Maria, flieg auf!* – 'Fly up Mary!'

As I lay dozing a sentence came into my mind: 'I want to go swimming over there in the shade of the trees.' There was no water anywhere there, only shade; but in my semicomatose state the wish seemed perfectly reasonable.

The three attic rooms are the best. When the family gets too noisy I retire into the smallest, the one that faces north.

The room diagonally opposite is where Marie-Jeanne plays her cello. But between us there's the stairwell, the corridor and the open attic space, three doors altogether. I can't send my daughter and Bach and Fauré down into the cellar.

The attic room facing south is the guestroom, seldom used; only the toilet and the shower get used occasionally.

Eva usually reads until deep into the night, I watch old films. Eva normally gets up late, I often get up very early. Eva sleeps deeply and snores, I awaken at the slightest sound.

Why always plug one's ears with memory foam? The blockhouse, the hut on Lake Walden, Mark's Reef, or the luxury of being alone.

From my attic room I can see across the treetops to the mountain.

"We're going to catch wasps. Are you coming?" Lydia asked her sister.

"Of course not, it's much too stupid," said Marie-Jeanne.

Now they'd be sitting in the Aaregarten or in the Gambrinus, sipping their Cokes, bored, but with a lot of important things to tell each other at the tops of their voices. And they'd be catching wasps with the empty Coke bottles; it seemed to be the latest craze.

The empty bottles were placed upside-down in the holes for parasols in the middle of the table tops. Attracted by the scent of Coca-Cola, the wasps flew into the bottles and, as they persisted in fleeing upwards towards the light, couldn't find their way out.

The game was pursued as a competition, table against table.

"Cruelty to animals," said Marie-Jeanne.

"You poor little sensitive creature," said Lydia.

They've gone through several phases, all my daughters have! Frayed jeans ripped at the knees accidentally or on purpose; white ankle socks that absolutely had to be from Esprit. The coke-chips-ketchup phase started early, and it's still not quite over. For a while Lydia went riding – girls and horses, a worthy topic for an Andereggian analysis. Black T-shirts, black leggings, even the wristbands were knitted in black, a new pair almost every week. And when Lydia started to keep a diary Marie-Jeanne made haste to do the same although she'd hardly learned to write. However, their fads seldom overlapped; while Marie-Jeanne was still at the chewing-gum stage, it was the Parisienne cigarettes stage for Lydia; the one was still reading Daddy Long-

Legs *and* Pippi Langstrumpf, *while the other was on* Anna Karenina. *Only Marie-Jeanne's cello playing has outlived it all.*

So this year catching wasps was all the rage among the young people here. At least it's better than having noses and lips pierced with fake jewellery; not to speak of other piercings.

And there was no shortage of wasps this year. The windfallen fruit on the roads around the library was full of them.

"What about going jogging, Dad?" Marie-Jeanne suggested.

"A good idea, yes," said Eva. "Come along next time. You'll be very welcome."

"With you and old Kupferschmied?"

"I'm sure she wouldn't mind. Of course we'd be very considerate to start with, we can't have a man like you coming in last."

"No need for your indulgence, I wouldn't dream of running through the woods with you."

"But a little walk, that'd be something."

"A walk? What for?"

"What do you think, you old bore! You spend the whole week on your bum between bookshelves, a bit of exercise and fresh air would do you good."

"Ten press-ups in a draught are just as good."

"What rubbish! Come on, let's go out! Only a quick walk up to the Crag. Who's coming?"

Who indeed! Our exemplary daughter, Marie-Jeanne. I didn't want to be a spoil-sport. The family marching in formation through the neighbourhood on Assumption Day: afternoons like that should be abolished.

"You're not serious, are you, I mean about China?"

"I'm not quite sure, it just slipped out, in the heat of the moment. What about you, are you going?"

"Probably. It's the last chance I've got of meeting up with Isabelle there. She'll hardly want to stay a third year."

"Well then, go."

"Most likely I will."

"And perhaps I really will go with you, for once. Or would it put you out?"

"Put me out? On the contrary, it'd be lovely."

"Well, perhaps, it might be worth thinking about."

"Harder backs down! It's always the same."

"No, no. I just want to give it some more thought. I'm taken by surprise myself."

"Well, you haven't got much time for thought. At least the flight has to be booked soon. – By the way, is your passport still valid? Go and take a quick look."

2

Against youth – For passion –Table manners

"Young people today: weird, shrill, flashy."

"Occasionally forward, full of vitality of course, or simply more cheerful than you, that's how I'd put it."

"Disco, techno, all styled and dressed up. Either spoilt or neglected. Or both at the same time."

"Stop it! It's age."

"Whose age?"

"Yours, dear husband." Eva laughed. "You can't stand young people any more, it's as simple as that. At least that's what it sounds like, listening to your drivel. But you don't believe what you're saying yourself."

"But it has to be said, anyway it's what everyone thinks."

"What rubbish! Are your daughters spoilt, neglected, cheeky, vain? And the folk they go around with, are they? There, you see!"

"They're noisy though, admit it."

"Marie-Jeanne, noisy? You couldn't even say that about Lydia. And what about you? Were you always well-behaved, and quiet, and modest, and retiring?"

"Definitely quiet – very quiet, even! All that noise gets on my nerves, all those loudly laughing popcorn chompers at the cinema, those boasters at the library. Why do they all have to be so obtrusive! Why can't they make up for their insecurity in some other way – or somewhere else!"

"Anything else? Do you feel better now?"

"Why should I feel better?"

"Just be careful who you say things like that to. Not everyone understands a joke."

"But I mean it, honestly, I'm serious."

"Honestly? Seriously, you sound pretty grumpy."

"The crazy thing about it is that they take me back to when I was young myself."

"Aha!"

"Very much so."

Admittedly, at times those same young people went to great efforts in the library. They'd search eagerly, and if they happened to find anything they were quick to declare it 'awesome' or 'wicked'. It was a joy to help them.

Eighteen when I kissed my first girl, in midwinter, beneath the projecting roof of the shooting range shelter. Wasn't that early enough? It had seemed much too late at the time. And then again, what a long time it took for Real Life to begin! Erica, my first! Had all the time before – from fourteen to eighteen, from eighteen to twenty-two – really been an inferior period? The idea's absurd: in fact, those were the most eventful years of my life. My head was filled with plans, impassioned hopes, and passionate disappointments. I felt outraged by so many things! I could fly into a fury without considering for one moment the possibility that such outbursts might do me harm. Such insouciance – I could even feel depressed for several weeks and not be bothered. And every day was unique, it was all stage fright and first performances. These days I look back on those times in Gonten and Appenzell with amazement. Everything was so much more intense, so much more inspiring. Now all I can manage is the occasional fit of anger – at least that, that at least.

"The way you eat! It's disgusting," Eva said to Lydia.

"Typical family! Only mothers think they have the right to tell their eighteen-year-old daughters how to hold a fork. What exactly am I doing wrong?" She challenged Marie-Jeanne mockingly, poking her with her shoulder.

Marie-Jeanne, straight-faced, demonstrated the way her sister ate with both elbows on the table.

"But that's perfectly all right, I don't know what you're on about. Instead of raising my arm I bend my head down to the plate. What's so special about that?"

"It doesn't exactly look nice."

"But it's practical. I'm not at a restaurant after all, there's nobody watching."

"What about us?"

"You don't need to look. Really, you're all mad. Dad, admit it, you're mad."

"We mind our manners here, Eva taught me that. Now she's teaching you. It's only fair."

"Manners, manners! I'm not that bad! I've seen worse. Your workmate, Dad, whatshisname – what is his name? – he smacks his lips, really, it's so loud it bursts your eardrums, and he slurps so noisily that his dog starts howling under the table, honestly."

"Yes, and what about Anderegg?" said Marie-Jeanne.

"What about him?" I asked.

"Ah yes, you're right. There's him too," said Lydia.

And Marie-Jeanne demonstrated the way she thought Anderegg ate: very fast, very fast indeed. I'd never noticed.

"And where might you have seen that?"

"Last autumn in Paris, don't you remember? The man spends four hours in the kitchen cooking the most complicated dishes you can imagine, then he sits down at the table and wolfs it all down as though he hadn't eaten for days."

"And that's exactly what you're doing now," said Eva. "You'd think you were an excavator, the way you shovel rice into your mouth! If you don't mind my saying so, it looks awful."

Now she was licking the spoon she'd used to serve herself another portion of fricassee, but at least she didn't place it back in the dish – that at least.

"Why get all worked up about it?" I said. "Young people have the most peculiar eating habits anyway. Cucumber salad in the early morning, midnight snacks of tuna fish salad together with Nescafé sweetened with six spoons of sugar; and instead of a normal meal at lunchtime they stuff themselves with three nut croissants, a bar of chocolate and two hotdogs."

"Slightly exaggerated," said Marie-Jeanne.

"Completely off the mark," said Lydia.

"I've seen it with my own eyes," I said. "And you've seen it too, the raw and the cooked, I'm an unerring observer of family life."

"What does 'unerring' mean?" asked Marie-Jeanne.

If that's not crazy! I'm a herdsman in Appenzell for the cattle drive up to the alpine pastures; a roadsweeper every Tuesday morning here in Wangen around the library; a teller at number three polling station, flummoxed when the numbers don't tally in the final count. I'm the teacher who's afraid there won't be enough money for all three children to go to university; I'm the man from the town works who comes to read the gas meter; the plumber who's just been given his notice; the office girl, broad-hipped, cheerful, too old to find a husband; I'm this one and that one; I'm the drunken painter at the Sternen carrying on about the Allied landing in Normandy fifty years ago; I'm the post office lady with the narrow face and the powerful hand wielding the rubber stamp; the police constable, about to be pensioned off, grumbling because of the new regulations requiring him to wear his uniform, including his pistol, even when he's only in his office; I'm the florist in the house opposite who comes home late at night, switches on the lights in all the rooms and, with windows open, runs through all the rooms singing; the newspaper kiosk woman, the woman with the dog, the driver, the dentist, the male nurse, I'm everything, I'm nothing; a bit of everything, hardly anything. But I was the one who got Anderegg to read old Whitman, so that he could make hay of that grass too: Not youth pertains to me, Nor delicatesse … flood-tide below me on Brooklyn Ferry … And the following week already Anderegg gave me the explanation: it was the exuberantly healthy variety of a type of insanity, the centre of the world and the outer fringe; the psychiatrists at the Hôpital Hôtel-Dieu had been doing research on it for years. Apparently, according to them, youth too was nothing but a short phase of insanity. Yes indeed, in Gonten and Appenzell too you'll find loonies walking through the hilly countryside, nothing in their heads, everything in their heads, their brains like sweet butter inside their skulls.

"This place looks like a junk-shop. You'd better do a bit of hoovering before you get an attack of asthma."

She simply dropped everything on the floor: pullovers, CDs, blouses, books, exercise books, messed up with trainers and sandals.

I never interfere, I've always left it to Eva to bring up the children.

But since her trip through the south of France Lydia seemed to be keeping a diary again. The usual untidiness and the not so usual habit of writing everything down. What exactly did she write? Far be it from me to want to know. It was astonishing that the custom still prevailed among the youth of today. Old-fashioned egocentricity, age-appropriate therefore harmless.

As it was, she read a lot and liked writing; in the rue Lacépède kitchen, she'd always seen someone reading and writing, vide Anderegg, vide mimicry: city girl Lydia.

186

And Marie-Jeanne, a country miss. Just now she was in the model-daughter phase, tidy, well-behaved. She enjoyed everything, even school. She was extremely diligent, not only at the cello. Quiet but not entirely withdrawn.

Besides, about a year ago she'd discovered the cinema. Previously on her occasional visits it had been dolphins, whales, dinosaurs, Kevins and Batmen. But now she got acquainted with presidents of the United States, CIA agents, Mafia bosses and cops, single mothers of supertalented children, innocent jailbirds, serial murderers, the people next door so to speak. Tall and self-assured: she'd have had no trouble getting in for any film, whatever its rating. However she preferred to be accompanied.

A new fatherly feeling: going to the pictures with my daughter. The phase won't last long. ,

3

Dinner at the boss's – Homeric birth – Küng, Boff & Drewermann

"Actually the baby wasn't due for another fortnight," she began. We were sitting out on the roof terrace having dessert, coffee and schnapps, and it was the turn of my boss's wife, Ursula, to give us an example of the usefulness of books in everyday life.

"I'm sure you've already told them that story half a dozen times," said Odermatt.

"Not as far as I know," she said. "Or have I really?"

"No, I'm sure you haven't," Eva reassured her. "Not to me, anyway."

So Ursula continued: "According to the doctor, it wasn't due before the beginning of January, at the very earliest. Of course my dear husband had already been urging me for ages to get my suitcase packed so that everything would be ready, just in case. But as there was no hurry I kept putting it off. And anyway, we wanted to celebrate Christmas properly beforehand, with all the trimmings – no small matter in our family. Then, on Christmas Eve, in the middle of the afternoon, I suddenly felt something. You know how it is: even though you've been expecting it all along, it still comes as a surprise. I immediately rang the doctor, only to find that he didn't at all appreciate being disturbed during the holidays. Admittedly there could be no talk of regular pains. No need to worry, Mrs Odermatt, you can celebrate Christmas, and New Year too, he said. Fine, that's all right with me, I thought, and went back to the kitchen to bake another cake. Then our boy came home from school, full of excitement: school beginners always have a lot to tell, and twice as much on a day like that. So I listen to the child, take the cake out of the oven, do the cooking, and am all ears again when my husband comes home for a quick break at noon.

Why the library has to be kept open on the afternoon of Christmas Eve is something I've never been able to understand! I had no choice but to act the efficient housewife: wash up, keep the child busy, tidy up, shop for the last few things at the Co-op, everything on my own, with my protruding belly, awkwardness personified. Later on, on top of all that, we had to pay your parents a visit. There are days when it's all family duties, and I caught myself thinking that if I could be taken to hospital there and then I'd escape all the fuss and kerfuffle of a family Christmas, just this once. Excuse me, my dearest, it so happens that your wife sometimes has thoughts like that. Perhaps that was what made me suggest taking a little walk after we'd left your parents' place, although the area down near the football ground isn't exactly inviting, particularly in winter in the fog and the dark. So I stumbled along on my husband's arm down the dirt track to the river. Gynaecologists aren't infallible either, I thought, and at least I can try to get something going."

"Aristotle, long ago, said that a pregnant woman's whims should be indulged," said Odermatt.

Ursula continued: "I was disappointed and at the same time relieved when I noticed that nothing seemed to have been set in motion. Besides, it was really dreary down by the stadium; the glow over the town only intensified the gloom. We hurried back to the car and home into the warm! Our son could hardly wait to see the candles burning on the tree, and the gifts in their wrappings under the tree. And then, at long last, the candles were lit and the gifts could be unwrapped, the whole business ushered in and accompanied by the traditional Odermatt rituals. I was so caught up in the joy of the moment that I almost forgot the other business. Until my husband came up with the idea of going to Midnight Mass. Do you remember?"

"Midnight Mass that starts at ten," said Odermatt.

"At ten, eleven, or twelve, whatever," Ursula continued, "it was too much for me. I was tired. And anyway, attending Holy Mass on Christmas Eve in a highly pregnant state is symbolically charged, don't you think? Almost kitsch! We squabbled a bit, not for long:

189

I was too tired to argue, I just gave in. Our boy enjoyed it, of course. It's surprising how full the churches can be on such occasions! Obviously, it's still better than the telly, *in dulci jubilo*, nothing was missing. There was even a sermon – you can have three guesses what it was about – embellished with current issues like wars, the crisis, unemployment, foreigners, fringe groups, that all went perfectly well with the search for shelter, the stable and the straw."

We were sitting out on the roof terrace in the semi-dark: marvellous to find oneself in the middle of winter on a warm evening at the end of August! It seemed to me that I'd heard the story before, albeit in a shorter version. Probably the Grimms' Dictionary would come up now. I was right. At long last, said Ursula, the child was in bed, exhausted and happy, surrounded by his presents.

"And the other person who was surrounded by his presents was my husband." She reached across the corner of the table and squeezed his arm briefly. "The Grimms' Dictionary, remember? It was that Christmas I hit upon the idea of putting those one and a half metres of paperbacks under the tree for you. Later on you also bought the thing for the library. And of course he couldn't help leafing through one volume after the other till long after midnight; the origin of words, the history of words, it was something that had always fascinated him. You read out one quotation after the other: A, the noblest of all sounds, ringing out roundly from breast and throat, oedema, ox, ox-eye daisy …"

"Look!" Eva cried out. "There – what is it?"

It flitted over the terrace toward the chimney.

"There, look! Again!"

"Bats," said Odermatt.

"What? Are you sure?"

"We have a lot here. They roost in the roof of that old monastery over there. We often see them at this time of night."

"Yes, bats," Ursula confirmed. "Quaint creatures. But please don't change the subject. We were talking about the Grimms, not Brehm's *Life of Animals*."

"Who changed the subject?"

But Ursula was adamant: "The Grimms under the Christmas tree, as I said. At any rate, it had already got much too late for a Christmas-night birth. It wasn't until the following day – it must have been ten o'clock already – while I was starting up the coffee machine, that I felt something again. I didn't say anything, just breakfasted calmly with the others, enjoying all the things that go to make up a late and festive breakfast. I'll just boil the ham, I thought, so that the family has something good to eat for the first two days; after that, my husband can look after things by himself. And while the meat was simmering in its stock I gathered up the things I needed and packed my suitcase. Only then did I phone. And would you believe it, although he was seriously inconvenienced by my call, the doctor came to the same conclusion: not surprising as the waters had broken, or so I thought. I should get someone to take me to the hospital, said the doctor, he'd be there in ten minutes. It was a false alarm, of course. Nothing happened. Nevertheless they kept me there.

My husband had to take the child to my parents-in-law, so for a while I was left to wait on my own. And then there was someone in the room next door, groaning, you know, from really deep down inside, and stammering 'Jesus Christ, Jesus Christ', a woman's voice, very guttural, moaning, stammering, groaning – she must just have had an operation, an emergency case – or perhaps she was also waiting for delivery! Don't lose your nerve Ursula, I told myself. So I started to read, something or other, a novel I'd packed in a hurry and that now turned out to be quite unsuitable for the occasion. No television in the room. On the radio, either classical hits or a silly play. So all I could do was read – I couldn't just lie there listening to a stranger's wailings.

Late that evening my husband came by again. Nothing new had happened; nothing was to be expected. I sent him back home.

The next morning, Boxing Day, I was finally given an infusion to induce labour. Now it was the doctor who'd become impatient; probably he'd planned to go skiing with his family in the Bernese Oberland. For this, my second birth, I didn't want gas or an injection, I didn't want to be anaesthetised or even slightly numbed. I'd bought two books on childbirth without pain and knew what I had to do. And when the pains started, my husband was back with me again. He sat down at the head of the bed, then at the foot of the bed, he stood in the middle of the room, then near the window, looking completely at a loss – there's no other way to describe it. And I did my breathing, the way I'd learned – more or less by heart – from the two books. You can see, I'm coming to the point now, books really do sometimes turn out to be useful.

And now my husband took heart. He remained seated

where he was, well out of the way between the foot of the bed and the window, took a book from his pocket and started to read out from *The Iliad*, the fifth canto. I kept up my breathing, breathing, straining to relax. What else could I do? Induced is induced, the doctor wanted to go off on his holiday. From time to time, then more and more often, the midwife poked her head into the room. Everything was going perfectly. The *Iliad* recitation continued. Now and then I understood a verse, or at least I imagined I understood a verse, for the rascal was reading it to me in Greek. It sounded archaic, fearfully beautiful. And he was in his element; he'd livened up visibly and didn't look half as dejected as before. Now the midwife stayed in the room and started to help me. I panted and gasped, pushed, relaxed, pushed again, and everything thrust in one direction. I was fully occupied, I had no time to heed the pain – childbirth without pain my foot! The inventor must have been a man, the one who invented the square circle!"

There was laughter on the roof terrace: Ursula, a classical scholar, still bright and sparkling. Only the boss, slightly embarrassed, remarked with a smile that she was exaggerating: it had been her idea to have him read to her to help pass the time during labour. "You asked me to provide effective distraction. That's what I did, rather reluctantly of course – after all, rhapsodising on Greek atrocities in a hospital ward is not everyone's favourite activity, as you'll admit."

"Of course, but the two things go well together," said Ursula.

Once a year Eva and I, together with our daughters, are invited to dinner at the boss's; once a year Eva invites the boss and his family to our place. At the end of this August it was our turn to go to the boss's.

Marie-Jeanne had come docilely; Lydia had something important on – obviously, considering it was Saturday evening.

"Education's never in short supply at the Odermatts'," I said as we walked across Squirrel Meadow on our way home.

"Why are you being so sarcastic?"

"I'm not being sarcastic. Besides, I like Ursula. Having to spend a whole evening with the boss on his own would have been relatively tiresome."

Küng, Boff & Drewermann: a celebrated company in our library here. Odermatt believes in the reformability of the Catholic Church, and it is this belief that explains the purchase of the books which, a few years later, Rome will see fit to condemn. Theology and research, oh dear! For the Holy Hierarchy in Rome there's no doubt that theology today is no more than applied science: there's no need to concern oneself with fundamentals any more, that was all settled a long time ago; at the most, there might be some call for contributions concerning up-to-date ways of spreading the truth. So Catholic theologians are simply PR men whose job it is to find out how best to disseminate the truth, right? If that isn't modern! And if en passant they happen to discover something that doesn't accord with the truth, they are asked in all kindness to correct their findings, to recant, and preferably to be silent in future. And if they're not prepared to do so – who, these days, likes amending, recanting, keeping quiet! – their licence to teach

194

is rescinded. If, on the other hand, the university at which they teach is not directly under Rome's jurisdiction they're in luck: where there's an intermediate lay authority, heretics may continue to teach – nothing true and Catholic any more but at least minor subjects such as Comparative History of Religions, Christianity and Tradition, Christians in China, etc. As a classical scholar my boss knows the old pagans and heretics and finds them interesting. That's why he has books by the new heretics bought too, all of them, without exception, as far as possible. On coming out they're much in demand and are often borrowed from the library. After a time public interest abates. One day it's Küng, then it's Boff, and after that it's Drewermann; it's a long time now since Câmara had his day; now it's Gaillot. Fashions change, Rome remains, the big boss is always right. But this firm belief in the reformability of the Catholic Church is somehow touching, walking upright through clouds of incense, in a house of breath, and all roads lead to the confessional. I too was pious in my youth!

The old established Odermatt family: building contractors, brewers, lawyers. My boss was the first classical scholar in the family; his younger brother took over the building business; the elder one is a district court presiding judge; a cousin manages the brewery, one of the last small independent breweries in the Mittelland.

In former times, anyone in Wangen named Odermatt was Catholic and conservative. It wasn't until the three brothers came along that there was a slight change. I don't know if it was intentional or just happened. The lawyer is a Social Democrat who became a judge years ago with the support of the Christian Democrats, an amiable comrade. The manager of the building business and its affiliated real estate company is a Free Democrat, of the neo-liberal variety. My boss and his cousin are the only ones to have remained politically Christian conservative, my boss, however, in 'inner emigration', secretly hoping for pagans and heretics.

Eva and he have known each other since childhood. To him Eva is a heretic.

Ursula: "Yes, it did hurt. You think it'll tear you apart, quite literally, the head that wants to get out, out, out. And then it's over. And I got this feeling – a feeling I've never ever had since: You've done it, the job's done, and it's a job well done."

What else was there in the hitparade that late Saturday evening in August on the terrace at the Odermatts'? The way one thing leads to another, and from there on to something else. One thing I'm sure I didn't neglect to mention was the birth in Faulkner's *Light in August*:

Lena walking south, barefoot, for weeks, in search of the father of her unborn child; how there was neither a midwife nor a doctor to help at the birth, only an old defrocked minister to come to her aid with doctor book, razor and string; that's how things like that happen in Jefferson. Farmers and sheriffs and judges and niggers and nigger-women and the white mob and the woman who's just given birth in the hut, and pride and patience and despair and confidence: anything less won't do, Faulkner doesn't concern himself with trivial things in Jefferson.

"You and those old Americans!" said Eva.

And I listed all the different things you could learn from books like that. For example, it was from Steinbeck, in *Sweet Thursday* – or was it *Cannery Row*? – that I learned that big-bosomed women make efficient wives whereas flat-chested women make efficient prostitutes; where else, if not in American literature and thanks to a Nobel prizewinner, could I have acquired such a valuable piece of information! So many useful things you were taught just en passant: how to roast buffalo hump, how to escape from one's Red Indian pursuers; how to survive shipwreck on a reef in the South Seas, or the antarctic winter when seal hunting, or a forest fire on the Susquehanna River – Cooper could be relied on for good advice. And the formula that said the safest place to hide was where you were most likely to be found came from Poe and had since been used in several gripping films, for example by Redford, the CIA bookworm in the thriller *Six Days of the Condor*. And how someone who was an Italo-American could become Jewish – Malamud knew all about it. But also if you wanted to be a hotelier, a secretary, a prison director, a successful preacher and the leader of a sect, you could rely on the Americans for generous advice. Not to forget Hemingway's collected handbooks on fishing, and the erotics manuals by Updike, Bellow, Roth & Co.

"Where have the kids got to?" Ursula asked.

They'd left long since to go rollerskating somewhere in the neighbourhood. Marie-Jeanne had wanted to give it a try; apparently the Odermatt children were ever so good at it.

We, the older generation, stayed put with our schnapps, our mineral water, our old stories, book dust. Man, the addictive reader.

Now and then bats in blind flight over our heads. In

the halo of the streetlamp a shimmering whirl of gnats and moths. And when for a change no one was talking, the ticking and fizzing of the lawn-sprinkler could be heard from down in the garden.

4

Love stories – Dream roast – Books at bedtime – Window seat

Yvonne in a grey T-shirt, grey jeans, surprisingly low-key. At first I didn't even recognise her as she came out from the reading room to the lending desk.

Had she been in Willisau last week, I asked.

"Last Saturday, yes. In fact I'd have liked to have already gone on Friday evening but I couldn't make it." Then, pausing in surprise: "But how did you know?"

Why not admit it? A jazz concert live on DRS2 before and after midnight; just by chance I'd switched on the radio to listen to the news. Hadn't she told me she went every year?

"In that case we heard exactly the same thing, you on the radio and I right there in Willisau. By the way, it was a marvellous concert, don't you agree? That woman, the American, the things she can do with her voice, quite crazy you know. And the pianist, the Frenchman, he was fabulous too. Ever so creative, both of them."

And how were things otherwise?

"Stress," she said. "I've got too much on at the moment. I can hardly get away from my drawing board. Never go out, not to the pub, not to the pictures. At best I flop down exhausted in front of the TV and watch crime.

198

– But now the first delivery's off my hands. And I'm busying myself with other things, as you can see." She shoved her pile of books over to me and handed me her library card.

It occurred to me to ask her if any rubbish, as she called it, had been left over again.

"Oh yes, any amount, as always." She laughed, even blushed. And we exchanged a few friendly remarks. She didn't seem to be in a hurry.

With a yawn Eva stretched out her arms to the ceiling. I beckoned her with my finger to come to the kitchen table. She came and I put my right arm around her hips, pushed my left arm between her legs and clasped my hands around her bottom. I leaned my head against her stomach and midriff; thus I sat and thus she stood while the coffee maker purred.

"Have you heard anything yet from our little women?"

"It's Sunday. Let them sleep. Lydia had the light on till late last night."

Three pots of jam: apricot, fig, red cherry; also honey; bread already sliced, butter in its dish.

"Anything new?"

"Not as far as I know. Only love stories, the usual ones. Just imagine, last night I was with Simon, you remember that man I had a crush on in Paris ages and ages ago when I was doing my semester abroad. I never tried to find out what became of him. Suddenly the fellow turns up, incredibly present – as far as a man who looks exactly the same as he did more than twenty years ago can be said to be present. And we started snogging straight away, including nearly everything, without shame, in public, the Jardin du Luxembourg, near the pavillion, bare trees, summery warmth. No one paid any attention to us, in spite of our provocative gymnastics. In fact, in those days, Simon was very tame, even prudish. What a joke!"

"Not a nightmare, at least."

"The opposite, not bad at all really. What you once missed in real life is supplied years later without your asking. In any case I woke up in a good mood. Funny isn't it?"

"Sad is more like it."

"Yes of course, sad too."

When Lydia was still small she used to get up at six or half past every day. It was the same later with Marie-Jeanne. But for some time now we have our peace on Sunday mornings.

"I'm beginning to worry about the condition of my aging brain."

Eva just laughed.

"Old age is a disaster."

"No, a debacle."

"Both, if you want."

"But we're neither of us anywhere near that stage yet."

"The beginnings are noticeable, unfortunately."

"The beginnings of memory loss can also be seen in our daughters. The things they forget!"

"That's something else: youthful absent-mindedness."

"I see."

"It doesn't count as an excuse for us."

And once again nothing came of the overtures to the afternoon of a faun.

200

"Awful, our indolence."

"You shouldn't force yourself to do something you have to pull yourself together for."

I've been set down on the dinner table as the roast. The whole family is seated around it, that is: my old family, not you and the girls, none of you are there. But my parents are there, my sister and my brother are there. And I eat with them, I'm the Sunday roast and I eat the roast – please don't ask how that could be! There I am, lying appetisingly on the table amid the accompanying dishes and at the same time sitting at the table eating with the others. And while calmly using my knife and fork I say to myself: Just look at that, I've got a lovely back, it must be admitted, a beautiful shoulder. It sounds abstruse, but in my dream it didn't seem all that bad; there was simply a fine roast lying there and I knew that it was my shoulder. Gruesome I know, but dreams are dreams, you can't do anything about it. It would be good if we had someone like Anderegg here at the moment, he'd surely be able to give us a detailed interpretation. The woman of the family offering herself as food; love that goes through the stomach. It makes me think of that story by your Anderson, do you remember, about the woman and the wolves. Or were they her own dogs?

Maple leaves in the gusts of wind, the branch bends and bends again, swings back, bends again, the rushing sound so loud that it almost drowns the noise from the ring road. I could have asked what colours would be in fashion the following year. And what designs. Dozing, not to be confused with pondering, man the being addicted to reminiscence. In the Froschaugasse near the Predigerplatz there was no tree in front of the window, but in the autumn the smell of smoke in the air like in Appenzell.

201

"Do you want to? Or rather not? It would be nice if you came. But you must decide now. I'm going to book the ticket this week. And we also need visas."

Not the Maghreb in Belleville, or Chinatown behind the Place d'Italie this time. Autumn is the best season to visit Beijing according to the guidebooks – *Polyglott*, *Merian*, *Baedeker*. It was confirmed by Isabelle in her last letter to Eva.

I wasn't scared of flying. "We must get window seats," said Eva, "otherwise it might get boring. Take enough stuff to read anyway."

Even the boss helped with good advice. He'd always got himself window seats in advance, he'd never waited until the check-in. All you had to do was ring up a fortnight before the flight and say in a concerned voice that you knew it wasn't possible to reserve a particular seat as early as this, but you were travelling with children, and children on the plane on such a long flight, you'd done it before, it was difficult, and it had always been best if the seats weren't somewhere in the middle of a long line in the centre of the plane but right on the side, near the window. That had always worked, the best seats, always at least one of them next to the window.

Classical scholars, how worldly-wise they are!

I'd never have managed to organise something like that. Luckily there was Eva; she too has the touch of arrogance that's needed.

"What was the film like?" she asked, putting the book down beside her on the bedcover.

"Rubbish, it wasn't worth it. What about you? What did you do all evening?"

"Verena rang up, she can't come jogging tomorrow.

Then I corrected the proofs of the winter courses progamme. Then I had a shower, had a glass of beer and chatted with Lydia."

"What're you reading?"

She picked up the book and held it up to show the cover.

"So?"

"A serious book: three thousand years of Chinese ideas of happiness; perhaps it's too serious. Did you know that over there lukewarmness and half measure were once pronounced to be the highest ideals? Here, listen to this: 'Boats at half-sail sail the steadiest, and horses held at half-slack reins trot best.' Everything's fine when things are just so-so; sixteenth century, postmodern."

She explained.

I listened. Pleasant to have someone to read books for me.

"Are you going to go on reading for long?"

"Just these few pages."

"Okay. I'm going upstairs. Reluctantly though: leaving you all alone in a bed that's much too wide. How easily someone might get the idea to take a lover for a change."

"Don't worry, I like being all alone in this wide bed for a change."

She pursed her lips mockingly.

"Nice and dry," she said and we touched lips several times.

A smack on her nightgowned shoulder, cotton, pale yellow, machine washable at 95 degrees, Calida: married life.

5

'I'd prefer not to...'

Durkheim Today, fourteen essays, and he's the editor and – at an age when most professors no longer write anything more than prefaces – the author of the longest article. An article that I enjoyed for its stolidity.

I'll write to tell him that, I thought. Strangely enough he'd remember me, although I'd only met him once since submitting my Paris paper, it must be a dozen years ago by now. I'd write to say I'd read his latest book and … what exactly? Stimulating … still seminal … bearing in mind … as a sign of life …

An aging man to an older aging man. For weren't the first signs perceptible in my case too? I didn't understand young people any more, least of all the older young people, precisely those who should have been closer to me. Is that the result of … the result of what? Random questions came up, no real train of thought. But what with all the old love stories from my Zurich days gathering around my desk, it wasn't surprising that I should also remember the professor, not without affection. I'd never told him how much I appreciated him; it wasn't the done thing. And anyway I wouldn't have known how to say it.

That distant time when I was working serenely; Elisabeth, the quiet beauty in Basel, only in Zurich at weekends. The fixed and the flexible, discipline for six days and then from the evening of the sixth day on: love at the weekend, the best time of those good times.

Not a bit of it! Toil and tiredness, that's what it was,

and the permanent worry that I'd never ever get to the end of those Tibetans.

"Did you know," asked Eva, "that Etiemble also wrote a couple of books about China? An interesting man. When he was asked what he'd wanted to be when he was young he's said to have answered: *professeur* at some provincial lycée. Of course he'd rather have been a real professor at a university, he admitted – or rather a real professor in the style of Nietzsche, Bergson, Schopenhauer, something of that calibre. That – or preferably nothing at all! And since he was just not talented enough to be exceptional, he plumped for mediocrity. And he really was a grammar school teacher for a while."

Etiemble, Granet, Gernet, Gifter, Johnson: Eva seldom goes to sleep before she's read a chapter of clever text. The books she reads are seldom recent publications, ten years storage time on average. By that time the books are usually no longer available in the bookshops. That's what libraries are for.

Do what you can, and do it with discipline and dedication – how easy it sounds! Yet even just knowing what you're capable of doing is difficult. Have you really got the ability to do what you'd like to do? What you admire about other people: How can you be sure that you'd be capable of doing the same? You can only find out by doing it, or trying; and you'll only ever get started if your urge is really strong. And since beginnings are always uncertain it'll take a long time for you to get to know if the ability you thought, hoped you had is really adequate. And even if the beginning turns out to be easy and you make rapid progress, there's still no guarantee.

Can activity stand in for talent? Isn't dogged work on a task per se already the talent? If success was a sure sign I'd now be a sociologist with a lectureship at some university, or the editor of a learned journal, or an expert on youth problems. Keep plugging along, you'll be awarded a gong! Would I have been capable? I don't know. Of course I have my doubts. Not being certain is what's most certain. I didn't consciously choose mediocrity; on the other hand I've remained true to it. There are enough people without self-doubt. And then there's nothing worse than being successful with the wrong things. Propelled by praise and criticism, idiot, you think you're following your star, but the star is only your nose.

That's how I'd set it out for myself, I don't remember any more what made me do so. Probably it was during my humble period, sometime between Assumption Day more than a decade ago and Assumption Day in the year of the wasps. Scribblings, scribblings.

I'd never found academic writing easy. I never had the feeling the job could be completed fast, effortlessly. I also didn't really have enough ambition. Sudden bursts of ambition, perhaps; but with long periods in between not knowing what use it all was. Just the petit bourgeois plebeian virtue of finishing the job you've taken on: a start's a start, in for a penny, in for a pound …

A particular aptitude for sociological thought? Where's it to be taken from if not stolen, Durkheim, help! The idea that moral issues should be regarded as a thing like other things remained foreign to me. And my choice of ethnology had been just as haphazard. Everything had been chosen in youthful ignorance.

And whenever I managed to solve some little problem

I was surprised. Naturally I was also delighted. On the other hand I'd also have been satisfied so long as I hadn't clearly failed. And when real success came it was unexpected and it unsettled me.

Staying power, even obstinacy, they were qualities I'd always possessed. Also the odd conviction that the job could be done somehow or other, as long as I got started, got started and didn't stop, the confidence that every day thus employed would produce a tiny result and that those tiny results, strung together and taken as a whole, would suffice in the end to produce an overall result that was just about acceptable.

That's the way things were for a long time; probably already back in Appenzell, certainly in Zurich, and also in Paris. And all along I had this strange, initially scarcely noticeable feeling of tiredness..

My fatigue seemed to be harmless, but it increased. Since each day had to yield its tiny result – important results were a priori unlikely – I could hardly ever allow myself a day off. In all my time as a student in Zurich I took only one holiday: I went down to Provence with Erica, and even then I carried two boxes of index cards in my rucksack.

Can it be done? It can. But it's no wonder I got tired. Only seldom – usually late at night – did I feel a kind of buoyancy while at work, something drawing me along, surging towards me, something vast: associations were revealed, suddenly and briefly I saw something new in bright light. It probably only happened because by that late hour I knew that my daily quota would shortly be fulfilled. And at the end of such a day – and my days were all alike –

207

I'd creep under the sheets, curl up tightly and say to myself: There you are, Harder, you got it done after all!

Sociology-lite would have been the right thing for me. Now it's the library. No need to scoff! No great findings to be made here. But then it's also not required.

Blood, urine, cardiogram, everything's normal. Almost neurotically so, said the doctor. Absolutely average. So the tiredness must be part of me. Not that it's ever really worried me, I hardly ever even think about it. It's only in the early afternoons, in summer as well as in winter, that my chronic weariness becomes acute, and as long as I'm not on duty at the time, I can't help taking a nap. Not that it's much use, unfortunately – after waking up I usually feel even more lethargic than I did an hour earlier. That's one reason why I've always tried to make sure to be at the lending desk in the early afternoon. Users who want something from me keep me awake. It would be difficult to get through the first part of the afternoon alone in my office. Didn't Isabelle write in one of her letters that working hours are very long in China? Shops stay open during the lunch hour and until late in the evening; sometimes when you go into a store you'll find the salesgirls asleep, their heads on the counter, and if you want to buy something they only serve you grumpily or, occasionally, slowly and with a smile, like sleepwalkers.

... acquired by study, laborious study. I've never had a quick mind. Stolid slowness, not to be confused with conscientiousness. Staying power perhaps – that would go with the stolidity. And always what's known as 'diligent'. But diligent without any real inclination, a diligence more stolid than enthusiastic. Exactly: once I've set myself a task, I stick to it. How airily, almost casually,

Marie-Jeanne plays her cello! Unconcernedly, without qualms, serenely …

"Midlife crisis or something?" Eva once asked.

"I've heard of it, but I've no time for it."

"In that case you're in for a surprise!"

6

The great leap forward

"As far as I'm concerned they can all die, then the problem will be solved. All those junkies and stoners and coke-heads, they'll be the end of Western civilisation. But I won't live to see it, it's not something I need worry about. In twenty years there'll be nothing left of us, then you'll see the light, you young people, poor you!"

A retired bank clerk at the polling station, he'd been rubber-stamping ballot cards for the past hour. Clearly he was addressing me as I sat beside him extracting the voter identification cards from their envelopes and checking them. Another man came along to give him a hand; he was also a member of the polling station, an insurance agent, not much younger than I, about forty.

"Giving them heroin for free helps," he said, "especially if it's laced with strychnine."

They both nodded smugly.

Was that the Bratwurst and Beer Party?

I asked them if they'd also poison the drug market profiteers.

They had no objections. Weren't they all foreigners anyway?

And what about strychnine in people's daily beer, I asked. I couldn't think of anything nicer to say.

They dropped the subject, slightly embarrassed in spite of the majority appeal their opinions probably had.

Father, Dad, husband, town librarian, colleague, comrade, a member of number 3 polling station in Wangen, a motorist, a pedestrian, a cinemagoer, a one-time jogger in the Jardin des Plantes and almost a scholar, yesterday that, tomorrow this, a man like everyman, a collector of trivia. Only concerning oneself with small things. Is that small thinking, faint-hearted sensibility? Do the big things never come to me except in small things?

"*Kussecht und vogelfrei* – where in heaven's name did they get that from?" mocked Eva. "And here's our dear party chairman with a lecture on how we're to interpret it. The lips with the beauty spot symbolise closeness, warmth, *joie de vivre*; and the little bird – how charming – is meant to show that our dear old Socialist Party is agile, light, upbeat, a party with vision; and *kussecht*, kissproof, means well made-up, but at the same time without make-up, unvarnished; and people who call themselves *vogelfrei* are nonconformists like William Tell, Robin Hood, witches – and like us, the Social Democrats. Logical, isn't it? The man who's trying to make us believe all this is a lawyer. And, as far as I know, the election committee that concocted it also included a Germanist, a graphic designer, an historian and a sociologist – a colleague of yours, so to speak. This time our young academics have taken the biscuit, not only that, they've taken a whole tin of biscuits."

We were talking about the upcoming cantonal parliamentary elections. I wasn't involved – all I'd have to do was sit in the polling station for a couple of hours, tick the lists and then add up the ticks in the columns. I leave the canvassing to our academic youth. It's nice that I haven't got any political ambitions myself; being a polling official is not a sought-after job.

"Quite remarkable the way the eggheads now want to sell us as some kind of kissproof lipstick," Eva continued to mock. "Social democracy and first-class cosmetics: if that isn't playing honest!"

"I never thought of it like that; self-irony is a rare thing."

"And look at the seductive curve of the lips," she continued, pointing at the logo. "Lydia immediately thought of Madonna. Taken together with *vogelfrei* you can't help seeing all kinds of ambiguous associations … I wonder if the eggheads thought of all the implications – or was it born spontaneously out of youthful enthusiasm?"

"Oh well, one more dirty joke in the ads won't do any harm."

"True. But they could at least have looked up the word *vogelfrei*. No need for it to be Grimms' Dictionary, the good old Duden would do."

"The best thing would be for you to run for election yourself next time, with you nonchalant and topless in a picture captioned: 'To paradise with Eva'."

"At least that wouldn't be ambiguous. Nice and frank, no gratuitous sleaze."

"Exactly."

"What idiots they are!"

The weather in northern China could be relied on to be dry in autumn, a bit on the cold side occasionally. How many shirts? What about long johns? Would cotton ones do or would I have to change to one of those new waterproof, breathable fabrics? Or was it breathproof, waterable?

Four-day trips to Paris had also always required lengthy preparation.

I bought a pair of black trainers, Rabbit brand, at The Red Boot to serve as spares, nice and light. When I unpacked them back home I noticed the label 'made in China' on the bottom of the box. A pure coincidence!

Eva decided we'd use rucksacks; at least we already had a selection of those to choose from.

But I had to go and find a new jacket, one with a lot of pockets and a removable lining, something modern but nothing that would make me stand out in a crowd. It wasn't easy to find; people don't walk around in camouflage any more.

Two cameras? No, one would be enough. Binoculars? If I never actually got onto the Great Wall, at least I'd want to view it magnified from a distance. In the end we used them to see details of the Beijing Opera performance at the Qianmen Hotel.

Three visits all in all to Tschan, the travel agency: the place ought to be named Gordon Pym – for where exactly was the journey taking us?

And we had to send our passports twice to the Chinese Embassy to get our visas: the first time Mr Tschan had given us the wrong application forms.

Eva managed everything efficiently and with gusto. I never stopped feeling slightly uneasy. What had I let myself in for? But it was too late to beat a retreat now. Our daughters observed us with interest and good humour.

"Don't worry, just go. Go on, we'll manage all right."

What were the two of them planning? Why were they so pleased to be alone for three weeks?

"Super that you're going away together for once. We can cope, of course we can, don't worry."

You can't change the habits of a lifetime. All doors open to courtesy. When the cat's away, the mice begin to play. *Kussecht und vogelfrei*, pouting lips and the brains of a sparrow, to paradise with Eva.

VI

The almost girlfriend or The journey through China

'I am talking about love, the man said.
With me it is a science.'

Carson McCullers, *A Tree, a Rock, a Cloud*

It wasn't only my cold that brought tears to my eyes: once more those earth-coloured plains, criss-crossed with rows of poplars, drew past me, the train journey to Changchun, from Changchun to Shenyang, and the long night journey from Shenyang to Chengde; and that afternoon in the three-windowed guestroom, so brutally short, came into my mouth like honey-and-vinegar sauce, the sunshine in the room, hawkers' cries up from the road, the shattering of window panes down in the courtyard; and the early morning of our departure, as we stood at the open gates waiting for the car, the porter in his blue overalls, Eva, Isabelle, and then the two of them embraced, and Isabelle put out her hand, fox-woman, accomplice, such a lovely time and have a good trip; dumpling aftertaste. Why fight it, ah, it was simply the effect of the two small bottles of wine, and the voice of Kathleen Ferrier, heart-piercing, '... *vom Reif bezogen stehen alle Gräser* ...' and I, old fool, didn't fight it, bliss above the clouds, wide awake amid dozing passengers. The flare of a match, a puff and it's over, and there you are fretting about little nothings, what though the Boeing spin out of its powerful flight and go down, down ...

Then the Ferrier voice was gone, replaced by something else on channel eleven Classical Choice, *The Flying Dutchman* or a string quartet, Barber's *Adagio*, *Westside Story*, something or other, no longer the three-windowed room in the guesthouse and that heart-piercing afternoon: somewhere else and other strange times, and never in those days would I have thought that one day, at a thousand kilometres an hour, above Siberia or whatever it was, homewards, home; a courtyard, narrow, and the two-storey house in the middle with its greenish copper roof and the roar of the city coming in through the window, rue Lacépède, rue Linné, the pigeons, a crackling transistor radio and water running down my cheeks. Yet now it seemed to be a kind of overflow: where from, where to? Masked by inflamed eyes, squeezed in as I was between Eva and the wall of the plane, headphones on, gazing obliquely down onto craggy clouds, for hours and hours already through dusk into an evening that refused to turn into night: no, the maudlin movie wouldn't continue much longer. A bright glow inside me from the wine, and aspirin with my Swissair dinner, barren land down below, tundra, forest or whatever it was. And now, what had changed? Gently, almost timidly it came to me, some time or other the voice will ask quietly, firmly: and where do we go from here? How far? Was that all?

Eva was asleep; many of the passengers were dozing, digesting their Zurich-style veal stew, and the hors d'oeuvres, the cheese, the desert, the coffee; homewards, home …

Take-off in Beijing; it should have been at half past two. But there was still a convoy of baggage carts standing beneath the right-hand wing, bluish grey the mountains in the distance, pale grey the sky above them. An air hostess came down the gangway with reading material; Eva chose

Le Monde, I took the day before yesterday's *Tages-Anzeiger*, but I immediately put it aside. A terrible cold, my own fault: I'd chosen a bad time to wash my hair, had gone to eat dumplings at the Ritan Fanzhuang with wet hair, in bright sunny weather with a cold wind.

A second hostess distributed the earphones and the entertainment programme. And at last we started backing slowly away from the building. Nearby, two other airplanes were taxiing across the tarmac. They looked ungainly and fragile. And the wing of our Swissair plane, silhouetted against the afternoon sky, was wobbling precariously. However, the radar tower across the way was revolving regularly, so no doubt everything else would be all right too.

Rumbling in a broad curve onto the runway. A cartoon on the screen, furious cat versus man and canary, along with Wagner's *Flying Dutchman* in the headphones, at least it sounded very much like a sailors' chorus. Both interrupted now by a film on emergencies and safety. Outside, blinding sunlight reflected off the wing.

Four o'clock. The plane was stationary again, only the choir continued to sing, Ho! Hey! Hey! Ha! Helmsman, here … And a woman's voice broke in again to apologise for the delay, in German with a Swiss accent, in French, in English, and no, not in Chinese.

And then, at last, a great roar of engines, jolting, juddering; hangars and sheds passed by, Hussa hey! Helmsman ho! Fence posts raced past – the ground disappeared; all I could see now was the wing, and it wasn't until the plane veered to the right that I got a clear view down: Beijing suburbs, the chequered pattern of the residential districts, merging into farmland, canals, ponds. One thousand five hundred and twenty, two thousand and sixty, two thousand six hundred and thirty, higher and higher; hardly anyone was looking out, blasé nearly all of them, smugly engrossed in their newspapers. The yellow maize on the roofs, every single house clearly visible, far down and yet so near, so near; we veered slightly left – then right again, ascending, still ascending, to over four thousand metres within eight minutes; with meticulous precision the information appeared on the screen: seven hundred and twenty-two kilometres an hour; another ten hours and twelve minutes to Zurich; outside temperature; flight schedule: Ulan Bator, Irkutsk, Novosibirsk, Solikamsk …

But we hadn't got as far as that yet. Below us for the moment, a small section of the Great Wall in a delicate line across the mountain range.

We'd never seen it close up; but towards the end of our train journey from Chengde to Beijing Eva caught sight of it way off in the jagged landscape – to the amazement of the Chinese people in our carriage who hadn't believed us, maintaining that there was no Great Wall in this region, whatever the map or the guidebook said.

No, I'd never seen it close up; instead I'd seen plenty of other things: department stores, children's playgrounds, hairdressing salons, overground district heating pipes, tricycle cabs, the fifty-eight balconies opposite the Sports Hotel; the old quarter with the one-storied houses near the Ritan Hotel; cabbage neatly laid out to dry for three days on the pavements; bicycle lanes wider than the adjacent traffic lane; female street-sweepers wearing white face-masks; free German beer in front of the Friendship Store; everywhere thermos flasks with hot water; birdcages on bicycle carriers, birdcages hanging high up in the trees; the shop assistant taking his afternoon nap on his bed behind the counter; Eva in the queue at the ticket-office in Shenyang; bare mountains in moonlight, full book-shelves in neon light; a general, a nymph, a princess, an emperor, a student, a monkey king, a daoist nun, a pantomimic boat trip down the river; kites high above the geology museum, rice fields, threshing floors, steam engines, television aerials, popcorn cannons, et cetera. Wouldn't that do? And now once more I saw the clouds from above, not autumnal swathes of fog cloaking the ground, clouds of all shapes and sizes with large gaps in between, casting shadows on the beige-coloured countryside. No villages now, not the regular pattern of roofs and roads and fields – only a straight line starting and ending in the invisible, the railway line somewhere betwen Beijing and Ulan Bator.

And now the air hostess came along with the drinks trolley, Swiss comfort above the Gobi, it was too late for coffee, too early for an aperitif, I chose a red wine from Beaune, Bouchard Père & Fils; back here we'd always be the last to be served; but at least we'd managed to get a window seat. The *Flying Dutchman* with the Vienna State Opera choir was still on, or on again; I could have changed the channel, folk ensembles from Graubünden or the upper Basel region, an army brass band from Geneva.

A couple of days fasting wouldn't have been such a bad idea; in the past three weeks we'd eaten copiously, even if it had usually entailed a lengthy trek before we found a restaurant I considered looked hygienic enough; Eva was less fastidious, and anyway, without Eva's travelling skills, I'd often have had to live on bananas, pasty breadrolls and tea.

For our supper on the First of October we'd also spent hours walking through the old quarters, heading from our hotel near the Temple of Heaven roughly in the direction of Tian'anmen Square and the Gate of Heavenly Peace. Actually we'd wanted to take it easy on our second day in Beijing, sleep off the seven-hour time lag so as to be refreshed for the train journey to Changchun; as Eva knew from Isabelle, the trip was likely to involve some stress and strain. Finally we found ourselves sitting in a high-ceilinged hall with pale green walls, single-child families to left and right, behind and in front of us. Bowls to mouths, slurp of noodles, click of chopsticks, steaming dishes being carried to the tables, much to smell and much to see: but no one served us. It was only after Eva had gone over to the kitchen counter herself and spoken to the woman there – volubly, though haltingly – that we finally got served. And it was exactly what Eva had said we'd have: chicken cubes with peanuts and hot peppers, tofu, green vegetables, rice, beer. "They must have been embarrassed that they didn't know English. They acted as if we simply weren't there."

But now they were twice as friendly; the manageress herself came with the bill: she saw us to the door, chatting and nodding. Welcome back, see you again in China, in

Beijing, in Ling Dang Lane at our Pianyi Fandian; long live international friendship and canteen food. A pity I didn't understand anything.

Back outside, walking through the crowds; shoulders, arms, backs; simple clothes, blue, grey, coloured; slim, short-legged, lithe, the women in trousers and jackets; and all those faces, high cheekboned, eyes turning our way. The First of October, everyone walking towards Tian'anmen, they must be putting on some sort of show there today, so onward, follow the flow.

A reddish glow; the distant façades opposite hung with flags; single street lamps high above the crowds, tiny in the square's expanse. No grandstands, no military marches, no fireworks, nothing at all, only people, people. We moved along, pushed onward by the crowd; Eva knew roughly where we were, pointed to the Great Hall of the People on our left, to the Museum of the Revolution on our right. A leisurely throng, a great family affair. Hold hands so as not to lose each other; on my own I'd hardly manage to find my way back to the hotel. Sumptuous underpass beneath the avenue separating the square from the Forbidden City, down and through and back up to the pavement; three TV vans, surrounded by the crowds – wasn't there perhaps an official reception after all, inside the building? In through the Gate of Heavenly Peace.

Imperial edicts: this was where ministers had kneeled to receive them, said Eva. And she knew more: this was where the uprising against Japan had begun, where the republic had been declared; demonstrations had been held here, demonstrations for and demonstrations against, and always spearheaded by students; school reports had been burnt here, the red book waved for the Helmsman, the Three Leaps of Wang, the Leaps of Lun; the papier-mâché statue of liberty, then the rattling of the tanks, blood, and the square closed on holidays for months thereafter.

Their necks, their shoulders, their backs, patient people.

When we crossed the square again the following day we saw dozens of kites wriggling about on their taut strings high up in the wind while children raced their remote-controlled cars on the paving below.

The inner part of the wing in the shade, its tip in the light. A man with a telephoto lens squeezed in between the seats to take a snapshot of some greenish blue stretches of water. "*Et là-bas il y a une rivière!*" That was an exaggeration, nothing but scree, rocks, ochre-coloured aridity; there had been a river there once – but when was the last time? On our outbound flight a blanket of clouds, now a sandpit world down below. And on channel three, oldies from *Pretty Woman, When Harry Met Sally, A Hard Day's Night*; I'd seen all three films in their time so I must have heard the hits before; they were easier to put up with than the soundtrack of the Mickey Mouse film that was on at the same time. And Eva was looking forward to Wangen, for the first time in three weeks, and had an urge to talk: her adult education college, Lydia, Marie-Jeanne, keeping house, et cetera. We were sure to land on time, no fear, the roar of the motors sounded reliable. And we'd also make up the lost time, O Captain! my Captain! the winds were favourable, he said. Again a bright green lake, its banks lined with salt.

The older hostess with the short haircut came up with the food trolley; a younger one, friendly and efficient, helped her. But hostesses are by no means all long-legged and elegant any more; on the outbound flight already I'd found them stocky and staid; Cecilia must have been the great exception, she didn't need support stockings and I'd never noticed a ladder either.

Then we were served: venison and hazelnut terrine with cranberry sauce; Zurich-style veal stew with broccoli and noodles; cheese, cinnamon apple mousse, coffee – on a doll's tray, super-hygienic, everything at once, each portion luxuriously small. Even when I'm ill I don't lose my appetite; add coal to the fever fire! Plus another small bottle of Beaune; I felt warm, comfortable.

Outside, the sun should have set a long time ago. The main film would be starting soon. However, I didn't want to miss Ulan Bator.

En route to the classless society there can be no talk of first or second class, not even for the railways, so it's 'soft seat' or 'hard seat'. Isabelle urged us to take soft seats but Eva only managed to get hard ones, albeit in a sleeper, they call them 'hard sleepers'.

So we were sitting on the train, and it was the right train and the right carriage too; we'd already handed over our tickets and passports to the ticket collector, control is imperative on the way to the classless society, on the way to Changchun.

The doorless compartment was open to the corridor; the six bunks were all fixed, the middle ones couldn't be tipped back either, but you could still sit comfortably on the two bottom ones. Two Japanese students and a Chinese couple with their child. The man immediately started talking to me, he didn't notice for quite some time that I was not the one who understood Chinese. He was a doctor at a hospital in Changchun; as soon as he learned from Eva that we were going to his city to visit someone who had been teaching English at Jilin University for the past year he started explaining China to us.

All the things we saw from the train: the greenhouses, the fields of vegetables around Beijing, then the rice fields, the maize fields, the modernisation of farming life, the villages, the architecture of the single-storey houses and how they consistently faced south according to the theory of wind and water (that he also explained), the solar water-heating systems on isolated rooftops, the brickworks, the railway system, the one-axle carts with their donkeys and the carts with their one-axle tractors, the rice sheaves and the lined up stooks of rice sheaves, the maize stalks, the maize stalk bundles, the avenues of freshly planted poplars. He talked about progress, the rural exodus, electricity generation, bridge building, private initiative.

His wife sat beside him in silence listening, it seemed, with kindly indulgence to the flow of words.

Eva listened with close attention. For the most part she had only a vague idea of what he was saying; she asked a lot of questions, tried to find out what he was talking about. Misunderstandings didn't bother the man, he responded eagerly to everything Eva said.

He explained the school system. Their little daughter would be going to school in a year and would be doing

English from the start, at the moment she was still at a kindergarten for acrobatics. The little girl showed us the splits, handstands, and all kinds of fearsome contortions, sometimes her head seemed to have disappeared, or one of her legs seemed to be missing, circus acts on the bottom bunk. We were astonished, and her father, a doctor, an anatomist, briefed us on tendon and ligament stretching and the untapped potential of the knee joint, on the flexibility of the spinal column in early years; he was proud of his daughter and she was keen to show us what she could do.

The two young Japanese fellows in our compartment had been in Beijing since spring studying Chinese; this trip to Changchun had been organised for them because there were a lot of Japanese things to be seen there. While they were both out in the corridor the doctor explained that too. Puyi the Last, Japan's puppet emperor of China, had had his residence in Changchun. Not only was the palace with the imperial yellow tiles still to be seen, the Japanese had also constructed many other things besides: administration buildings, factories, hospitals. But there was also a grand monument there now, in People's Square on Stalin Avenue: a military aircraft atop a stone column – as a reminder that the Russian paratroops had chased the Japanese back out of China. It was something every single Chinese was happy to remember.

The doctor wanted me, too, to understand what he said, he wanted Eva to translate everything immediately, and so she did; and then I nodded to him so that he could go on. A crash course in Chinese, Eva was getting her lessons.

At half past eight, thoroughly exhausted, she climbed

up to her bunk directly under the curved ceiling. At nine all the lights were put out. Below us in the dark the doctor continued to talk at the two Japanese. His wife had lain down long before, with the little girl beside her.

I dozed, fell asleep, woke up, dozed, fell asleep again. Cold shoulders, the right one, then the left one, cold legs, cold back, I rearranged the blanket – and felt cold again each time I awoke. How on earth did I land up here! On this joggling night train with all these strangers I couldn't understand, yet among whom I felt so strangely at ease.

At a stop long after midnight two men came and sat down on the tip-up seats in the corridor, raised beer bottles to their mouths, a pastry in their other hand; they chewed and they drank. "Hello," they both said when they noticed that I was awake. Laughing silently they looked up to me: the three of us, keeping vigil in the dim light that came through the train windows from a station hall.

At four in the morning they weren't there any more. Loud rattling from the end of the corridor. Someone must have left the door to the next carriage open.

When the lights came on I was the first in our compartment to get up. In the washroom two old Chinese men were already washing their faces and necks, spluttering; vigorous hawking and spitting was also part of it.

I sat down on one of the tip-up seats and gazed out at the dawning countryside. The land was flat. Fields of maize, most of them already harvested. A man on a bicycle on a perfectly straight road. Wind ruffling the willows behind a small station. Freight trains laden with tree trunks. Again the single-storey farmhouses, small, in rows, each with its walled-in courtyard. Again the yellow maize cobs on the roofs.

Eva sat down on the tip-up seat beside me. A railway employee was mopping the corridor with a wet mop. Another came to replace the empty thermos flasks with full ones.

The sun rose. Fog patches. Birds.

The distance between the villages grew smaller.

Droves of cyclists.

Pylons, blocks of flats, sheds, factory stacks, hangars, lorries, buses, mist and fumes. So this was Changchun. Again the doctor drew our attention to this and that, Eva looked, nodded, asked questions. Apparently the city's name meant 'Eternal Spring'.

The gloomy station. Wasn't this where Isabelle had arrived, on the Trans-Siberian via Moscow and Irkutsk over a year ago? "Look around a bit," said Eva, "she knows we were on this train, perhaps she's waiting for us."

She was standing at the station exit. And on the square in front of the station, in with the taxis, there was a university car waiting for us. "I told them you were the director of the Wangen *Gongren Daxue*, the Adult Education College. That impressed them. They wanted to do things in style. Still, I didn't manage to find a brass band, there aren't many here." It wasn't until we were sitting in the back of the car that she admitted she'd been joking. However, it was true that foreign teachers were entitled to use the university taxi service.

At any rate, we were allowed to stay at the university guesthouse; the manageress herself conducted us to our

229

room on the first floor. It was a big room, three windows, a balcony, a private bathroom. The house was one of those the Japanese had built during the years of disaster. Now the fancy plasterwork in the ceiling was crumbling and the windows and doors had become ill-fitting and draughty. But it still had a kind of antiquated charm, and it was convenient as well: Isabelle lived right next door in one of the two side buildings.

And where, at long last, was this Novosibirsk? Nothing but thinly wooded mountains and the occasional river. Then, after I'd been peering down intently for almost half an hour, something like a road – a couple of houses – and then, again, nothing. The almost full moon behind us; no, you didn't get to see much of this now free Russia. Wasteland upon wasteland – China had looked tidier, more Swiss, so to speak: wherever there's a stretch of land it's cultivated: even on the occasionally flooded river banks near Changchun there were little fields of maize, vegetables and sunflowers. Suddenly the moon was no longer in the distance behind me but large and pale on my right; so we'd veered north. And all the time people passed us on their way to the toilets, and Brahms, orchestral variations on a theme by Haydn, Karajan, and wisps of cloud rushing away beneath us; the desolate land and the powerful flight above it, and still more than six hours to go before we got to Zurich.

And now a pattern of stripes down in the purplish plain, and then repeatedly, again and again; mysterious though it looked, chariots of the gods had certainly not landed here – post-kolkhozian agriculture seen from above. And pinpoints of light, more and more, a village, then another, small towns, they merged, they coalesced; a tangle of lines, floodlit warehouses and squares; power stations, industrial sites; broad rows of residential blocks, clusters of lines that seemed to come straight off the drawing board: Novosibirsk, techno-city down there in the barren land.

Half past seven, Beijing time, not local time. The film had already started, *Bodyguard*; I glanced occasionally – not exactly new, but years ago at the cinema I'd liked Costner's impassive manner, except that now, with Classical Choice and Karajan-Haydn-Brahms on channel twelve, I was on the wrong soundtrack; the lips and teeth and gums of the pop singer in the role of the pop singer looked oddly bare on the monitor; and we flew on and on, a shimmer of sunset glow still on the curved front of the wing, on the engine nacelle; no night flight, still an evening flight, the world down below us sparsely lit.

"He's an idiot," said Isabelle. "Come from Paris to Changchun to write a paper on birthrates, and after a fortnight he thinks he knows all there is to know, and that without knowing a single word of Chinese. He maintains that fundamentalism will come to China. It's a normal stage in the historical development after communism, he says. Like in Algeria. A true idiot, I can't say anything else!"

What a mocker! Eva here, Isabelle there, it must have been the wine, my third small bottle all to myself, and a second aspirin, and the bodyguard moved across the screen with exemplary composure, accompanied by

Brahms' variations in full orchestral blast; not quite the thing for flights over Novosibirsk with those horribly low outside temperatures, what a world! So there I sat, with a running cold, in my shirtsleeves, separated by just a few centimetres from sixty degrees below zero, little man, nearly nothing, triumphantly crossing Siberia, as if I'd only been so sleepy all those three weeks in China so as now finally to be wide awake up here, whilst the other passengers around me were starting to fall asleep. Eva too stretched out in her seat. "Do you want to read *Le Monde*? I've finished."

It wasn't thanks to me that the carapace had become as thin as an eggshell; but at least it was something and not nothing, not a trifling matter either actually, in fact it might almost have become too much for me the moment I became aware of it; wake up Harder, you can't lose what was never yours. And the fact that she'd sent me packing – for it was she who'd sent me away, I'd have stayed – really didn't make any difference; I hadn't fled, I hadn't made the slightest move to flee, and even if it had ended some other way, miserably, it would still have been the most blissful of Thursdays, although I didn't know why, had no idea why. And in the night train from Shenyang to Chengde, in that long night alone with Eva in the four-berth compartment, a soft-sleeper this time and very luxurious, I kept pondering, Isabelle and Changchun and Eva's excursion to the nunnery in Nong'an and the woman glaziers at the guesthouse and the dust and the lack of space in the library and the Chinese cabbage everywhere on the streets and Eva's telephone call to say that she and Kate had missed the last train, and the four-table restaurant with the concrete floor where one of Isabelle's female students was a waitress, and the noise of the Chinese in the guesthouse opposite and the evangelising Americans and Kate's boyfriend, the Chechen, a former paratrooper in the Russian army, and the German professor who had got his students to translate Seneca – indirectly via English – into Chinese, *On the Happy Life*, and Confucius, communism, capitalism, corruption and really existing hell down at the bottom of the borehole, and the first book of Moses, Adam's bone, Eve-apples, and this and that and then something else: it went through my mind in variations, even without earphones and the mighty Brahmsian orchestra, and I suddenly knew where the lightness came from: no doubt about it, I'd have stayed if Isabelle hadn't sent me back to the guesthouse, in spite of the noise and all the other reasons, but no, why look for reasons, any reason will do. And the lightness persisted, not a hint of fright or anything like that, no attempt to flee, no panic; and though Isabelle might be a terrible mocker, she wouldn't betray anyone, or anything, you could count on that. And what if she did? It kept running through my head all night long on the way to Chengde; on the way home, homewards, a week ago already, drunk without wine or beer or rice brandy, as I gazed out of the train window into the night where I hardly saw anything, just as I was looking out now and seeing just as little.

Trailing the setting sun at nine hundred and seventy-eight kilometres an hour – or whatever speed it was; we'd never catch up with it: celestial mechanics. I looked out along the wing to the flashing light, then down obliquely to streaks of cloud, and further down to the dark countryside. Shenyang to Chengde, the train journey through the night; then too I'd looked out steadily, although there was even less to see; I'd been as keen then not to miss the Chinese night out there as I was now not to miss Siberia down below. Never again, not once, would I travel along the foot of this mountain, past this station with its two strips of neon lighting, then for ages nothing but the embankment, tree trunks flashing by in the headlights of the train as it curved to the right; the carriages rolled noisily through the dark, their rumble slowing down as we went uphill, quickening as we went down. Eva was asleep, I was awake, with my pillows and covers stuffed under my back, behind my neck and my head, so that I could see out; never again, not even once, will I travel through these parts, catching glimpses in the fleeting light of embankments, walls, tree trunks, shrubbery, pebbles in a dried out river bed, telephone wires along the railway lines. I looked out intently although there was hardly anything to see, rheumatic twinges in my knee – just the same as now, squashed in between Eva and the wall of the airplane, I looked out onto the ever same wing section, the bluish grey metal with its dotted lines of bolts, the pink shimmering on the edge of the wing, the almost invisible vibration. On and on we flew with a monotonous roar.

"I don't know enough about it; I see those pagodas, the roof figures, the lions at the gateways, and all the time I can't help thinking: when, where, how, who, why? For each detail there at least two books you could read, it's discouraging. I prefer to go in front of the geology museum at six in the morning and watch people dance the tango to music from their transistors, and the foxtrot, the slow waltz. The music sounds so poignantly stale as it wafts across the square. Or nearby, beneath the fir trees there, the slow-motion gymnastics – *qigong*, you called it? Allow breath to stream through your body? The breath of energy, I see – with cosmic vibrations perhaps?"

Nong'an, no, I didn't feel like going and seeing yet another monastery, especially not seventy kilometres out in the country, a day trip. I preferred to stay in town. I liked it in the guesthouse; I liked sitting on the balcony here, the gardens, the courtyards, the other balconies nearby, and all the people going about their daily business; lorries passed, whole families on a single bicycle, coal merchants, horse-drawn carts, student couples: there was plenty to see here.

And besides, my knee was hurting. "I'll take a break just this once," I told Eva. "But don't let that stop you going; you'll enjoy it, on the train you can talk with Chinese people all the time, I only get in the way. Once we're in Chengde we'll do everything together again." "Let him stay, if he doesn't want to go," Isabelle interceded. "I'll look after him if necessary; he could come and take a look at our library for example, that wouldn't demand much effort and perhaps it'd be more interesting for him than yet another monastery. Take Kate with you, she's been meaning to go to Nong'an for ages."

Kate didn't have any lessons that Thursday and was pleased to go along with Eva. That settled it.

So I got to have a day in peace. It was peaceful to start with anyway.

Kate came early in the morning, at seven, to pick up Eva. I left the house with the two of them, they turned left in the direction of the railway station, I turned right in the direction of the geology museum, where for a while I watched the Chinese dancing the foxtrot. Back in my room I read the *China Daily*; it was delivered to us every day in the dining-room: textile exports had increased again, by thirty-nine per cent in eight months; karaoke had conquered Chinese homes; the rich and the poor regions were helping each other; Tibet was enjoying social stability, economic development and national unity; on the last page there was an advertisement for a building complex in Beijing that was to be named 'Manhattan Garden', the perfect thing for 'business people'.

Shortly after nine there was a knock on the door: comrade chambermaid in her red jacket, beside her a young woman in blue overalls, her toolbox in one hand, a hammer in the other. Neither of them wasted time with explanations I wouldn't have understood anyway; the one in Mao blue went straight to the windows, opened one of them, sat down astride the sill and pointed with her hammer at a cracked pane in the wing opening outwards. And already the pane had been knocked out – the sound of breaking glass came up from the courtyard.

And soon the clink and clatter and hammering came in through the open door too; the woman hadn't come alone, there was a whole team of glaziers – all women – noisily at work in the guesthouse. Two of them, bent over a board on trestles by the stairs, were busy with glasscutters and

L-squares. Shrill shouts issued from the various rooms into the corridor where they were repeated, presumably they were measurements for the window panes: measure, score, break. In our room the woman in Mao blue was already cleaning the empty frame: removing the splinters, pulling out the nails, scraping out the putty. Then, with furious panache, she positioned the glass and fixed it with the old points. The new panes fitted perfectly, there was not one that had to be recut. A handful of putty was shaped into a sausage, held vertically in the fist and spread across the crack, then the knife was pressed down and the putty smoothed with the angled blade; for each pane the procedure was repeated, briskly, skillfully – and that was that. A smile, and off to the next room.

A pity that Eva was away: she'd have liked those woman glaziers. "And my father would have been astonished too," I said to Isabelle when she came to pick me up for lunch. "I never saw either him nor any of his workmates insert and putty a window pane so fast." "Nice you've found something to praise," she said. "It's not always easy here. Lots of shoddy work. The maintenance team – all women too, by the way – have fixed the toilet flushing in my flat at least three or four times. Admittedly, they were always very quick."

From the guesthouse dining-room across to the university library. "Are you sure you've got the time? As you can see, I'm not bored on my own." She waved my protestations aside: she had to go there some time this week anyway.

She greeted the young woman at the entrance desk

with cheerful courtesy and they exchanged a few words. I was introduced; and now the Chinese woman nodded several times to me too. And I was allowed to go with Isabelle into the stacks. It's a privilege only foreign teachers have here: the right to meander through the stacks without supervision. "You can't find anything in the catalogue, at least it's impossible for us foreigners. I really tried hard to understand the system, but it's hopeless. Somehow they realise that. That's why they let us come and see the books here."

The stacks were tall and close together; overladen, even the space between the tops of the books and the next shelf up was crammed full. Numbers, ideograms in the neon light. "Your fingers will be black, you'll see. In winter, with twenty degrees of frost, all the coal fires. The day after a snowfall the snow looks as if it's been gritted with soot. And the ice in the park is black. But even in summer there's always lots of dust from the countryside all around, and some of it gets into the library."

We crooked our heads sideways to look at the book spines, we crouched, we stood on our toes. "Masses of things like Dickens or Balzac," she said. "Almost all the Russians too, in English as it happens, I've no idea why. Strangely enough there are also quite a lot of things in German; probably bought by the Japanese. I've also come across some rarities, for example Joyce's *Chamber Music* – and your Warren is there too, *All the King's Men*, a book I hadn't read before, by the way; astonishing, isn't it, that you have to get to China to find the time to read books like that!"

She left me alone for a while.

"Sociology? Yes, of course. Wait a minute, I think it's over there." She led me to one of the rooms in the rear.

Durkheim's *Rules of Sociological Method* was there too, in the original French and freshly bound in strong marbled paper. "I told you there were things to be found here," she said, "not only Mao and Marx. With luck you'll find what you're looking for."

Or with patience. What a muddle! In the midst of sociology classics Heine's collected works, next to Heine a couple of volumes of Freud, the English translation, but also a thick textbook on the diseases of dogs. "Particularly useful in Changchun," said Isabelle, "especially since keeping dogs is strictly prohibited here. I've never seen a dog since I got here. Not that I mind."

After poking around for an hour I still wasn't sure if the books had been arranged by topic, by subject or by date of acquisition. The Chinese official on duty at the card-index cabinets was not familiar with these criteria. She listened with interest to the colleague from the country of watches, mountains and Schindler lifts. But she didn't understand my English very well and I didn't understand hers any better although Isabelle helped us both.

"You see," she said as we were on our way out, "that's why, if for no other reason, I have to stay on here – till all the librarians know enough English to catalogue foreign books properly, at least the English and American ones. On the other hand, just imagine how long I'd have to stay on to be able to arrange the Chinese books here in such a way that the Chinese could find them!"

We separated in front of the building. "One more double period," she said. "What time shall we meet for supper tonight? Eva's bound to be back long before seven. Just come along and pick me up. – By the way, how's your knee?"

The coal pile in the park, the student dormitory buildings. Demolition bricks, planks, timber, buckets, baskets, barrels, crates, nothing was thrown away; everything was piled up beside doors, in stairwells, on balconies. Bunches of leeks dangled from pieces of string next to washing hung out to dry. And again I passed through the dusty grove near the pond; between the tree trunks a few old people posed grotesquely as if in imitation of Chinese characters; a man slashed at the air in front of him with a sword. On the pavement of Dongzhonghua Road cabbage had been spread out to dry, leaves green, stalks yellow, row upon row, unguarded. Tinkling from the droves of bicycles through the early afternoon.

Now the glaziers were working in the side building. I couldn't see them from my room, only heard the clatter of panes being thrown down into the courtyard, the sound of hammering. Comrade chambermaid must have cleaned up while I was at the library with Isabelle, there were no bits of old putty on the floor any more.

The water in the thermos had gone lukewarm. I fetched some hot water down on the ground floor. Maxwell Instant Coffee, made in Shanghai, with dried milk and sugar already added. I took a chair out to the balcony and sat down in the sun. In the adjacent private gardens too there were rows of neatly laid out Chinese cabbage. "It takes about three days," Isabelle had told me, "and then they bury it. Yes, even here in the town centre, in the garden or next to the front door, wherever there's a strip of untarred ground. Last year the kitchen staff dug a pit over there between the two moon gates. We were eating cabbage from that supply up until the end of January."

In front of the house directly opposite my balcony a woman was sitting on the bottom step shelling beans. A man in front of the next house was scrubbing and rinsing pots. Chickens pecked at grain from a bowl. A girl was mending the inner tube of a bike. The honk of car horns from afar, bicycle bells and shouts from nearby. Behind the flat roofs of the apartment buildings the iron structure of the television tower jutted into the sky.

The hectic doctor, his wife and their acrobatic daughter came to my mind; our arrival in the morning here in Changchun, the hoards of taxi drivers in front of the station; our first lunch at the guesthouse, Isabelle, Kate, a few other young people from America; the walk through the university campus; all the kites above the park of the geological museum, paper buzzards and owls and butterflies high up in the steady wind, held by old men with thin strings you could only make out for the first few metres.

Back to my room; to brew another cup of instant coffee, the right thing for the foreigner in the guesthouse; I ought to have drunk green tea, but tea didn't keep me awake and I did want to stay at least half awake. *De vita beata*, on the happy life; the lefthand page in the original Latin, on the righthand page the translation in Chinese characters, a pale yellow paperback, thread-bound, with commentaries and an afterword in Chinese. A colleague of Isabelle's, a German classicist, had given it to us, 'For

Eva and Antonius with best wishes …' An Institute for the History of Ancient Civilisations: that too was to be found here in the former Manchukuo Empire, with young Chinese people studying Assyriology, Egyptology, Hittitology, and obviously Greek and Latin. I could already see how astonished my boss in Wangen would be when I told him about his German confrère in Changchun who'd been at work for years with his students translating the Romans into Chinese. Indirectly via English of course.

English, or rather American, is the Latin of the twentieth century; and there's no danger that this might change in the near future. Even for China, America is the model and radiant monstrance for progress, popular television and the public good. That afternoon there was no Beijing Opera on television, there were no Kungfu films either; instead, they were showing instalments of *The Denver Clan* – and commercials, commercials: bottles of alcohol, refrigerators, ginseng farms, cigarettes, cigarettes, and again alcohol as though it was an elixir for long life, male potency and family harmony. Then something else came on after all: people in heavy armchairs, teacups on the tables in front of them, political poker faces, disciplined clapping – no news programmes without meetings like that, either propaganda or commercials. Ah well, soon there'd be nothing but commercials, inventive progressive creative and offbeat, like in the West, in the whole world, the true Internationale.

The haze over the roofs grew thicker. The kitchen crew crossed the courtyard. Later Isabelle came in through the entrance gate, rounded the porter's lodge and disappeared in the side building. I sat, drinking coffee, looking out; I

242

took a few steps on the balcony. Soon Eva and Kate would be back from Nong'an.

From five o'clock on I started waiting. After six I grew uneasy.

Some new guests had arrived, noise out in the staircase, noise in the rooms next door. Twice, elderly Chinese men opened my door by mistake and apologised profusely; unfortunately we couldn't understand each other.

At a quarter past seven Isabelle came over.

Eva had just phoned. "They missed the train in Nong'an. Now they'll have to wait till tomorrow morning for the next one. Luckily they've found a hotel, a kind of Friendship Hostel near the station. What shall we do now?"

We went out for a meal.

On our way Isabelle reproached herself for not having helped plan the trip properly, she shouldn't have left it all to muddle-headed Kate. "On the other hand, Eva will at least see now what it's like in cheap hotels. As a tourist you're spoilt, you don't get to know normal living conditions. In the last winter holidays, when I was travelling with Kate and Friedrich through Henan Province we usually went to bed in all our clothes, and not only because of the cold. In winter, when there aren't any foreigners, they don't change the sheets. Oh no, we didn't get lice. Even if the rooms are dirty it doesn't mean that the guests are dirty too. Especially people's hair – I'm sure you've noticed how the Chinese like parading their freshly washed hair, and not only the women, the men too. Hair salons are the trendiest establishments around here."

It wasn't far to the restaurant near the Children's Park where one of Isabelle's students occasionally served. We'd already been there once before, Eva, Isabelle, Kate and her boyfriend, plus the classicist; we'd half-filled the place.

"Scatterbrain Kate, I should have known, I travelled around with her long enough last winter. Every day at some moment or other she'd keep us waiting, see something, get all enthusiastic about it and forget everything else. Charming, self-centred, spoilt. But perhaps it's only the generation gap. And it's to her credit that she doesn't belong to the super-pious American gang. It's pure chance, by the way, that she's in Changchun at all: she was on a tour in China with her student choir so she made use of the opportunity to visit a fellow student from Yale – and got herself employed as a teacher. Spontaneous, carefree. When I consider what it took for me! And now she's staying another year. Friedrich, her winter boyfriend, left in July. She takes it all in her stride, and the difference between her old boyfriend and the new one could hardly be bigger. There was Friedrich, the sinology student, a booklover, twenty-seven and already very much the German scholar – during our travels in the loesslands and on the holy mountains we really benefited from his knowledge. And now the Chechen: an ex-paratrooper full of mysterious scars, here on a university course in equally mysterious business studies. Both of them suit Kate. Oh dear, young people with their express love stories! Quite incredible the dramas Kate and Friedrich staged every day on that winter trip, with me in the role of the detached, impartial third-party onlooker."

The following spring, in the May Day holiday week,

Isabelle had gone on a second trip, this time on her own. Beijing, Lanzhou in the far west, a two-day journey along the edge of the Gobi, dunes, camel caravans. From Lanzhou a hair-raising trek in buses that were always trying to overtake each other so as to be sure of having enough passengers at the next stop: free enterprise the Chinese way.

Finally, Labrang Monastery: a high plateau, fresh snow every night and by midday the snow had melted away; yaks, sheep, herdsmen on bicycles; adobe buildings and monks in purple robes laying bricks; monks blowing alphorns, and monks debating learnedly in chorus, crowds of novices.

"Oh yes, I certainly enjoyed it. Still, even all those exotic carryings-on won't make a believer of me. Lama monasteries are very popular again just now. Even outside the tourist season you'll find loads of foreigners in those places. Tao, Buddhism, shamanism, you name it, it's in; even the wise teachings of our Hudson Bay Indians are all the rage now. A guilty conscience, who knows? In Datong an American woman got on the train; she introduced herself as a Buddhist; she'd been on the road for almost a year, in India and Nepal, from one holy place to the next. We quarrelled amiably – that is, first of all we talked for a long time, then we quarrelled for a long time. That mix of boyscoutism and egotrip – nirvana in pill form; pilgrimaging with their dollars throughout the wretched world. Try to find yourself, okay, and perhaps even find yourself. But losing yourself for a change mightn't be a bad idea either!"

Pork cubes and beansprouts with chives and fried

245

noodles and beer. For a long time we were the only guests and the host had enough time for the occasional chat with Isabelle.

"I seem to be making myself useful here. There's no one waiting for me in Wangen. Or in Quebec for that matter. Incidentally, I got to know a couple of Canadians in the guesthouse here last summer, agricultural engineers. They were here for three weeks, two women and three men, on invitation from the university. Apparently the climate in Manchuria is much the same as in southern Canada; so advice from there is likely to be sound. However, it was only with the greatest difficulty that the Canadians managed to talk their agrarian colleagues out of buying the big sowing and harvesting machines. The comrades want to go from donkey carts to whole lines of combine harvesters in a single leap. Which only results in ruining the soil. The latest, the biggest, prestige. They ought to be smarter by now, their great leaps have landed them in a mess often enough. You only learn from your own mistakes – and most of the time you probably learn nothing at all, unfortunately."

Yes indeed, as I was sure to have noticed for myself already, there were quite a few things to criticise here, and not only the things the Americans and the Swiss usually mentioned first: Tibet, the death penalty, censorship, et cetera. However, she was cautious, if only because of her students.

"I don't want to get anyone into trouble. The Americans maintain that they're being spied on, crackling sounds on the phone, things like that. Probably persecution mania. In fact they're astonishingly tolerant here as far as the

Americans are concerned; the people from the university must know, must have known for a long time, that a lot more gets taught besides a little bit of English. Of course it's done with the very best American Baptist conscience. After all, the yellow race must be converted for their own salvation; otherwise, as Confucians, communists, materialists, they'll burn in hell. I've read the Baptists' lecture notes on Western civilisation and culture: the Bible is the most important book in the world, oh well, if they say so, listing most important books in the world is nonsense anyway; but it gets really funny when the First Book of Moses is held up as the most important textbook for world history – it's all in there, you don't need any of your old history books any more. I've discussed it with Kevin, the red-haired computer scientist, a nice fellow in other respects – it's hopeless, he really believes it, takes it literally. The world was created in six days, on the seventh day the boss reviewed it and found everything okay, the first president of America I presume, long before George Washington. Advanced Western civilisation, that's it then. What's good enough for a Baptist course in the Midwest is excellent for Chinese people. The world was created four thousand and thirty-eight years ago, precisely calculated from information in the Bible. Over there, in the US, those people are computer scientists, accountants, nurses, insurance agents, lab assistants; and here they have to teach the students English conversation – which is what they do, but at the same time they have to spread the truth. Just as well, then, that the Chinese, including the young ones, are resistant: they just sit there with embarrassed smiles on their faces. Calling the First Book of Moses history is pretty

247

steep – Yankee crassness – and if I was the boss here I'd have read those pious guys and dolls the riot act a long time ago. On the other hand, it's only because those young people are so pious and stick together in their sectarian way that they manage to survive at all in Changchun. Which doesn't mean that life is particularly difficult here for foreigners. But difficult for Americans, that's for sure! Often there's not enough hot water for a shower. Or the water's red from the rusty pipes. Or there's a power cut. And in the autumn the heating only comes on after room temperatures haven't been above fourteen degrees for days on end. Such un-American things, you see. And you can't get cornflakes either, or peanut butter, not to speak of cheeseburgers."

The arrow on the screen showed that we were approaching the Urals. Plus the usual other things: outside temperature, altitude, speed, flight duration to Zurich; the only thing that was missing was the local time. I still had Beijing time on my wristwatch, a quarter to ten, almost time for a nightcap, and yet it was still twilight. Dark twilight if I looked out to my right across the wing tip and to the north, bright twilight if I looked ahead to the west: orange and yellow and yellowy green and green and greenish blue and blue and bluish grey and grey, one colour flowing into the next, their sheen reflected in the matt metal of the wing.

Inside the plane, the Costner film was over and nearly everyone was dozing, except for a couple of readers here and there and, in the centre row next to us, a notebook freak; I hoped his fumbling wouldn't disrupt the flight electronics.

A tugging sensation between my nose and my right eye, the aspirin was taking effect. On the flight to Beijing there'd been a loose connection in my earphones; this time it was different, unimpaired inflight entertainment on thirteen channels, everything perfect, I had the choice. '... *Herbstnebel wallen bläulich überm See ... vom Reif bezogen stehen alle Gräser ...*' recorded some time aeons ago, remastered and digitised by Bitstream. If it had been sung by a man it would hardly have moved me; but that heart-piercing voice, Kathleen, Cecilia, whoever ...

"What do you want to go over to the guesthouse for?" said Isabelle. "Stay here. The Chinese people in the rooms next to yours will all be smoking and drinking and chewing nuts, they want to enjoy themselves. They'll make a noise all night, you'll see. Sleep here. It's an offer. I won't seduce you. Although ... that would be something! To wake up in the morning with a man at one's side, just for once. Can you understand that? No you can't, or only wrongly. Never mind. Anyway, does it really have to be my best friend's husband? What a crazy idea! It's the rice liqueur, rice liqueur after beer has turned me into a fox woman, dreadful. Pardon me. And I pardon you. You're Catholic aren't you? Lucky for you. In thought, word and deed, you're familiar with that aren't you? In thought often, in word seldom, in deed never. So may we both be granted absolution. And as an act of repentance let's drink a cup of green tea together, that has a sobering effect doesn't it?"

Isabelle's flippant beer mouth. We'd only each had two little cups of rice liqueur as an extra offered us by the landlord after our meal at that four-table restaurant in the something something Road or Lu next to the Children's Park.

"How does one flirt?"

"You're not managing too badly."

"And who started?"

"No one, of course, it was more or less inevitable – which makes it all the more suspicious, don't you agree?"

Stimulating enough for a night of cinema-in-the-head between Shenyang and Chengde. Eva in the narrow bunk above me, her snoring drowned in the rattling of the train. Indian summer, Canadian autumn, Hudson Bay; *Tents in the Wilderness* is the first book about Red Indians I ever read, long before *Leatherstocking* or *The Wept of Wish-Ton-Wish*.

"If it weren't for Eva," she said. "If Eva weren't my friend. And if you weren't her husband. Oh, any kind of man, how nice that would be! In my life here there's hardly any choice, practically none at all. Students are out of the question; my Chinese colleagues are all married, sentimental and respectable. And the few foreigners around here are also married – with the exception of crass eccentrics. And my missionaries of course. Imagine starting an affair with one of them, good God! In any case they prefer to keep themselves to themselves, they don't want to be exposed to the danger of having outsiders cast doubts on their faith. It's all in their Book of Genesis, it's definitive, no commentaries please. They even found proof of the existence of hell in one of their absurd newsletters: absolutely dreadful wailings had suddenly been heard coming up from old boreholes in Abu Dhabi. Of course, blazing oil rigs and hell back home in Texas won't do, hell has to be in the Middle East, that's the true proof, they found old Noah's Ark somewhere around there too, didn't they? Clever people blinkering themselves with the Bible! Hellish howls up from the empty borehole, just imagine the scene. And then imagine lying in bed with someone who believes in such things! You might drink a friendly cup of tea with him, why not? But go to bed with him – never! In any case, they're all much too young for me. A mature woman, overripe, already gone squishy. No, don't say anything, I know what I know; married, divorced, single in China, Changchun, hopeless. And then all those Wangs here! Did you know that every fourth Chinese is named Wang?"

A hug, you might also say a tight embrace. Like the Bosch figures in Purgatory, but with all our clothes on. Infatuation plus necking plus Tao divided by three, like in the distant days of youth when passion was mighty and experience minimal. Face to face, breast to breast, belly to belly, we held fast to each other, shoulders, ribs under pullovers.

"We'll be full of bruises, both of us."

"So what? That's the minimum. Less would hardly be flattering. But you must go now, go."

She shoved me towards the door. Hang your head, demonstrate deepest regret.

"Sleep well,"

"You too."

"Forget it."

"Certainly not."

Out onto the landing in the stillness of the night, then down the steps and across the courtyard. Dark the porter's lodge over to the right of the entrance. Shards of glass in the moonlight. I found my way.

The Chinese guests next door really were still making a noise. Laughter came out through their half-open door; it also came in through the wall. Sleep was out of the question anyway.

It was only during the long night in the train from Shenyang to Chengde that it dawned on me: I'd felt no alarm, not a trace of alarm, I hadn't made even the slightest move to flee – all I'd felt was frustration, trivial and suprisingly nice.

Variations on the night journey to Chengde. My knee was still painful, a calcified joint or something. As morning started to dawn and I gradually began to see more than just the embankment and treetrunks and telephone poles flashing past in the light of the train, I felt refreshed by the rising brightness and was all the more determined to stay awake.

An hour on my own by the window, then two more hours with Eva beside me. No one else had joined us in our luxury compartment. We drank tea and ate the rolls we'd bought the previous afternoon in Shenyang.

Ricefields on terraced hill slopes, pussy willows along the stream, birch trees; villages, far away from nothing, with thin wreaths of smoke floating over the roofs.

"The library there is much nicer than the one here, really. You'll go and take a look at it, won't you?" Isabelle had said. I'd have taken her word for it even if I'd known she was lying.

We went there on our first day. Eva mustered all her travel skills to try to obtain admission: she enquired at the main entrance gate to the park, she asked at the kiosk by the lake, at the antiques shop, at the calligraphy supplies store, she asked three guardians in succession. Each one listened attentively, pointed earnestly with head and hand in one direction or the other, not one of them said no, but each seemed glad to send us on our way. We never found the person who might have been authorised to make an exception for a library specialist from the 'Land of the Brave Mountain Soldiers'.

We circled the house a couple of times. Astonishing how small such imperial buildings are. A curved main roof, a heavy porch roof, grey unrendered brickwork on the two narrow sides, the long south side built of wood: painted green and pale blue and red, with characters on the beams, small-paned windows. And up there, beneath the porch roof, the hidden middle floor, trompe-l'œil. I knew that the stacks had been empty for a long time; all you'd have seen would have been dusty shelves. And in any case, the Wenjin Ge Library here was only a late copy of the Tianyi Ge Library in Ningbo, and that was probably not the first of its kind either.

Chinese tourists trailed in single file through the rock garden. Here, in moonlit nights, the emperor would read in the pool of light under the paper lanterns. And on the fifteenth day of the eighth month, the Mid-Autumn Festival, when the full moon rose from behind the Eastern Mountain, the emperor would stand on the highest point of the rock garden and gaze at the celestial body. "Where did you get that from?" asked Eva. Other sources say he simply used to lie there comfortably and lose himself in reverie, more likely moon mania than reading mania.

Leaving the Wenji Ge Library we passed through a little wood and crossed a meadow to a pagoda – this one was closed too. In its stead, a Mongolian Holiday Inn: neat rows of concrete yurts, each of them with air-conditioning. We'd hoped for a cup of coffee, but the restaurant was closed in the afternoons; we'd have been welcome as overnight guests.

We picnicked on the edge of the artificial lake; everything looked strikingly natural: here a flat shore with a pebble beach, there a shore with a sandy beach, a steep shore with cliffs, deep bays, various peninsulas. Adalbert Stifter's *Indian Summer* in Chengde; no roses, but plenty of lotus flowers.

On our second day the sky was overcast, the air cool. But instead of swathes of mist, clouds of dust were floating over the roofs towards the river: streets of old housing were being demolished. Two excavators were rumbling around on the site. Builders were knocking the old mortar off the bricks, sorting out the beams and planks. Huddled close together, a few single-storey houses; on the other side, the first six-storey buildings: without stone lions in the doorways, without inner courtyards, without curved roofs. Blocks of flats like the ones in Changchun: with bathrooms and balconies – and the following spring the balconies would look like hanging gardens or garden sheds suspended from the façades, filled with potted plants, climbing vines, cluttered up with baskets, cupboards, bicycles, birdcages.

We crossed the river again and reached the fields. In Nong'an Eva had got out into the countryside. She wanted to do so again. "This time, we don't have to worry about missing a train," she said. After the bridge, through sparse woods up to the weir; a real river, not part of the miniature China whose 'Great Wall' stretched out along the other side of the river. We walked for a while on the embankment, then we turned right towards the hill. A pit latrine beside the road, children coming from the village to use it; as they trotted back to the houses, they cried out "Hello!" and nudged each other giggling.

We'd come to see farmers at work and suddenly we found ourselves surrounded by farmers seeing us at leisure. Eva spoke to them; the people were interested, Eva was kept busy. One of the women led us to her house; all the others followed. We sat down on the *kang*, the woman offered us each a large slice of water melon. No, they weren't farmers, they were in one of the units responsible for road maintenance in the town, without much work at the moment – is what Eva understood. And they sold vegetables, vegetables from the farmers here in the village, they took them to market three times a week. Yes, they did have a bit of land of their own, not much. Just spit the melon seeds on the concrete floor, that was quite all right and polite, they assured us.

Oh, I'll remember that: us sitting there on that heatable bed, the *kang*; seven people quizzing Eva and giving her information; and the way the whole group escorted us along the field path all the way down to the road.

And then? What else?

In the end we didn't visit the mini Potala Palace in the hills behind the town after all.

It took Eva the greater part of the following morning to get us the train tickets for our return to Beijing.

In the meantime I settled down in the turmoil of the waiting room to write our postcards, at last. Chengde's miniature China was a suitable subject; however I couldn't find a card showing the imperial library.

Again we passed through the bird market, again we passed the snack stalls, to delve once more into the department store with its overflowing shelves.

Just as in Changchun, young people were at work painting all the town's tree trunks waist–high with white paint.

Just as in Changchun, cabbage had been spread out everywhere on the pavements.

Swarms of pigeons, wheeling like huge fans, flew between the blocks of flats.

And all that wind in the acacias, the alders, the birch trees, the willows.

And then this too, of course.

Young men in fashionable suits, a cell phone in one hand, a briefcase in the other. We'd seen them on the train to Changchun; we'd noticed them on the train from Changchun to Shenyang; and there were some of them here in Chengde at the hotel bar.

"It's a species that's vastly on the increase," said Isabelle. "The new man. What's the magic word? The separate path? The forked tongue? Comrades, get rich!"

I find it difficult enough to understand Wangen. How could I presume to say anything appropriate about China and the millions of Wangs. Turncoats of the world unite.

The silk vest, pale yellow embroidered with red dragons. "The flabbier the skin the finer the underwear." Eva's remark. And ginseng syrup, stalk celery: folklore, folklore.

Staring through the safety glass out onto the wing, to the control flaps and the blinking light; there was nothing I had to do as yet, no obligations, nothing. The long holiday was over, the last evenings in Beijing too, the long walks; one late afternoon we went through old neighbourhoods on our way to the Beijing Hotel where we had dumplings, green vegetables and all kinds of other things in the most beautiful restaurant I've ever been in; another time we walked to the Liyuan Theatre to see selections from Beijing opera, *Classical Choice* so to speak. How quickly you get used to luxury, to honey-glazed yams, to hot candied apples, to the beer that's served at state banquets, rice wine, *maotai* sorghum spirit.

And those Chinese women everywhere, flat-breasted, high cheek-boned, the true aphrodisiac applied to the eyes in tiny doses, day in, day out. You couldn't call it wild, unusual at the most; celery as good as ginseng, potatoes as good as celery, all it takes is for you to be full up and in a state of drowsiness; masses of Chinese women, a perpetual proletarian fashion show, on squares, in parks, through alleys, in department stores, at street kitchens; no, not long-legged, but graceful and supple, it must have been that.

How faraway now that period of fasting in Paris, cramp-reliever, you mocker! And the beige-coloured, sweeping countryside with the rows of poplars even on our last day on the drive out to the airport: so that in spite of my running nose and tickly throat I felt so incredibly light of heart, more so than for years past; and it wasn't just due to those three small bottles of Swissair Beaune.

High flights of the imagination are rare. Fasten your seatbelts for landing – the world down there full of folderol. We circled above Schaffhausen, waiting to land. I saw the Rhine Falls, could pick out the street lamps, saw cars crawling across intersections and squares. The elation had gone. The Boeing swayed. Two other heavy planes were moving close by. Ten minutes later we approached Zurich airport. Dropping, rumbling, no further incident.

Local time: half past six in the evening. My watch said half past one after midnight, Beijing time. Actually I should have been tired, tired a long time ago. But I wasn't. Tiredness would come of course, and how! Wait for the luggage; passport control.

Behind the glass partition in the hall outside, on the shiny tiled floor, two people we hadn't expected to see there were waiting for us: gangly, in carefully-casual attire.

"So, Dad, what was it like?"

'I am a thief and a thief is not to be trusted …'
Philip Roth, *Deception*

… Sherwood Anderson, *Winesburg Ohio: A Group of Tales of Ohio Small-Town Life*; Louisa May Alcott, *Little Women*; Saul Bellow, *Herzog*; James Fenimore Cooper, *The Pathfinder, The Prairie, The Pioneers*; Thomas Stearns Eliot, *The Waste Land*; Ralph Waldo Emerson, *Friendship*; William Faulkner, *Light in August, The Sound and the Fury, Pylon*; William Goyen, *The House of Breath*; Ernest Hemingway, *A Farewell to Arms*; Sinclair Lewis, *Babbitt, Main Street*; Bernard Malamud, *The Assistant*; Edgar Lee Masters, *The Spoon River Anthology*; Herman Melville, *Moby Dick, Bartleby the Scrivener*; Arthur Miller, *All My Sons*; Henry Miller, *Quiet Days in Clichy*; Carson McCullers, *Short stories*; Eugene O'Neill, *Long Day's Journey into Night*; Edgar Allan Poe, *The Purloined Letter*; Ezra Pound, *Cantos*; Philip Roth, *Portnoy's Complaint, The Anatomy Lesson*; William Saroyan, *The Human Comedy*; Upton Sinclair, *The Jungle*; Betty Smith, *A Tree Grows in Brooklyn*; John Steinbeck, *Sweet Thursday*; Henry David Thoreau, *Walden, Autumn*; Mark Twain, *Autobiography*; John Updike, *Rabbit Run*; Kurt Vonnegut, *Hocus Pocus*; Robert Penn Warren, *All the King's Men*; Edith Wharton, *The Age of Innocence*; Thornton Wilder, *Our Town*; Walt Whitman, *Leaves of Grass*; Thomas Wolfe, *The Hills Beyond* …

and

… Peter Bichsel, Jean Paul, Adalbert Stifter, Walter Schenker, Arno Schmidt …

and

… Anna, Anne, Ann, Barbara, Bernath, Brigitte, Prof. Bourdieu, Cécile, Christa, Dibo, Edith, Eva, Eva, Franziska, Prof. Gifter, Goren, Guggenheim, Hanna, Held, Helena, Jauslin, Prof. Jurt, Kleinmann, Kretz, Prof. Levy, Lina, Madeleine, Margret, Marie-Louise, Maya, Meienberg, Prof. Mutschler, Nicole, Nina, Prof. Oechslin, Probst, Reckel, Regina, Renée, Rickenbacher, Rosmarie, Ruth, Sandra, Silvia, Schmid, Prof. Staiger, Ursula, Ursula, Ursula, Veronika, von Arx, Wang, Wirz, Wolf, Wormser, Yu, Zita, Zumbrunn

The Author

www.erhard–von–bueren.ch

Erhard von Büren was born near Solothurn, Switzerland, in 1940. After a PhD in Psychology and German philology from Zürich University and study stays in France he worked as a teacher in advanced teacher training.

He has had three novels published in Switzerland: *Abdankung. Ein Bericht* (Zytglogge Verlag, Bern 1989), *Wespenzeit* (Rotpunktverlag, Zürich 2000), *Ein langer blauer Montag* (verlag die brotsuppe, Biel/Bienne 2013).

After *Epitaph for a Working Man, Wespenzeit* is the second of his books to be published in English.

Erhard von Büren has won various literary awards including the Canton of Solothurn Prize for Literature in 2007. He lives in Solothurn.

The Translator

Helen Wallimann was born in 1941 in the UK. After her MA from Edinburgh University she worked in publishing in Munich, Paris and London. From 1973 to 2001 she was employed as a teacher of French and English at the Kantonsschule Solothurn. She taught English at Chinese universities for two years.

Literary translations that have been published in book form include: *Legends from the Swiss Alps.* MCCM creations, Hong Kong 2009 (trans. from German); Leung Ping-kwan, *The Visible and the Invisible. Poems.* MCCM Creations, Hong Kong 2012 (trans. from Chinese); Erhard von Büren, *Epitaph for a Working Man.* Matador 2015.